The
CARVING
TREE

THE CARVING TREE

TERRY BOWMAN

Mill City Press,
Minneapolis

Mill City Press, Inc.
322 First Avenue N, 5th floor
Minneapolis, MN 55401
612.455.2293
www.millcitypublishing.com

ISBN-13: 978-1-63413-231-2
LCCN: 2014921332

Cover Design by Colleen Rollins
Typeset by Mary K. Ross

Printed in the United States of America

MAY 14, 2005

🍃 CHAPTER ONE 🍃

Sadie Hopkins paused on the top porch step, cocked her head, and studied the Carving Tree. She touched a finger to her lips and slowly scanned the old beech. Located one-third of the way down the grassy hill and in full view of their home, the massive tree dominated their front yard. Its thick canopy, like a giant parasol, cast a cool shadow on the ground beneath. The plush green carpet of fescue abruptly ended at the tree's drip line and exposed the red piedmont soil. She knit her brows. The foliage was not its normal dark green color. Perhaps, the dry spring was taking its toll on the ancient beech.

She left the steps and headed down the dirt driveway for a closer inspection. Japanese honeysuckle consumed the old woven-wire fence next to the road. The white and yellow tubular blooms of the wild vine gave off a sweet scent. Her eyes traced the two well-worn ruts of the driveway. They were separated by a dark green median of grass. After forty-five years of marriage, she and Jake had grown to be a lot like those two ruts—well worn, always running side by side, and always headed in the same direction.

She stopped under the protective shade of the Carving Tree and admired the landmark. With its four-foot diameter and massive canopy, everyone agreed that it was by far the most majestic beech around. She walked to the base of the tree and stood between two large roots that extended outward three feet before disappearing into the red clay. She ran her fingers over the smooth gray bark and marveled at the numerous names and carvings that had been etched decades before. Many of the scars bore the names of people she'd never known. The letters had broadened and grown distorted with the passage of time. She placed her right palm on a large heart-shaped carving, closed her eyes, and inhaled deeply.

Jake Hopkins leaned against the garden hoe to regain his balance. His breathing came in shallow pants, and his racing heart pounded in his ears. He looked at Buckshot, his devoted canine, who was lying between two nearby rows. "Old boy . . . must be . . . getting old . . . twenty minutes of gardening . . . never winded me so." The dog rolled his large brown eyes toward him and softly patted the soil with his tail.

Jake wiped his brow with the back of his hand and glanced at the sun. What a scorcher for the middle of May. He admired the half-acre garden while he rested. The plot, twice as long as it was wide, formed a perfect rectangle. The neatly plowed rows looked as if they had been set with a surveyor's transit.

Two battalions of crows hidden in the treetops on either side of the clearing called back and forth across the garden. Buckshot swung his head like a pendulum as he followed the crows' conversation. Jake squeezed the rough wooden handle and wished the tool was his shotgun. Most assuredly, the feathered bandits were plotting to steal the corn kernels that he'd planted earlier.

He counted the remaining tomato plants on the row and decided he would quit when he reached the end. He cleared a smoker's tickle and resumed hoeing around several young plants. He pushed the crusty, red dirt away from the tender plants and then pulled fresh soil back around them. The sun-baked earth released a dusty odor.

Within moments his pulse quickened, and his breathing became shallow. His arms grew heavy, and he dropped the hoe. Light-headed, he bent and rested his elbows on his thighs. A pack of cigarettes fell from his shirt pocket and spilled on the ground.

Sadie held the cherry-stained frame against the den wall above the desk and frowned. The collage did not look right against the oak paneling. Yet, it deserved a special place. After all, much of her adult life was captured in the photographs.

She caressed the frame and admired its smooth glossy finish. She laid it on the desk and surveyed the walls. With the stone fireplace, large floor-to-ceiling bookshelves, numerous windows, and existing pictures, there wasn't a suitable place in the den to hang it.

She slipped on her reading glasses and inspected the collage. She smiled as several photographs brought back fond memories, but a void filled her chest when she read the bold-lettered phrase, "Best Wishes on Your Retirement." Her lip quivered, and tears rolled down her cheeks.

The porch door creaked, and she brushed the tears from her face with the back of her hand. She forced a smile when Jake entered the den. His discerning brown eyes revealed he'd already seen her tears.

Jake removed his dusty shoes and placed them near the door. His short-sleeved button-down shirt was soaked with perspiration. He lit a cigarette, and the strong odor of burning tobacco filled the room. "Baby, perhaps you should put off retirement for a while if it upsets you that much."

She slipped off her glasses and let them hang from their beaded lanyard. "And leave you here all alone? I've waited a lifetime for the opportunity to spend all day every day with my husband." She cocked her head and studied him. "You look awfully pale. Do you feel okay?"

He puffed a smoke ring, and the transparent halo expanded and dispersed into the air. "Just got a bit overheated at the garden. I'll be as right as rain as soon as I cool off."

She pulled the cigarette from his lips and extinguished it in an ashtray. "Jake Earl Hopkins, cigarettes are going to be the death of you."

Sadie slipped into a knee-length navy dress, inspected her appearance in the bedroom mirror, and nodded with approval. The dress was one of her favorites—modest and neat.

"It's ten minutes after nine," Jake yelled from the den. "We need to leave or we'll be late for church."

She gently rubbed her hand over her hair one last time and rushed to the den. Jake stood near the stone fireplace with his foot on the hearth. He was dressed in his dark gray suit and burgundy tie—her favorite.

He extinguished his cigarette and ambled toward her. "My, baby, don't you look lovely. You'll be the prettiest girl at church."

She stepped close to him and batted her eyelashes. "You're just biased." She fluffed the handkerchief in his chest pocket. "You know, honey, you're pretty outstanding yourself." With his full head of hair and tanned complexion, he remained the most handsome man alive. She cinched up his tie, buttoned down his collar, and ran her fingers through his wavy silver hair. "In fact, you're not half bad for sixty-five."

The mantel clock chimed, and she jumped. "Goodness. We'll be late." She spun around. "Zip me?"

He placed his hand in the small of her back and tugged at the zipper. She felt the dress tighten, but before she could turn, he slid his arms around her waist. She locked her arms over his and tilted her head back against his neck.

He squeezed her tenderly. "You're the best thing that ever happened to me."

She turned and poked him in the chest. "And you had better not forget it."

He pulled her close. His forceful embrace, the gentle touch of his lips, and the pleasant scent of his aftershave made her knees go weak.

He grinned and his deep brown eyes sparkled. "Want to skip Sunday school?"

Jake waited patiently with three other men in the shade of a large black oak located thirty feet from the front of Glendale Baptist Church. The congregation filed down the front steps like fire ants vacating their mound. The numerous voices produced an unintelligent chatter. He took a draw from his cigarette. "So, when will the project start?"

Leroy Davis shrugged. "I'm not sure. I need to talk to the Habitat for Humanity folks."

Jake loosened his tie and watched Sadie walk down the wooden steps with two other women, the "M and M" twins, as he liked to call them. They stopped at the bottom and continued their conversation. Sadie was probably acting as referee again. It seemed as if Mabel and Maude were always fussing.

He glanced at Leroy, flicked the ashes from his cigarette, and eyed the women.

David Simmerson jingled the keys in his pocket. "How many men from our church do you think will help?"

Jake ignored the question and admired his lifelong companion. She was petite with small shoulders, and her collar-length hair was slightly curled and colored to match her brunette color of younger years. Even at sixty-three, she held her head high and conveyed an air of sophistication.

Their eyes met for a moment, and he winked. She responded with a playful glance. He wilted. Those striking green eyes . . . he could get lost in those eyes.

"What about you, Jake?" Leroy snapped his fingers. "Jake!"

"What?"

"Can we count you in?"

"Oh, uh . . . sure."

Sadie smiled at Clyde and Erma when the waitress set a basket of homemade biscuits on the red and white tablecloth. The elderly couple seemed mesmerized by the hot steaming bread.

The waitress placed four menus on the table. She appeared to be in her mid-twenties, plain but pretty. Her face was flushed from rushing about. "I'll give you a minute to look over the menu," she said as she scurried to the next table.

Sadie glanced around the restaurant. The diner, smothered in the pleasant aroma of a bakery, looked like it had been transported to the present from the 1950s. The aged walls were adorned with baskets and ancient cooking utensils. Oak tables and chairs complemented the hardwood floor, and the curtains in the windows matched the gingham tablecloths. However, what Juanita's Diner lacked in sophistication was more than offset by the wonderful food. She buttered a hot biscuit, and her mouth watered. "Most people come to Juanita's for the home cooking, but I come for the homemade biscuits."

Jake picked up a menu. "Judging from the church crowd here, I would say a lot of people like Juanita's home cooking."

Clyde nodded.

Erma grinned. "Law, honey, I love to poke a hole in the end of a biscuit and pack it full of these peach preserves." She took a bite and then spoke with a mouthful, "Mmmm . . . it's pure heaven."

Sadie laughed at her plump eighty-year-old friend. Erma wore a flower-print dress with a matching hat. Her teeth were stained with the same red lipstick that was caked on her lips. The small amount of hair that had escaped from beneath her hat was jet black—dyed, of course. In spite of Erma's peculiar appearance, Sadie considered Erma to be her best friend.

Jake flipped through his menu. "What are you going to order, Clyde?"

Clyde tilted his head. "What was that?"

Jake spoke louder. "What are you going to order?"

Clyde scratched the top of his bald head. "The usual—country-style steak and gravy." He waved a boney finger in the air and preached in his high-pitched voice, "Why risk ordering something I may not like?"

Jake nodded. "Sounds like a wise choice."

Sadie glanced at Jake. His eyes sparkled in good humor. They both knew Clyde was as predictable as the sunset right down to the clothes he wore: plaid shirt, blue jeans, and the ever-present World War II military medal prominently pinned to his shirt.

The waitress returned with her pad in hand. "Are you ready to order?"

Jake nodded. "Are you ready, Sadie?"

Sadie closed her menu. "Why I certainly am, Mr. Hopkins, dear."

The waitress placed her hand on Sadie's forearm. "Mrs. Hopkins . . . You're Mrs. Hopkins, my fourth grade teacher. Aren't you?"

Sadie handed her menu to the waitress and smiled. "I sure am." She braced for the next question. She'd heard it a thousand times.

"Do you remember me? I'm Kelly Jones. You taught me fifteen years ago."

Sadie nodded. She'd taught more than 1,100 students during her career, and this attractive waitress surely didn't resemble any awkward-looking ten-year-old girl she'd taught. She lied. "Why, yes, Kelly. It's been a long time, but you do look familiar."

Kelly's smile faded, and her eyes reddened. "I'll never forget what you did for me." She wiped her eyes. "Making three new dresses for me, and all. Why, I'd never had anything but hand-me-downs. The beautiful new dresses made me feel like I really belonged."

Sadie swallowed hard. Indeed, she did remember the girl. Her family had been among the poorest in the county, and she had worn the same brown tattered dress every day.

Kelly broke into a huge smile. "It's very good to see you. I can't wait to tell all of my friends." She shifted back and forth from one foot to the other. "Is it true you retired this year?"

"I made it official a few weeks ago on my sixty-third birthday." She reached across the table and patted Jake's hand. "Somebody needs to keep Jake out of trouble."

Jake grunted and picked up his menu.

Kelly momentarily covered her mouth. "I'm very sorry. I got carried away. You guys would probably like to finish ordering."

Sadie glanced around the diner to see if any other customers were staring at their table. Jake and Clyde were engaged in a loud conversation about a recent stock car race. Their voices drowned the background babble of numerous conversations. By now, everyone in the restaurant knew all the details of the race.

Oblivious to the spectacle, Erma leaned close. "How is the retired life treating you, shugah?"

Sadie shifted in her seat. "So far it's no different than any other summer break, but it's exciting to think about all the possibilities."

Erma picked up a biscuit. "Y'all need to get active in Lamp Lighters. We're going to Gat'inburg in October to see the fall colors."

Sadie nodded. "Sounds fun. Jake and I have always talked about taking some bus tours across the country. I want to see firsthand some of the great national landmarks that I've taught about over the years."

Erma poked her thumb in the biscuit. "I always had my heart set on seeing Ni'gra Falls, but we've never even gotten outside the Ole Tar Heel State."

Sadie nodded. "And Grand Canyon . . . the Redwood Forest . . . and Smithsonian."

Erma looked puzzled. "Smith who?"

"The Smithsonian Institute—our national museum in Washington, DC. I always wanted to take my fourth graders there, but"—her voice wavered—"that's not going to happen now." She wiped a tear from her cheek. "Nearly my entire life has been wrapped up in teaching."

Erma laid the biscuit on her plate and placed a hand on Sadie's. "Well, honey, I'll keep you in my prayers."

Jake laid down his dessert fork. "What did you think of Pastor Nolan's sermon on God's faithfulness?"

Clyde's forehead wrinkled, and he cupped a boney hand to his oversized ear. "What'd you say?"

Erma leaned toward Clyde and shouted, "Pastor Nolan's sermon—what did you think?"

Clyde hooked both thumbs in his red suspenders and shouted, "God's been good to me. Kept me alive in the big war and always sent a good tobacco crop."

Sadie felt her face blush. She glanced around to see who was looking.

Jake nodded. "He's blessed us with good fortune for many years."

Sadie clenched her teeth.

Erma's eyes sparkled. "God has always been faithful to keep his promises to us. He's always met our needs and answered our prayers." Erma turned toward her with an expectant look.

Sadie let out an exasperated huff and slid back her chair. "Excuse me. I need to visit the ladies' room."

☙ CHAPTER 2 ❧

A blanket of peace settled over Sadie while she finished the breakfast dishes. It had taken five days of deliberation, but she finally knew what she'd do with the retirement collage. She dried her shriveled hands, removed her flowered apron, and marched to the linen closet. She retrieved a musty bedspread from the top shelf and headed for the den desk. She slipped on her glasses and studied the collection of pictures encased within the delicate cherry frame. They represented a long and rewarding chapter of her life. But now she needed to move on.

She and Jake had long awaited this phase of life. They had worked hard, been good stewards of their income, and been disciplined to build their retirement nest egg. Now the time for which they had long planned had arrived. Employers would not govern their weekdays. Her evenings would not be consumed with grading papers and developing lesson plans. They would be blessed with free time. They could go to bed early and get up late. They could travel and see the country. But best of all, they would have more time to share with each other.

She carefully wrapped the collage in the old bedspread and placed it on the top shelf of the hall coat closet. She needed to start a new chapter in life—retirement life with Jake. She needed to charge full steam toward their future and not constantly be looking back at her past. Someday, when the grip of the past did not pull as hard, she would get the collage down and hang it.

A sense of premonition pricked the back of Sadie's neck as she stepped out on the front porch and noticed a dark ominous cloud. She immediately recognized the cloud's anvil shape. She would have told her class it was a *Cumulonimbus incus*, and this classification of cloud often brought severe thunderstorms, hail, and occasional tornados. Her father would have taken one look at the threatening cloud and warned all who would listen, saying, "Good things never happen in such weather."

The moist and heavy air carried the fresh smell of rain. They could use it, but an early morning storm during the month of May was rare. Storms usually occurred in the late afternoon spawned by the midday heat.

She looked down the long driveway that descended to the state-maintained gravel road and sighed. The road, like ivy, grew longer every day. She slowly picked her way along one of the reddish ruts, careful not to spill the freshly squeezed lemonade she'd prepared for Jake.

She paused at the Carving Tree and frowned. Many of its leaves had turned yellow as if the tree had confused the seasons. Certainly the ageless beech had seen many dry springs and would survive to see many more. Perhaps the approaching storm would refresh the tree. She left the landmark and headed for the rickety old mailbox at the end of the driveway.

She set the glass of lemonade on the horizontal wooden arm that supported the metal box. The rusted hinges gave way when she opened the mailbox, and the thin metal door came off in her hand. "Great. Guess I'll add this to Jake's to-do list. Funny thing— he's only been retired two months, and he's busier now than he was before."

She laid the door on the ground at the foot of the post and reached into the box. Good. Ernie Simmons had already delivered. He usually started his mail route later on Saturdays. She reached for the reading glasses that normally hung from her neck, but she'd left them on the kitchen table.

She held an envelope at arm's length and squinted. The text came into focus, but the words were too small to read. She sighed at the curse of old age. From the logos on the envelopes, she deduced that several of the letters came from credit card companies. She shook her head. One would think the credit card companies would wise up and stop sending offers to retired couples.

She examined the large print on the third envelope. She could barely make out the name of their insurance provider. She returned the door to the mailbox, tucked the mail under her arm, and retrieved the lemonade.

A large raindrop pelted her head. She glanced up at the dark cloud above. Should she make her delivery or head back to the house? She continued to the garden. Jake would appreciate the cold drink.

Located across the road and behind a stand of hardwood trees, the garden occupied a half-acre clearing. Two black crows abandoned their feast of newly planted seed and took flight when she entered the field. Their annoying call made it clear they were not pleased with her presence.

She scanned the garden. The familiar red clay resurrected not-so-fond childhood memories of chopping up dirt clods in her parents' garden. She wiped the perspiration from her brow with the back of her hand. She was glad she wore no makeup. In the heavy humidity it would probably clump on her face like the large clods of clay.

The freshly turned soil provided evidence that Jake had been there. But where was he, and where was his faithful canine? She smiled. How many times had she seen Buckshot lie between nearby rows while Jake hoed?

Perhaps Jake had sought refuge from the sun. She headed down a long row toward the Resting Place, a small grassy spot under a shade tree at the back corner of the garden. Halfway down the furrow she found Jake's hoe haphazardly lying across two rows of tomato plants. Several tender plants had broken under the weight of the hoe.

A wave of apprehension washed over her and her throat tightened. Jake wouldn't just drop his hoe in the middle of the garden. She hollered toward the Resting Place, "Jake!" Buckshot immediately raised his head above the tall grass. The fear that clutched at her throat relaxed its grip. Jake could not be very far away as Buckshot always stayed by his side.

She continued toward the Resting Place, her eyes searching for movement along the tree line that surrounded the garden. She stopped abruptly when she saw a body lying in the grass.

Adrenaline flowed through her veins, pounding its way through her arms and legs.

She dropped the lemonade and the mail and ran toward the body.

"Jake! Jake!"

He didn't answer.

❦ CHAPTER 3 ❦

Megan looked up from her bank teller window to see who was next in line. The man looked away when she caught him staring. He wore faded blue jeans, a T-shirt with the Campbell University logo, a well-worn baseball cap, and large brown-rimmed glasses. He reminded her of the Harry Potter character.

She suppressed a laugh. "Next."

The man jumped to life, knocking over the chrome-plated stanchion. *Clang!* The metal stanchion rattled against the marble floor. He righted the stanchion, re-clipped the burgundy rope, and moved forward to the teller window. His face grew bright red.

She struggled to keep a straight face. "May I help you?"

"I'd like to make . . ." He dropped his deposit slip and stopped mid-sentence, bending to retrieve the slip.

She rolled her eyes. What a loser.

The man spoke with a slow country drawl, his face even redder. "I'd like to make a deposit."

She grinned, took the check and deposit slip from the man's hand, and began to process the transaction. She could feel his eyes fixed on her. "Cash back?"

The man stirred from his obsession. "Huh?"

She leaned forward and exaggerated her pronunciation, "Do you want any cash back?"

"No." He adjusted his ball cap. "By the way, I'm Daniel."

She ignored him and kept processing the transaction. Men—they were all alike. Any second now he would ask her for a date. She laid the deposit receipt on the cherry countertop. "Is there anything else I can help you with?"

The man took the receipt and put it into his wallet. He glanced behind, then leaned forward and softened his voice. "I thought . . . maybe . . ."

"Megan, you have a phone call . . . again."

Megan looked up at the branch manager of the Glendale Bank and Trust. Ms. Howser stood with her hands on her wide hips, a sour expression on her face.

"Yes ma'am. I'll be there in a second." She placed a "CLOSED" tent sign in her teller window and smiled at the man. "I've got to go. Have a pleasant day."

She headed to the phone in one of the windowed offices. She longed to occupy one of those offices as a loan officer or maybe as the branch manager. But that would never happen as long as Ms. Howser ruled the office. Ms. Howser resented her for some reason.

Who would be calling her at the bank on Thursday morning? She was going to get fired if she kept getting personal calls. She lifted the phone, released the hold button, and turned away from Ms. Howser's penetrating stare. "Hello. This is Megan Thompson."

"Miss Thompson, this is Paulette Jones, the school administrator at Little People Skool. Please come and remove Ethan from our day care immediately."

Megan squeezed her eyes shut and leaned back against the wall. Not again—he hadn't even been there a week. "Mrs. Jones, what has he done? Surely, we can work something out."

Megan heard nothing but heavy breathing on the other end of the phone. Where was she going to find another sitter for Ethan? "I need some time to find another . . ."

Mrs. Jones interrupted. Her voice was as cold as the winter's wind. "You need to come and get the monster now and don't bring him back." The phone clicked, and the line went dead.

Megan continued to hold the phone to her ear. She gasped and covered her mouth with her free hand. What had Ethan done this time? She looked up and saw Ms. Howser standing with her arms crossed and tapping her foot. "She is so going to fire me when I tell her I need the rest of the day off," she muttered under her breath.

Daniel claimed a corner table at the Glendale Roaster, booted up his laptop, and awaited the moment of truth. The small coffee shop was quiet for a Thursday morning. He inhaled the aroma of freshly baked pastries, an assortment of recently brewed coffees, and a variety of flavored additives. He tapped the tabletop and gazed at the hourglass on the screen. Observing the laptop's boot-up process was like watching a lawn grow.

The image of the gorgeous young bank teller came back to his mind. Her long brown hair streaked with blonde highlights fell across her shoulders in a gentle wave. She had dark brown eyes and an olive complexion. Her nametag had read Megan Thompson, but her name was not familiar. She had to be close to his age, yet he didn't recognize her from high school. He definitely would have remembered a girl with her figure.

He took a sip from his coffee and opened the Campbell University website. It had been almost two weeks since his last exam. Surely his grades had been posted. He swallowed hard. He felt good about all of his classes except Constitutional Law. He'd spent more time on that course than the others combined. Yet, he'd struggled with the course from the first day of the semester. He had to pass. It was a prerequisite for several other courses.

The webpage finally opened. He nervously scanned down the screen and read the grades in a whisper: "Civil Procedure II, 'B;' Contracts II, 'C;' and Torts II, 'C.'" The grades met his expectations. "Property II, 'B.'" Awesome—he must have aced the final exam. He glanced at the last grade posted and his heart sank. He sighed heavily and propped his forehead in his hand. An 'F'—how could he tell his father that he'd failed Constitutional Law?

Megan's stomach churned as she pulled into the Little People Skool parking lot. The red-brick building sat several hundred feet from the road with a neatly maintained lawn. The fenced playground behind the building lay dormant due to the midday heat. She stopped the car and sat in the driver's seat with both hands fixed on the steering wheel. Her heart ricocheted against the walls of her chest. She desperately needed to persuade Mrs. Jones to let Ethan stay because she was running out of child-care options. She released her grip on the steering wheel and dried her palms on her bright red skirt. She sighed deeply and opened the door. The smell of freshly cut grass greeted her. "Oh well, here goes nothing."

She'd barely gotten out of the car when the front door of the day care center opened. Mrs. Jones stepped out with Ethan in tow. She had a commanding grip on the child's wrist and pulled him along forcefully like a farmer dragging a stubborn mule. She carried his small backpack in her other hand. The defiant three-year-old leaned back and pulled against her with all his might. As Megan knew well, the three-foot child could put up quite a fight.

As soon as Ethan saw her, he charged past Mrs. Jones. "Mommy!" His abrupt change in direction nearly toppled the woman, and she let go of his wrist. He made a straight line for Megan.

She stooped and swept the child up in her arms. "Hey, darlin'." He buried his freckled face against her neck. A cowlick on his head tickled her chin.

Mrs. Jones arrived out of breath. Her face looked tight, and the veins in her neck stood out. "I thought you would never get here."

Megan forced a smile, trying to disarm the school administrator. "Mrs. Jones, what in the world has Ethan done to get him kicked out of your day care?"

Mrs. Jones narrowed her eyes and extended her arm with his backpack. "What hasn't the little brat done? He won't listen or obey and talks back to the teachers. He is downright mean. He bites the other students and kicks the teachers in the shins."

Megan had heard it all before and knew further protest was pointless. She took the backpack. Obviously, Mrs. Jones had already made up her mind and was determined to see the little boy leave her school.

Mrs. Jones pointed at the pack. "You'll find a check in the top compartment. The school is being very generous in that you're not being charged for the last three-and-a-half days."

Megan's first impulse was to tell the lady where she could stick the "generous" check, but she desperately needed the money. She swallowed her pride, and it left a bad taste in her mouth.

Without another word she turned and headed back to her car. She put Ethan down and used both hands to pull open the stiff-operating rear door. The beat-up '78 Corolla had more than three hundred thousand miles on it. She leaned into the car and repositioned the car-seat harness. She really needed to get a larger car seat. Ethan had outgrown this one. She turned to pick up Ethan, but he had disappeared. "Ethan!"

She rapidly circled the car but found no sign of him. The highway . . . he might be in the highway. She swallowed the rising panic in her throat and rushed toward the road. She frantically scanned the area through tear-blurred eyes and repeatedly screamed, "Ethan!" He didn't answer. Relieved at not finding his small body in the road or ditch, she wheeled around and surveyed the school property—the front lawn, the bushes next to the building, the entranceway, and the long chain-link fence that surrounded the playground. Finally, well down the fence line she saw him climbing the chain-link fence.

The tone of her voice changed from panic to irritation. She stood with her hands on her hips and yelled, "Ethan, you get down and come here." He ignored her call and continued climbing. Concerned for his safety, she rushed over and snatched him off the fence.

"No," he screamed, kicking and flailing both arms. "I wanna play!"

"Not now, Ethan. We've got to go. We'll come back some other time."

"Playground."

She lowered him to the ground and looked him in the eyes. His face was smudged with dirt. "Not now, darlin'. I've got to find someone to keep you so Mommy can go back to work."

He squirmed unsuccessfully against her grip. His face grew crimson red, his eyes narrowed, and then . . . he spit in her face.

A pulse of blinding rage surged through her body. The child let loose a pitiful blood-curdling scream, and she realized she'd slapped his face. She remained motionless for several seconds, shocked by what she'd just done.

She pulled the wailing child close and embraced him. Everyone in the school probably saw her slap Ethan. She felt a wrenching sensation in her chest like her heart was being ripped out, and the tears flowed. "What have I done? What kind of mother am I?"

As she carried Ethan back to the car, it started to drizzle. A convicting thought haunted her mind. "I'm not even fit to be a mother," she muttered softly.

❧ CHAPTER 4 ❧

Sadie stopped pacing when Dr. Gordon entered the ICU waiting room. "How is Jake?"

The small man in the white lab coat laid a reassuring hand on her forearm. "His condition is stable." He looked around the crowded room and pointed his clipboard in the direction of the hall. "Mrs. Hopkins, can we take a brief stroll?"

She examined his eyes. Her father had always said that people bearing bad news avoided eye contact. The doctor's eyes were unwavering. "Sure."

The frail doctor pushed open one of the swinging doors into the hallway and held it. The brightly lit hall was full of activity. A nurse's station located a short distance down the hall looked like a beehive as nurses, doctors, and orderlies darted back and forth. Unlike the waiting room, no one stood still long enough to overhear their conversation. She turned and faced the doctor.

He held up his hand like a policeman halting traffic. "Mrs. Hopkins, we have ruled out heat stroke."

She felt her mouth drop open. "If it's not heat stroke, then what is it?"

Dr. Gordon rubbed his goatee. "I'm not certain, but given all the symptoms, I believe it may be heart related."

She gasped and covered her mouth. "His heart? Jake hasn't been sick three times during our entire marriage."

Dr. Gordon glanced at his clipboard. "I ordered a complete battery of blood tests. The presence of a certain protein can indicate if Jake has had heart damage."

Her knees went weak. "Heart damage." She propped against the wall to steady herself.

Dr. Gordon reached for her arm. "Do you need to sit down?"

She shook her head. "I just need a moment."

Dr. Gordon released her arm. "We don't know if Jake has suffered heart damage. The results of the blood work are not back yet. It's just a standard diagnostic test we run to pinpoint the problem." He stroked his goatee. "The electrocardiogram during his stress test showed normal electrical activity. However, Jake couldn't finish the stress test. So, there's something abnormal going on. I ordered an echocardiograph for later this evening. It will show the blood flow through his heart and the efficiency of the chambers and valves."

She swallowed hard and tried to breathe slowly. "When will we know something?"

Dr. Gordon tucked the clipboard under his arm. "We should get the results sometime in the morning. As a precaution, I want to keep Jake here overnight and continuously monitor his condition."

Sadie stood next to Jake's hospital bed anxiously awaiting the doctor's return. Smaller than Frank's bedroom and twice as congested, the room also contained a well-worn recliner, a small table, a metal chair, and a rack with equipment monitoring Jake's vital signs. The tight quarters would have given her claustrophobia had it not been for a small window that overlooked the hospital parking lot.

She wiped the sleep from her eyes. The uncomfortable recliner and the constant sound of the monitoring equipment had made it a long, torturous night.

She stroked his arm and listened to his restful breathing. She admired his face. It was a strong face—a tanned leathery complexion with thick silver stubble. She looked out the window and saw it was raining. How depressing. She sat in the small metal chair next to his bed and kissed his forehead. She interwove her fingers in his, looked out the window at the morning rain, and waited for Dr. Gordon's verdict.

Jake raised the head of the hospital bed and yawned. His stomach growled from late morning hunger. A strong smell of bleach and pine cleaner permeated the air, and he heard the sound of a steady rainfall outside the window. Sadie sat next to the bed with her head lying on his hand. His fingers tingled as if injected with Novocain. He freed his hand and made a fist several times to restore circulation. He gently stroked her brunette hair and noted the numerous gray roots. He knew his antics at the garden had added to her gray. She stirred, and he spoke softly as he caressed her hair, "Baby, we're not spring chickens anymore. Time is catching up to us."

Sadie lifted her head and frowned. "Speak for yourself, old man. They say you're as young as you feel. Right now, I don't feel a day over a hundred." She dropped her head back on the bed, but immediately jerked to attention when someone knocked on the door.

"Hello. Dr. Gordon here. May I come in?"

Sadie quickly pushed her hair in place and patted it down. "By all means, Doctor."

The doctor pushed the door open. "It's kind of dark in here. Do you mind if I turn on the lights?"

Jake placed his hand on hers. "Go ahead. We were just making out."

Sadie rolled her eyes at him, and her cheeks blushed.

Dr. Gordon chuckled. "They say you never get too old for that."

The frail doctor had a warm smile. He sported a gray mustache and goatee that matched his thinning hair. He laid his clipboard on the foot of the bed and crossed his arms. "I've reviewed the test results. Your blood work looks normal. There are no signs of heart damage."

Sadie sighed. "Thank goodness."

Jake took a cleansing breath and exhaled slowly. "Great. So when can I take off this girly gown and go home?"

"Not so quick, Jake. Your stress test and echocardiograph revealed some abnormalities. Your oxygen levels are lower than expected, and the blood flow rate through your heart is less than desired."

He rubbed the back of his neck. "So, Doc, what are you saying?"

Dr. Gordon picked up his clipboard. "We really need an expert opinion. I'm going to refer you to a friend of mine, a gifted heart specialist at Duke Medical Center. My assistant has already made the arrangements. You'll be transported by medical van tomorrow."

Jake's pulse quickened. He feared very few things in life, but heart conditions could be life threatening. He remembered his helpless state at the garden. He spotted Sadie's tear-filled eyes. What about Sadie? She needed him. He couldn't afford to leave her. She still had some unresolved issues.

She took his hand. Her hands felt soft and warm. He always enjoyed her delicate touch. They could communicate with each other without ever speaking a word, one of many benefits from a long marriage. At this moment, she communicated warmth and comfort, the very things he needed.

Dr. Gordon took on a serious expression. "Jake, you're a heavy smoker. Aren't you?"

He cleared his throat. "Well . . ."

Sadie pinched his hand and responded. "Very heavy."

His face tightened, and he gave her a stern look. He didn't like where the conversation was headed.

"Jake, your smoking is likely the cause of your present condition," Dr. Gordon said. "Now is an excellent time to quit. After all, you aren't allowed to smoke in hospital rooms, here or at Duke."

Sadie wagged her finger at Jake.

Megan and Ethan finally arrived home at eight o'clock in the evening. She turned off the ignition and listened to the soft patter of rain. What a long and disappointing day. She looked through the rain-splattered windshield at the place she called home and frowned.

She wished for a cloud of darkness to hide the eyesore, but with her limited income, the dilapidated trailer was the best she could rent. The tall grass looked like a jungle around the small, rusty trailer, and several vinyl skirting panels were missing.

She let out an exasperated huff and stepped into a steady rain. Her thin blouse soaked up the cold rain like a sponge and prompted an army of chill bumps to surface on her back. She gently lifted Ethan's limp body from his car seat and hurried through the rain to the trailer. With any luck, he would sleep the rest of the night. She could surely use the break. She felt whipped after dragging Ethan around the entire day. Her remaining energy drained at the prospect of spending the weekend in search of a sitter. If she didn't find child care before Monday morning, she would have to find a new employer as well.

She struggled to hold Ethan in one arm and unlock the front door. She pushed the door open and flipped on the light switch. The single bulb in the den fixture momentarily lit the dark room and then blew. She cursed. She laid Ethan on the well-worn couch and found the kitchen light switch. The sudden illumination exposed three large cockroaches scurrying to the safety of the crack between the countertop and the wall. She gasped. "What a dump. I'm so sick of living this way that I can't take it anymore."

❧ Chapter 5 ❧

Sadie traveled home from the hospital in deep thought, a woman on a mission. She stepped through the mental checklist of things she needed to do before they left for Duke Medical Center. Buckshot needed fresh water and several days of food. She needed to shower, grab some clothes, get the mail, and—oh, yeah—get Jake's Bible. He wouldn't forgive her if she forgot it. He sure spent a lot of time reading from that thing. Apparently, he had an insatiable appetite for the Word that drove him to get up before sunrise every morning and read for an hour. She, on the other hand, labored to read the Bible and avoided it.

The rain had stopped during the night. She squinted as she drove toward the bright morning sun. Her mind shifted gears, and she thought about the doctor's preliminary prognosis—heart trouble—an unfair turn of fate. Jake had slaved for the last forty-seven years at the Glendale Furniture Factory, and now only two months into his retirement, he'd been stricken with this "heart thing." Why would a good and loving God allow this to happen? Had God himself stricken Jake for some reason? Her face tightened.

She stopped the car at the mailbox, retrieved the mail, and pressed the door back in place. It would be a while before Jake replaced the mailbox. Could it be he might never be well enough to perform such a simple task?

She looked up the long driveway toward the small one-story stone house. Located at the crest of a hill, their little castle provided a commanding view of their property. They had been gone for fewer than forty-eight hours. Yet, the place seemed strangely abandoned.

Buckshot stepped off the large covered front porch as she rolled to a stop. The old dog stretched one back leg and then the other. He fanned his tail in recognition.

She got out of the car, and the dog immediately rolled over on his back with his belly exposed. She couldn't keep the smile off her face. "Want your belly scratched, do you?"

She stooped and scratched the dog's belly. The canine grunted with gratitude as she ran her hand back and forth. "Bet you're waiting for Jake. Aren't you?" Her mouth tightened and her voice trailed off. "He won't be home for several days."

She stood and looked down the driveway at the Carving Tree. It grew more yellow with each passing day, and numerous leaves had collected on the ground beneath the tree. "Buckshot, what's going on with the Carving Tree? It's always healthy and majestic this time of year."

She walked down the drive, past the faint smell of dying honeysuckle blooms, toward the beech. Buckshot followed at her heels. She paused a short distance from the tree. Buckshot sat on one hip and looked at her with his tired brown eyes.

She spoke to the dog like one of her fourth grade students. "I don't understand, Buckshot."

He cocked his head and raised one floppy ear.

31

"Unlike most deciduous trees, the leaves of the beech usually stay pretty and green well into fall. Leaf abscission doesn't usually occur until early spring when the new growth pushes off the dead leaves." She lumbered to the tree and ran her hand over the smooth gray bark. She traced the arrow that pierced the heart-shaped carving. The deeply cut groove felt rough to her touch. It had expanded and deepened over the last forty-six years.

Sadie tried to relax in the hospital recliner next to Jake's bed. The strong smell of bleach reminded her of their present location. She lay with her eyes shut, feet propped up, and arms crossed. She certainly had not slept well the last few nights in the hospital. Though her body was tired, her mind was racing. She drew in a deep breath and exhaled slowly.

After two days of being treated like a guinea pig in Duke Medical Center, she could sense her easygoing husband had grown irritable. He didn't like being cooped up. He enjoyed the wide-open spaces and loved to do things with his hands. Above all, he didn't like for others to be in control of his life. Perhaps his unwillingness to obey the doctor's directives concerned her the most. How do you tell a man who has smoked all his life that he can't smoke? How do you place physical limitations on such an active person?

A loud knock at the door startled her from her semiconscious state. Her eyes snapped open, and Jake stirred. Was the knock a dream or the real thing? She heard a gruff voice. "Dr. Bradford here."

She battled to return the recliner to an upright position, smoothed her hair with her hand, and stood to greet the doctor.

"Yes. Please come in." The moment they had anxiously awaited all morning had arrived. Hopefully, Dr. Bradford would shed some light on the extent of Jake's condition.

The elderly doctor entered the room. His hair resembled retreating snow on a warm day. Tiny reading glasses were perched on the tip of his nose, and a stethoscope hung from his neck. He stood with badly hunched posture. Evidence, she thought, of spending too much time poring over medical books and too little time with physical exercise.

The doctor propped on the arm of a chair, half-standing and half-sitting, and opened the folder containing Jake's medical records. His bushy eyebrows rose and fell as he silently scanned several pages. Occasionally he said, "Hmm."

She tapped her fingers impatiently on a small table near the foot of Jake's bed and exhaled sharply. The doctor certainly had wonderful bedside manners and interpersonal skills. She admired the beautiful flower arrangement that sat on the table. The tag read, "Constantly in our prayers, Glendale Baptist Church."

"Ahemm." Jake cleared his throat. His brown eyes looked stern and darker than normal. She knew his patience had expired.

Through the open doorway Sadie watched two nurses standing in the hallway. They giggled as they shared some private joke. She wished for a more cheerful occasion like the birth of a new grandchild.

Finally, the doctor looked up over his reading glasses and said, "Mr. Hopkins, your LVEF is only 20 percent."

Jake frowned. "So, when can my L-V-E-F go home?"

She scowled at Jake and placed her index finger to her lips.

The doctor's eyes glared over the top of his reading glasses. His voice grew gruffer. "You have a condition known as dilated cardiomyopathy, and it's in a rather advanced state."

She leaned forward and fanned her face. She couldn't take the suspense any longer. "Dr. Bradford, we didn't graduate from medical school. Could you please speak English, and tell us what is wrong with Jake?"

Dr. Bradford closed the folder and laid it on the bed. He removed his low-riding glasses, folded them, and dropped them into the pocket of his white lab coat. His lips formed a straight line, and he looked directly at her. She felt very small all of a sudden.

"Mrs. Hopkins," he said in a very authoritative voice. "Your husband has a serious heart condition. Dilated cardiomyopathy is a weakening of the heart muscle that causes the left ventricle to perform at less than normal capacity."

She swallowed. At a loss for words, she stared out of the small hospital window at several gray clouds. She wanted to ignore the doctor's prognosis, but his words filtered through her brain and down into her soul. A serious heart condition—people often died from heart trouble. She'd heard that heart disease was one of the leading causes of death in the United States.

She needed more detail and turned toward the doctor. "What did you say about Jake's LV-something-or-other?"

The doctor walked around the bed closer to Sadie. "LVEF stands for left ventricular ejection factor. It's a measure of the heart's efficiency. The LVEF of a normal heart is 50 percent. Jake's LVEF is only 20 percent."

Jake cleared his throat. "And what does that mean?"

"It means your heart is not pumping enough blood. That's why you feel faint and weak when you overexert yourself."

Jake tilted his head back and stared at the ceiling. His jaw muscles flexed as he gritted his teeth. The room fell silent except for the doctor's loud breathing.

She placed her hand over her heart. This definitely did not sound good.

Jake broke the silence. "So, what's the fix?"

Dr. Bradford rubbed his eyes and then looked directly at Jake. "I'm afraid the damage to the heart muscle is irreversible. The best we can do is try to manage your condition."

She moved to Jake's side and placed her hand on his arm. "What exactly do you have in mind, Doctor?"

"I'm going to prescribe several medications that should help Jake's condition: an ACE inhibitor, a beta blocker, and a diuretic. The ACE inhibitor will dilate the blood vessels so the heart does not have to work as hard. The beta blocker will reduce the effect of adrenaline on the body. Studies have shown that beta blockers improve the survival rate of patients with heart problems. The diuretic, or water pill, will help reduce the excess fluid in the lungs that is responsible for shortness of breath. It will also help reduce leg swelling that often occurs in patients with dilated cardiomyopathy." He turned and looked at Jake. "We'll keep you in the medical center for a few more days, at least until we get the dosages regulated properly."

She gently stroked her husband's forearm. "Doctor, what caused Jake's condition?"

Dr. Bradford scratched his head. "It could be from any number of causes yet to be determined—coronary artery disease, a previous viral infection, diabetes, a variety of inflammatory diseases, or even heavy smoking." The doctor pointed a finger at Jake. "Oh, by the way, Mr. Hopkins, you must give up smoking. Do you understand?"

CHAPTER 6

Megan stealthily slipped out onto the front steps of the Grecian-style building and paused behind a column. Her eyes darted from side to side as she took in her surroundings. She scanned the sidewalks and the small park across the street. All was clear except for a man sitting on a park bench across the road reading the paper. She certainly did not want to be seen by anyone who knew her. It would be so embarrassing that she would die. She could hear it now. "Megan lost another job, and now she's mooching off the state." Ms. Howser had not treated her fairly and had fired her because "she took too many personal calls and needed too much time off." She couldn't help she had motherhood responsibilities. She suspected the reason ran much deeper. Perhaps, Ms. Howser's treatment stemmed from jealousy related to Megan's ability to attract men.

She studied the man on the park bench. Given his tailored suit and the expensive-looking briefcase sitting at his feet, he looked like a very successful businessman. The man noticed her interest and smiled. Her face grew warm. She pretended to be looking beyond him at something in the park. The man looked down at his watch, folded his paper neatly, and stood. He tucked the paper under his arm and headed down Main Street. She started down the steps. Then she saw it—the briefcase—still sitting under the park bench.

He must have been so preoccupied with some big business deal that he'd forgotten it.

She started to yell at him but decided not to draw attention to herself while in front of the unemployment office. She hurried across the street, snatched up the briefcase, and scurried after the man. The expensive case had shiny brass latches and hardware and had intricate patterns engrained in the leather. Fortunately the man walked slowly, apparently engrossed in some business strategy. She caught him before he reached the end of the block. "Excuse me, sir. You forgot your briefcase."

The man stopped, looked down at his empty right hand, and then wheeled around. His eyes locked on the briefcase.

She extended her arm with the case.

He smiled and took it. "Thank you very much. I can't believe I left it behind. I have some very important papers in it. It's most kind of you to return it to me." He sat the briefcase down on the ground and reached for his wallet. "Let me pay you something. You certainly deserve a reward."

She looked down at the cracks in the sidewalk. A reward— she sure could use the money with no job and a stack of bills piling up, but her conscience wouldn't let her take the man's money. She looked the man in the eyes. "Oh, no sir. I couldn't take any of your money. I didn't do anything to deserve it, really."

The man put his wallet back into his pocket. "I was just headed to lunch. At least let me treat you to lunch. It's the very least I can do."

She momentarily looked at his face and then toward the park. The attractive man, most likely in his late twenties, had a nice smile. "Well . . ."

"Say yes. I won't have a clear conscience unless you do."

She fiddled with the zipper on her pocketbook. "I guess it would be all right."

The man smiled. "Wonderful." He extended his hand. "I'm Jonathan Parrish. It's a pleasure to meet you."

She felt the warmth of his hand and the rush of blood to her cheeks. She smiled and forced herself to look directly at him. "I'm Megan Thompson. It's nice to meet you, too."

He glanced down the street. "Perhaps you could recommend a restaurant. I'm not from around here."

She looked up into the clear blue sky for a moment as she contemplated their options. "There are not a lot of places close by, but Juanita's Diner is around the corner. The food is pretty good."

"Then Juanita's Diner it is."

She suddenly became aware of the sweet aroma from the park's blooming rose garden.

Megan sipped on her sweet iced tea and scowled at the restaurant walls covered with old-fashioned baskets and cooking utensils. Mr. Parrish wouldn't be accustomed to the little diner's country atmosphere. He probably ate in places where the tables were covered in elegant white linens, not gingham tablecloths. However, the selection of restaurants was very limited in the small town of Glendale, and Mr. Parrish did not seem to mind.

She cleared her throat. "Juanita is known for her homemade biscuits. You need to try one."

Jonathan smiled and took a biscuit from the basket on the table. "I believe I will."

She studied Jonathan. He looked like the picture of success—neatly pressed long-sleeved white shirt, gold cuff links, and a five-hundred-dollar suit. She admired his smile and short brown hair. What brought such a good-looking and successful businessman to Glendale?

Megan savored the last bite of chocolate cream pie, thoroughly content with both the meal and the company.

Jonathan looked at his watch. "Megan, I still have a two o'clock meeting up the street. I've really enjoyed our lunch." He laid two twenties next to his plate and picked up his coat. "I own a flourishing modeling agency in Charlotte. I'm always on the lookout for young, attractive, and intelligent ladies." He pulled a business card from the pocket of his jacket and pushed it across the table. "If you ever want a fresh start, give me a call. I believe you have the look we're seeking."

She smiled. "Thanks. I just might do that." She watched him exit the restaurant into the brilliant sunshine. Such a gentleman— and he's good-looking to boot. She picked up the business card. The Right Look Modeling Agency . . . and he thinks I have the look they're seeking. She grinned and basked in his flattery. She pictured herself in an elegant evening gown parading before the top fashion brass and setting the latest trends. Wouldn't it be great to escape her past and start over in a place where people didn't know of her failures, broken relationships, and illegitimate son?

❀ CHAPTER 7 ❀

Jake heard a knock at the door and pulled the sheet up to his abdomen to cover the skimpy hospital gown.

Sadie answered the door. "It's Clyde and Erma."

He elevated the hospital bed to greet his old friends. Erma's hands shook as she handed a potted plant to Sadie. He recognized the early stage of Parkinson's disease.

Erma spoke in her typical Southern drawl, "We thought we'd come by and sit with y'all for a spell."

Sadie held the potted plant at eye level. "Oh look, Jake, a pink azalea. Isn't it gorgeous?"

He saluted Clyde. "Very nice. You can never have enough azaleas, especially in the spring."

Clyde returned the salute with a boney hand. "What'd you say?"

Jake spoke a little louder. "I said you can never have enough azaleas."

Clyde nodded and wiped the perspiration from the top of his shiny head with his palm. "Yeah, it does feel a heap lot better in here. Real scorcher outside."

Erma added, "Clyde rooted it himself, don't you know."

Sadie set the plant on the table at the foot of Jake's bed next to a large flower arrangement. "You're our third group of visitors today." She pointed at the large flower arrangement. "Pastor Nolan brought these on Monday. They still look fresh after four days."

Jake surveyed the leggy azalea. It looked out of place sitting beside the handsome arrangement. The elderly couple came and stood next to the bed. It seemed to him that they had been married forever. Clyde wore the typical attire of an old-fashioned tobacco farmer. The ever-present World War II medal adorned his shirt. Jake scratched his head. He wondered if Clyde pinned the Bronze Star to his pajamas every night.

Jake couldn't help but smile at Erma. She wore a black-and-white striped dress and matching hat. A large red pocketbook hung from the crook of her arm. The image of a plump zebra with large red lips passed through his mind.

Erma planted a big kiss on his forehead. "Well, bless your heart. How are you feeling, shugah?"

He felt the wet spot on his forehead. He didn't have to look in the mirror to know his face bore large red lip prints. Sadie's silly smirk confirmed it. "I'm doing well, thank you."

Erma turned up her nose and sniffed. "What's that awful smell?"

He lifted a silver plate cover on the hospital tray before him and pointed at the leftovers. "If I could identify what's laying in that plate, I could tell you what that strange smell is."

Sadie cleared her throat. "If you could identify what's *lying* in your plate."

He huffed at her. Her grammatical corrections, a symptom of too many years of teaching, seemed constant. "Yeah, like I said, if I knew what was *laying* in my plate, I could tell you what that smell is."

Clyde pinched his nose shut and tilted his head back. "Pe-u-wee! You actually ate that stuff?"

Jake nodded. "It's better than what they served for breakfast the past five days."

Erma twisted the gaudy red beads that hung from her neck. "Law, honey, I bet you're tired of hospital food. Just wait till you get home. Clyde and I will drop by with a big bowl of my famous nana pudding."

Jake returned the plate cover and glanced at Sadie. She rolled her big green eyes at him. Great, he couldn't wait for Erma's famous banana pudding. Last time he'd eaten it, the bananas had reminded him of rubber, and he'd picked pieces of eggshell from his teeth for two days. He forced a half-hearted response. "Please don't go to any trouble for me." He noticed Sadie remained silent on the matter.

Clyde hooked both thumbs in his suspenders and rocked back and forth. "I see they gotcha on one of those IV things and hooked up to a bunch of electronic gadgets. So, what does the doc say? When are you going home?"

Jake frowned. "He says I have dilated cardio-something-or-other."

Clyde cupped a hand to his ear. "What'd you say?"

"Dilated cardiomyopathy," Sadie yelled.

Jake sighed. "It must be serious. It takes a school teacher to pronounce it."

Clyde chuckled. "Sounds like something a pregnant woman would have."

Erma slapped Clyde's arm. "Clyde!"

Sadie frowned and responded in a serious tone. "It's a weakening of the heart muscle. The doctor says Jake's heart isn't pumping enough blood."

Jake cleared a smoker's tickle from his throat. "Doctor says I can go home in a few days, as soon as he can find the right dosage of medication to stabilize my condition."

Erma clutched Sadie's forearm. "Honey, I heard you found Jake lying in the garden. You must have been downright terrified."

Sadie nodded. "I was scared stiff. He was lying face down in the grass, and Buckshot was licking his ear. I thought he'd had a heat stroke or something."

Jake shifted in bed. "That's what I thought, too. I was hoeing around the tomato plants when my arms got heavy, and I couldn't catch my breath. I moved over to the shade, and next thing I knew Sadie was hovering over me."

"He's had several repeat performances while at the hospital," Sadie added. "I think he really alarmed the doctor during the stress test."

Clyde snapped a suspender with his thumb. "What caused the problem with your ticker?"

Jake scratched his head. "I don't think the doctor rightly knows what caused it. He said diabetes, kidney failure, an inflammatory disease, or a viral infection could have brought it on. I don't have kidney failure or diabetes."

Sadie shook her head and waved her finger at Jake. "Jake Earl Hopkins, you're ignoring the smoking." She turned to Clyde and Erma. "The doctor said his condition could have resulted from years of heavy smoking and that Jake must quit."

Jake suppressed a smoker's cough. Oh great . . . the cigarette thing again. "It's no big deal. I can quit anytime I want." The words rolled off his tongue easily, but going without cigarettes during the past week had been worse than the heart problem.

Clyde lifted his chin and spoke in a loud whiney voice. "You know, this place reminds me a lot of an army hospital I once spent two weeks in." He pointed to his right thigh. "I took some shrapnel right here in the leg. Have I ever told you how I rescued two of my fellow squad members?"

Jake rubbed the back of his neck. Oh no, not the Bronze Star story again. His eyes briefly met Sadie's weary eyes. He looked back at Clyde. "Yes, I believe you have. That was the reason for your medal, wasn't it?"

Clyde rocked back and forth on his feet. His voiced quickened. "It was 1941." His false teeth clicked as he talked. "I was a young whippersnapper . . ."

Clyde cranked the old F150 pickup and dropped his upper dentures into his damp shirt pocket. "These things are killing my gums."

Erma fastened her seat belt. "Try not to lose them again."

A bead of sweat ran down his back when he shifted the truck into drive. The old Ford didn't look like much, but it sure had given him many years of reliable service. He puttered up to the parking lot pay booth.

"Four dollars," the parking attendant said.

Clyde scratched the top of his head. "Four dollars! You mean it cost four bucks to park here for two hours?"

The attendant stared for a moment and then said, "I don't make the rules, sir."

Clyde sensed his lack of teeth disturbed the man. Why did a man's gums startle folks so? He paid the attendant and pulled onto the street. "It's a racket, ain't it? You got to pay to visit someone in the hospital. Somehow that jest don't seem right."

Erma nodded. "It's hotter in here than a tobacco barn during curing season. I wish you had AC in this old heap." She dabbed at her double chin with a hanky. "Sadie looked worn out. She looked worse than Jake. Don't you think?"

He grunted. He felt the medal flop against his chest when the truck hit a pothole.

Erma put her hand on the cracked dash to steady herself. "Land sakes alive—that was some pothole! They need to fix this road. I'm worried about Jake. This heart thing sounds very serious. Did I mention that Sadie looked worn out?"

"Uh-huh." The weight of the medal pressed against his chest. He stared at the road ahead and swallowed hard.

Erma took off her black-and-white striped hat and fanned her face with it. "Jake's been a heavy smoker nearly all his life, and now he's got to quit. Poor darlin' has a tough row to hoe."

He covered the Bronze Star with his hand. "Yep."

❦   CHAPTER 8   ❦

Sadie parked the car in the yard and smiled. Buckshot charged down the front porch steps and around the large azalea bed to greet her. His short, reddish fur glistened in the morning sun. He stopped at the driver side door. His tail fanned the air like a large furry whisk. She opened the door, and the dog's tail stopped. He whined and trotted to the passenger side door.

She frowned and got out. "Buckshot, you ungrateful mutt, aren't you going to welcome me home? I've been gone for two days."

Buckshot reared up on the side of the beige Impala and peeped through the window.

She scolded the dog. "Buckshot, get down!" What had gotten into the dog? They had taught him not to jump up on people's cars.

Buckshot dropped to the ground and walked toward her with his head hung low and tail tucked under. He looked at her with pitiful brown eyes.

She patted his head. "It's okay. It's been eleven days. I know you miss Jake." She scratched around the base of his ears, and the dog grunted. "The doctor says Jake will be coming home in a couple of days. I bet you'll like that. It'll be good to have Jake home again. Won't it, boy?"

The dog whimpered as if he understood her words.

Sadie took a refreshing shower, her first in several days, and put on clean clothes. She cherished her day at home, although being alone while Jake recovered in the hospital wasn't the way she desired to spend Memorial Day. This holiday was already difficult enough. She stepped out onto the front porch. Buckshot immediately jumped up from a sound sleep and charged off the porch into the yard.

"Get him, Buckshot."

The dog ran a squirrel up the Carving Tree. He circled the beech several times and then sat on his hindquarters and stared up into the branches. As if looking for approval, he repeatedly glanced between her and the tree.

She breathed in the fresh country air and enjoyed the beautiful morning. "Silly dog. You've been chasing those squirrels for years." She sat on the top porch step and watched the interplay between the squirrel and the dog. Buckshot would bark a "please come down" and then proceed to circle the tree. The squirrel would bush his tail, chatter angrily, and then change locations on the limb. His movement would start the whole process over again.

A layer of yellow and brown leaves nearly hid the red soil under the Carving Tree. In fact, the majority of the leaves on the beech appeared to be yellowing. She propped her chin in one hand and inspected the tree. The beech looked awful. She couldn't remember it ever looking this bad in the springtime. Its appearance was more like a beech in late fall. Two more leaves fluttered to the ground. The tree was sick . . . just like Jake. A startling thought came to her mind. The health of the beech had begun to deteriorate around the time she'd found Jake in the garden. It seemed like . . . The tears pooled in her eyes. She looked toward heaven. "Oh God, no. Not again."

A deep sadness flooded Erma's soul as she wiped clean the breakfast table. She'd felt it before. The sensation—an overwhelming compassion, a desire to help—stirred her to action. It resembled the sympathy invoked within her by missionary stories of starving children in foreign lands. She knew at once the Holy Spirit was prompting her to pray. She uttered softly, "Pray for whom?"

Just pray, the still small voice whispered to her soul.

She dropped the dishcloth in the sink and made her way through the den to her prayer closet. Clyde dozed in his recliner with the *Glendale Gazette* draped over him like a blanket. His head was tilted back, and his toothless mouth hung wide open.

A strong smell of mothballs greeted her nose when she opened the bedroom closet door. She flipped a switch and a single incandescent bulb dimly lit the small room. Clyde's clothing hung from a rod mounted to the right wall and her clothing hung from the left. Shelves above the clothes were loaded with large cardboard boxes that contained old clothes and mothballs. At the base of the rear wall rested two carpeted steps that Clyde had made at her request.

The closet served as her quiet place—a place where she could kneel before a mighty God, a God who answers prayers. Time and time again over the years, she'd witnessed His hand at work in response to her fervent, persistent, and often desperate petitions.

Numerous scriptural references had been carefully painted on the back wall of the closet. Erma wished her hand still possessed the steadiness required to paint the references. The one that caught her attention was Matthew 6:6. She recalled the passage. "But thou, when thou prayest, enter into thy closet, and when thou hast shut thy door, pray to thy Father which is in secret . . ." This very passage had prompted her to convert the rear of the closet into a prayer room.

She counted the creaking noises from her joints as she cautiously lowered herself to her knees. "Lord, if I get down here, you're going to have to help me up."

Just pray. The command was impressed upon her soul.

She poured out her heart to God. "What, Lord? Who, Lord? Why did you bring me to this place this morning?"

She heard a single word from the recesses of her mind, inaudible, yet strong and clear. *Sadie.*

Sadie had just leaned back in the recliner next to Jake's hospital bed when she heard a light tap on the door. "Hello. It's Maude. Are you decent?"

Sadie stood and glanced at Jake's bare leg. She gave him a smirk and pulled the sheet over his leg. "Come on in."

Maude peeped around the door. "Are you sure? I can come back later if it's a bad time."

Jake turned off the TV. "Nonsense. We're bored stiff."

Maude pranced into the room and handed Sadie a delicate flower arrangement. She wore a sleek pink dress that conformed to her slender body and carried a small purse to match. Her freshly teased hair and the strong smell of hairspray made it evident she'd combined her hospital visit with her weekly trip to the beauty salon.

Sadie placed the flower arrangement next to Clyde and Erma's potted azalea. "Such a pretty dress. Is it new?"

Maude stepped next to Jake. "Nothing special. Just something I found in the back of the closet."

Sadie's face tightened. She'd seen the dress in the display window of the Glendale Dress Barn a few days earlier. "Have a seat."

Maude touched Jake's arm. "Can't stay long. Just came by to check on my favorite hunk. How are you doing, honey?"

Sadie glared at Jake. Her single friend had a reputation of being man hungry.

Jake reached for the controller and raised the bed. "I'll be doing a lot better when I get out of this place and back in my garden."

A familiar voice called from the hallway. "Hi. Anybody home?"

Maude frowned and rolled her eyes.

Sadie slipped past her to greet the visitor. "Come on in, Mabel."

Mabel sauntered into the room holding a bouquet of "Get Well" balloons. She wore navy Bermuda shorts and a pale yellow blouse. A navy pocketbook hung from her shoulder. She stopped abruptly when she saw Maude. "Oh . . . I didn't know you had a visitor."

The small room suddenly seemed as cramped as an old-fashioned telephone booth.

Maude's eyes widened. "I was just leaving." She touched Jake's arm again. "You hurry up and get well. Okay?"

Jake nodded. "Thanks for coming by." He pulled his arm away and pointed at the flower arrangement. "And thanks for the flowers."

Maude cocked her chin in the air and marched past Mabel.

Sadie reached for the balloons. "Goodness. Are you two having another tiff?"

Mabel sighed heavily. "I guess you know Maude is on the hunt again. She has her sights on Sam Peterson."

Sadie placed the balloon anchor on the table. The balloons hovered above Maude's flower arrangement. "That's mighty quick. His wife only passed away six months ago."

"Maude has been dropping hints for him to ask her out for weeks. Well, last Sunday"—her gaze fell to her feet for a moment—"last Sunday, out of the blue, he asked me out." She fidgeted with the shoulder strap of her pocketbook. "Now she is accusing me of chasing him."

Sadie looked first at Jake and then back at Mabel. "Well, did you go out with him?"

Mabel's face reddened. "We had an innocent cup of coffee at Juanita's Diner along with her chocolate cream pie." She licked her lips. "That pie is to die for."

"Mabel."

"I couldn't help it. Sam is a good-looking fellow, and there aren't a lot of eligible bachelors in Glendale from which to choose. Besides, I have just as much right to date him as Maude."

Sadie swallowed hard. This argument promised to get real ugly, and she was caught right in the middle.

Megan looked at the water in the tub and sighed. She knew the final destination of the six inches of water—all over the floor. "That's enough water, honey."

Ethan sloshed back and forth in the tub and screamed at the top of his lungs, "More water! More water!" His carrot-colored hair was sudsy and slicked back. The freckles that speckled the majority of his skin highlighted his fair complexion. He slapped the water. The sudsy water splashed on her and the floor. "Boats need water! Boats want water!"

She wiped the soapy bath water from her face. It bore the strong fragrance of Mr. Bubble. She leaned forward on her knees. "I'll give you a little bit more, but you have to promise to keep it in the tub."

The child vigorously nodded.

Against her better judgment she turned on the faucet.

Ethan squealed with excitement, "Water, water!"

She stood and leaned against the doorjamb. Ethan pushed a small toy boat around in the tub and made motoring sounds. She scanned the small bathroom with disgust. Large sections of peeled paper hung from the wall, and the vinyl floor around the tub had dark stains where the floor had rotted. The run-down trailer reminded her of the slums in New York City. She sighed heavily, turned off the faucet, and stepped around the corner into her bedroom. She pushed the play button on the answering machine. "You have two unplayed messages."

She hurried back to the bathroom to keep an eye on Ethan. She propped against the doorframe with her arms crossed and the back of her head resting against the doorjamb.

"Message one." *Beep.* "Miss Thompson, my name is Jim Bollinger. I represent the Last Chance Collection Agency. You've apparently run up a very large debt on your credit card and have not paid the minimum payment in several months. Your credit card company has requested our agency get involved. I'd like to make an appointment with you to see what property can be liquidated to pay this debt. Please call me at 1-800-P-A-Y-B-A-C-K." *Beep.* "Received today, Tuesday, May 31st, at 10:20 a.m."

"Message two." *Beep.* "Hello, Miss Thompson, this is John Phipps down at Phipps' Convenience Mart. The bank notified me last Friday that your check for $20.36 has bounced. You need to come by and pay that amount plus a $25 fee for the returned check. Bring greenbacks because your checks are no good here." *Beep.* "Received today, Tuesday, May 31st, at 11:03 a.m."

She dropped her head to her chest and slid down the doorjamb until she sat on the floor in a fetal position. She buried her head in her hands and wept. What could she do? Where could she get the money to pay all these bills? The measly unemployment check wouldn't touch her debt. She was such a loser. She couldn't keep a job, couldn't keep a man, and couldn't provide for Ethan properly. Ethan's motoring sounds interrupted her thoughts. She wished she could be more like him, oblivious to everything and carefree.

Rrrriiinnnngggg! She jumped. The phone rang a second time. Did she dare answer it? Would it be more bad news? Her heart quickened. It rang a third time.

"Phone, mommy, phone," Ethan announced. She stood and leaned into the bedroom. The phone rang a fourth time and then the answering machine picked up. "Hi. This is the residence of Ethan and Megan Thompson. You know the routine. Leave your information and Ethan or I will get back to you as soon as possible."

Beep. "Miss Thompson." The familiar voice came slow and drawn out. "Sam Buckhalter here."

She stepped into the bedroom closer to the machine to hear her landlord. Just when she thought it couldn't get any worse, it had.

"Uh-hmmm. Got to have your rent money now. You're three months behind." He hesitated, and she stepped next to the machine.

The voice continued. "Ya need to pay up by the end of the week or git out." She heard a loud *click.*

She raked her fingers through her hair. There had been bad times before when life just seemed too big—like the time she told her parents and boyfriend about her pregnancy. Her parents had disowned her, and her boyfriend had left town. Her present situation certainly ranked right there with the worst of times. If she could just—

Ethan!

What about Ethan?

Her ears perked up, but she heard no sound from the bathroom—no splashing, no motoring sounds, nothing.

"Ethan," she screamed and ran back to the bathroom. She paused at the doorway hoping to catch a glimpse of her son, but did not see his small head above the side of the tub. An image of Ethan floating face down in the sudsy water flashed through her mind. She gasped and looked in the tub.

A wave of relief flowed over her, and she resumed breathing when she saw that Ethan had left the tub. Thank goodness. He hadn't drowned. But where had he gone, and what was he into? "Ethan, where are you?"

She turned and ran up the hall to the den. There he sat, completely naked, in front of the television. "Oh Ethan," she pulled the wet child close and hugged him.

"Mommy loves Ethan," he said.

She kissed his soapy scalp. "Yes, Mommy loves Ethan."

She fed Ethan and put him down for his afternoon nap. She sat on the couch to think. She had to figure out what to do about her debt, but most of all, what to do about her poor skills as a mother. Of all the things that had happened earlier in the day, her irresponsibility as a mother bothered her the most. Ethan could have easily drowned because of her negligence. In a period of just eleven days she had twice placed his life in jeopardy because of her carelessness. What was the matter with her anyway? She couldn't even protect him. Perhaps, as painful as it seemed, Ethan would be better off with foster parents—people who could provide him with all the good things in life, who could protect him, and who could teach him some discipline.

She reached into her purse to get a tissue to wipe her eyes. However, her hand found a business card instead. She wiped the tears from her eyes with the back of her hand and read "The Right Look Modeling Agency." A warm sensation spread through her body as she remembered the wonderful lunch she'd experienced with Jonathan Parrish several days earlier. But, most of all, she remembered his parting words, "If you ever want a fresh start, give me a call."

✿ CHAPTER 9 ✿

Sadie nervously looked at Jake and then knocked on the door of Dr. Bradford's study. After several moments she heard a gruff and rude voice. "Door's open."

Jake pushed the door open, and she stepped into the room. She felt the gentle touch of Jake's hand against the small of her back.

Dr. Bradford continued to pore over the documents on his mahogany desk. "Have a seat," he said without looking up. "I'll be with you in a moment."

She rolled her eyes at Jake, and he motioned toward two black leather chairs positioned in front of the desk. She sat and began to survey the doctor's study. The room, larger than their kitchen and den combined, contained floor-to-ceiling mahogany bookshelves along the wall to her right. Hundreds of medical books filled the shelves. A large black leather sofa occupied the left side of the room. Numerous diplomas and certificates covered the wall above the sofa. She looked back over her shoulder. Framed photographs, family she presumed, shrouded the entire rear wall. She frowned. Given the doctor's ill disposition, she found it hard to imagine *he* could have any family.

Dr. Bradford sat with his back to a huge picture window that provided a commanding view of the street six stories below. The high-back leather chair seemed to swallow the little man. His snowy white hair stood in sharp contrast to the black leather. His reading glasses were perched at the tip of his nose. His bushy eyebrows, like two furry white caterpillars, rose and fell as he read. He sipped from a steaming cup of coffee while studying the documents.

She inhaled the aroma of the hazelnut brew. Ummm. The doctor sure could use a lesson in hospitality.

"Uh-humm." Jake cleared his throat, and his tanned complexion grew red. She knew he had grown impatient with the doctor's rudeness. She held her finger to her lips to silence him.

Finally, the doctor removed his reading glasses and laid them on the desk. He looked first at her and then Jake. "Mr. Hopkins, given your condition, I felt it was imperative we have this little consultation before I released you. Your advanced state of dilated cardiomyopathy is quite serious. I've placed you on three prescription drugs that should help, and during the last few days I've been able to get your medication regulated properly and your condition stabilized. It's crucial you take this medication daily."

Dr. Bradford looked directly at her. "Mrs. Hopkins, you must make sure he takes his medication on a regular basis."

She glared at Jake. "You can rest assured. He *will* take his medicine. Won't you, Mr. Hopkins?"

Jake frowned. "Quit treating me like one of your fourth graders."

"While we are on the subject of quitting," the doctor's voice grew stern, "you must also give up your smoking habit, Mr. Hopkins. I can't say for certain, but a lifetime of smoking is the most probable cause of your condition."

Jake's jaw muscles twitched as he ground his teeth. She knew it would be difficult for Jake to overcome his addiction. He'd already been struggling from withdrawal. He'd been very irritable since entering the smoke-free hospital environment. He'd always told her that he could stop smoking at any time. However, a fifty-year habit had to be difficult to break.

Jake exhaled loudly. "Look, Doctor, is that really necessary? I've never been sick a day in my life."

"But"—the doctor hesitated for emphasis—"you are now. In fact, you're very sick. I'm not sure you understand the seriousness of your condition. Your heart's pumping capacity is only about 40 percent of normal. You need to be very careful that you don't overexert yourself. It could bring on ventricular fibrillation."

She gasped. Hadn't she heard that the term "fibrillation" meant an erratic heartbeat? "Doesn't the medication fix that?"

The doctor nodded. "It will help a little, but I'm afraid there aren't any miracle drugs."

Jake stood and walked to the large glass window. He seemed lost in the activity on the street below.

She watched her husband. This had to be very difficult for Jake, as he was the most active person she knew. It would be like placing hobbles on a racehorse.

Jake turned and faced the doctor. "I take it that this ventricular-fib thing is bad."

The doctor straightened a stack of papers on his desk and said, "Why don't you take a seat, Mr. Hopkins."

She found it difficult to swallow.

Jake placed his hands on his hips and looked the doctor straight in the eye. His large muscular frame and intense brown eyes had to be intimidating to the small doctor. "Shoot straight, Doctor."

She braced for the doctor's bad news.

The doctor drew in a deep breath, held it, and then exhaled loudly. "Mr. Hopkins, ventricular fibrillation is a rapid, chaotic arrhythmia that brings an immediate halt to all productive ventricular contractions. In plain English, all meaningful blood flow stops. This is followed by a loss of consciousness within seconds and then death."

At the doctor's words, her heartbeat became erratic and her breathing grew rapid and shallow. The room began to slowly spin, and the walls began to close in around her. The words "immediate" and "death" reverberated loudly in her ears . . . and then . . . all was silent.

Jake sat in silence and watched the countryside from the passenger window of the beige Chevy Impala. He was pleased to have finally left the hospital. Yet, the rainy countryside looked gloomy.

He glanced at Sadie. Her collar-length brunette hair looked like it had been caught in a wind tunnel, and her mascara had run down her cheeks. She seemed to have physically recovered from her fainting spell in Dr. Bradford's study. However, he knew she suffered from emotional shock. Except to insist that she drive, Sadie had hardly spoken the entire way home. The doctor had indeed dropped a bomb on them. They had long planned for an active retirement together. Now, two months after retiring from the furniture factory, he'd learned he would have to live the rest of his life—however long that might be—paralyzed by a bad heart. Where was the justice in that? He'd given the furniture factory forty-seven years of his life. He could count on one hand the number of days he'd missed work due to an illness. Now that the time had finally arrived to enjoy life, to travel, and to see the world with Sadie, every day would be a sick day.

He looked at an old cigarette butt in the car's ashtray, one of his for sure. It tugged at him like the pull of a magnet on iron filings. Boy, he sure could use a drag. He pushed the ashtray closed. He could taste the tobacco in his mouth and the warm smoke penetrating his throat and lungs. The doctor's stern words came back to him: ". . . a lifetime of smoking is the most probable cause of your condition." He swallowed the excess saliva in his mouth.

Sadie slowed the car to a crawl when they fell in behind a teenager riding a bicycle. When the oncoming lane cleared, she pulled around the cyclist. The boy struggled to pedal the bike up the steep hill in the misty rain. Jake sympathized with the boy. He struggled as well. How would he cope with his new limitations? He could never be content to sit around and do nothing. Someone had to tend to the house, the garden, and the forty acres. *Dear God, why is this happening to me? I don't understand. How can I possibly bring you glory with a bad heart? I won't be able to help people anymore. Who will mow Widow Cowan's yard? How can I take fresh vegetables to the residents at the nursing home if I can't hoe my garden? Who will make the carpentry repairs at church? Where are you in this, Lord? I simply don't understand why this is happening.* Isaiah 40:28 came to mind. He had been trying to internalize the verse—to memorize the words and to apply them to his life. "Hast thou not known? Hast thou not heard, that the everlasting God, the Lord, the Creator of the ends of the earth, fainteth not, neither is weary? There is no searching of his understanding." The last phrase bounced around in his mind. Could he be incapable of understanding God's omniscient wisdom, the wisdom of the Creator?

He watched as a silver Lexus passed them in a no-passing zone. "Wonder where they're going in such a hurry."

Sadie glanced at him and replied in a pinched voice, "Some people think they are above the law."

Her eyes, clouded with tears, made it clear she'd been contemplating the doctor's words. He reached over and placed his hand on her thigh. Instinctively, Romans 8:28 rolled off his tongue. "And we know that all things work together for good to them that love God, to them who are the called according to His purpose."

Sadie frowned and looked at him through squinted eyes. "I can't find anything good in this," she replied sternly.

He looked away from her penetrating gaze just in time to see brake lights in front of them. "Sadie, look out!"

✿ CHAPTER 10 ✿

The tires squealed, and Jake reached for the dash to brace for impact. With his other hand, he reached for Sadie like a parent protecting a young child. The Impala broke traction on the wet pavement and slid toward the rear of the silver vehicle. *Clunk.* He grimaced at the sound of the bumper-to-bumper impact.

He surveyed the car's interior. Sadie sat rigidly in her seat, her white-knuckled hands still locked on the steering wheel. Outside the rain had stopped, but a large cloud blocked the sun. The driver-side door of the Lexus swung open, and a sharply dressed lady emerged from the car. The slender woman wore a short navy skirt—a little too short in his opinion—a lacy white blouse, and a matching navy jacket. Her straight black hair, accented with silver highlights, reached her shoulders. He pulled the door handle.

Sadie grabbed his arm. "You stay here. I'll handle this." She brushed the tears from her cheeks. "The last thing you need right now is stress."

He fought the urge to snap back and state she was the main source of stress, but he didn't need to make matters worse.

Sadie climbed out and met the lady at the front of the car. He watched over the hood of the Impala as the scene unfolded. The young woman stood with her hands on her hips and shook her head as she looked at her car. He might have found her attractive if her face bore the slightest smile. But her sour scowl overshadowed any physical beauty. Sadie looked fragile. She held her left hand to her forehead as if she had a painful migraine headache. This didn't look good. Whether she wanted it or not, Sadie needed reinforcement.

The pungent odor of hot asphalt greeted him as he eased the door open. It reminded him of the hot, oily smell of new pavement. Sadie took a deep breath when she saw him exit the car. He touched his lips to silence her protest and walked to the front of the Impala.

The boy on the bicycle passed. He would probably reach his destination well before they did. Jake tried to assess the damage, but the cars sat too close. "Sadie, please back up our car a little." He couldn't help but compare the two cars. Their beige Impala, with its outdated body style, had sun-baked paint. The sporty silver Lexus, on the other hand, looked like it had been lifted from the latest cover of a *Car and Driver* magazine. Just like its driver, it reeked of money.

After Sadie moved the Impala, he squatted and inspected both cars. The Impala's tarnished metal bumper showed no signs of damage. He ran his hand over the sleek plastic bumper of the Lexus. The painted surface, smooth and even, contained one small scuff mark. He groaned as he straightened his stiff back and turned to the young woman. "No real damage. Just a small scuff mark on your bumper." He waved a car around the two vehicles. "I guess we should call the highway patrol though. Do you have a cell phone?"

The lady seemed a little less agitated. She fluffed her hair with her hand. Her manicured fingernails matched the silver highlights in her hair. "I don't think that's necessary. I'm already late for an appointment. Just give me your name and telephone number."

Sadie found some scrap paper in her pocketbook. Her hand trembled as she wrote down their contact information. She handed it to the lady and waited. The woman seemed to ignore Sadie as she pulled out a compact mirror and reapplied her lipstick.

He motioned another car around. "What's your name?"

"Kingsley. Vanessa . . . Kingsley."

"Can we get your phone number?"

Vanessa snapped the compact mirror shut and narrowed her eyes at him. "What on earth for? The accident was your fault." She turned and walked back to her car. She opened the door and raised her chin in an arrogant manner. "You can rest assured. I will be in touch."

Sadie nestled into her normal sleeping position next to Jake and tried to relax. Both lay on their right sides with their knees bent, his chest against her back, and his left arm draped across her side. His profile perfectly outlined her body. They called it spooning. After spending the last twelve nights in the hospital, she relished the opportunity to lie next to her husband and enjoy his embrace. She inhaled deeply and exhaled slowly as she enjoyed the smell of his aftershave. He'd worn the brand for as long as she'd known him. Even after forty-five years of marriage, bedtime remained her favorite time of the day.

A cool breeze blew across the bed through the open window and raised chill bumps on her uncovered arm. It ushered in a chorus of croaking frogs and chirping crickets. Jake's breathing, barely audible over nature's choir, grew slow and deep. She marveled at how fast he could fall asleep. She always needed a few minutes to let her mind slow down. Tonight her mind ran rampant. She stared wide-eyed into the inky darkness of the room and replayed the accident in her mind—wheels squealing, the car sliding out of control, and Vanessa Kingsley's parting words. She had a bad feeling about Miss Kingsley. She squeezed her eyes tightly shut and pushed Vanessa's face from her mind; but, the doctor's haunting words rushed in to fill the space and echoed through her head: "ventricular fibrillation . . . all meaningful blood flow stops . . . death."

The word "death" continued to bounce around in her mind like a rogue ping-pong ball. It drove her from bed. She quietly donned her housecoat and slippers and tiptoed to the den. Perhaps she would read the *Glendale Gazette* for a few minutes. The boring small town newspaper seldom failed to induce drowsiness.

She turned on a lamp, picked up the newspaper, and sat in the recliner. The headlines read, "New Highway Claims Historic Oak." She recognized the picture of the massive oak tree. The Glendale landmark would soon be cut down, all in the name of progress. She thought about the Carving Tree in their front yard. Something other than the highway threatened this landmark. Ever since Jake's initial attack the tree's condition had deteriorated.

Why would God let this stuff happen? A person would be hard pressed to find a better man anywhere than Jake. Yet, God had struck him with this heart problem. Why Jake? It wasn't fair. They had been faithful to regularly attend and give to the church. What more could they do?

What would life be without Jake? She shuddered at the thought. She had to make sure Jake hung around for a long time. But what could she do? She bit her lip. Dr. Bradford's words filled her mind again. She had to make sure he took his medication and never smoked again.

Why did God always let her down? Her face tightened, and she set her jaw resolutely. She wiped the tears from her eyes and tilted her face toward the ceiling. "If you can't make them better, then I'll do it. I'll nurse Jake and the Carving Tree back to health!"

✿ Chapter 11 ✿

A knock on the screen door woke Jake from his afternoon nap. He stared at the grain patterns in the den's oak paneling and listened intently. Why hadn't Buckshot barked at the visitor? Had he actually heard a knock or had he dreamed it? Sadie lay fast asleep on the couch. The last two weeks had been exhausting and difficult. He heard the knock again followed by a lady's voice with a strong Southern accent. "Yoo-hoo. Anybody home?"

He would recognize Erma's voice anywhere. He returned his recliner to an upright position. "Coming." His voice startled Sadie from her slumber.

He pushed the screen door open. Clyde and Erma stood side by side. Erma wore a bright yellow dress sprinkled with red polka dots and a matching red felt hat. It reminded him of a hat worn by one of Robin Hood's Merry Men. She held a fistful of daisies that had wilted from the early afternoon heat. Clyde, adorned in his usual attire, held a large bowl. Apparently, Clyde thought he would grow another four inches before his eighty-fifth birthday because his new jeans had been turned up to form four-inch cuffs.

Jake chuckled to himself. "Well, look here. It's Clyde and Erma."

Jake shook his head at Buckshot, who lay motionless on the porch. "Some guard dog you turned out to be. Not even a woof to warn us that we had company." The dog, too comfortable to pick up his head, rolled his eyes upon Jake, and lazily thumped his tail against the plank floor. Sadie stepped beside him and interwove her arm in his. Her touch quickened his pulse.

She exclaimed, "What a pleasant surprise!"

Erma extended her arm with the wilted daisies. "We brought you these daises, shugah, and seeing that Jake hasn't eaten anything but hospital food for the last two weeks, we brought y'all a big bowl of nana pudding."

Jake's stomach suddenly grew queasy. He forced a smile. "How thoughtful."

Sadie reached out and took the daisies. "Thank you. The flowers are very lovely."

Erma smiled. The color of her teeth matched her crimson lipstick.

Clyde offered Jake the pudding. "We thought we'd come visit a spell."

Jake took the bowl from Clyde. His stomach flip-flopped at the sight of the freshly made pudding. "Come on in and have a seat while I put this in the kitchen."

Clyde put his hand to his ear. "What's that you say?"

Jake pointed toward the couch and spoke louder. "Have a seat." He chased a dozen flies from the egg-white meringue while Clyde and Erma took a seat. At least the flies were enjoying the pudding, and they were still moving.

Sadie held up the daises. "Make yourselves at home while I put these in some water." She darted in front of him and disappeared behind the swinging kitchen door.

He followed her into the kitchen and set the bowl on the table. She walked over from the kitchen sink with the vase of flowers. They had already perked up from the cold water.

She looked long and hard at the pudding and then at him. Her green eyes appeared large and concerned. She whispered, "What in the world are we going to do with that pudding? We can't eat it. Last time it upset my stomach for three days. I know she'll want us to sample it while they're here. What'll we tell them?"

He rubbed the back of his neck. "Maybe it's better this time. The flies are still living."

Sadie frowned and responded in a hushed tone, "She doesn't even use a recipe. She uses whatever she can find in the kitchen. The only consistent ingredient in her banana pudding is bananas."

He looked up at the ceiling as if he would find an answer there. After a moment, he responded. "Let's tell them that we just ate lunch, and we're both stuffed. We want to save the pudding until we can appreciate it."

Sadie nodded in agreement and turned to leave. He reached out and grabbed her arm. "Not so fast, baby." He spun her around and pulled her into his embrace. "Have I told you that I love you?"

Her green eyes grew brighter. "Not today, darling."

"I do," he said. Their lips met. Electricity pulsed through his body. After all these years, her kiss still seemed magical.

Sadie broke the magic and his embrace. "You're crushing the daises. Besides, we've got company." She turned and pushed open the swinging door. He followed with his hand on her lower back as if to gently direct her through the doorway.

Sadie moved her parents' large family Bible to one end of the coffee table and placed the flower vase in the center. "Nothing like a few daisies to liven up the room."

Erma picked up the vase and sniffed the flowers. "Why, honey, I just love flowers. We were on our way over here in the truck, and I got to thinking. I said, 'Clyde, here we are a taking Jake a great big bowl of nana pudding, but we don't have a thing for poor ole Sadie.' I said, 'We need to take something for Sadie. God bless her heart. She's been through a lot over the past two weeks.' 'Bout that time we came to a pasture near the old Brunson Place that was covered plumb over with daises. I said, 'Clyde, stop the truck. Run out there and fetch some daisies for Sadie.' And he did." She closed her eyes, raised her double chin, and deeply inhaled the fragrance of the flowers. "Now, don't they smell good?"

Clyde snapped his elastic suspenders with his thumbs. "Old woman wouldn't let me pick the flowers next to the road." His loose upper dentures clicked as he spoke. "She made me go through the barbed-wire fence into the pasture. Said the flowers were purdier on the other side. Reckon I was real lucky I didn't step in nothing or get hung on a barb."

Sadie giggled and her brilliant green eyes danced. "I do appreciate your extra effort, Clyde."

He stood suddenly. "Say, speaking of barbed-wire fences and watching your step, did I ever tell you about the time when I went behind enemy lines?"

Jake looked at Sadie. She blew at a curl hanging down on her forehead. He reclined his chair and took a deep, cleansing breath. Just as well relax. This could take a while.

Clyde placed a hand over his war medal and began his story. "Our platoon had made a valiant push just before sundown and driven the Germans back . . ."

Sadie yawned and scanned the den while Clyde talked. She wondered what the den would look like with brightly colored walls instead of the dark oak paneling. Perhaps a tan leather sofa would look better with the hardwood floor than the brown tweed couch. She glanced at the mantel clock. Clyde had rambled with his war story for more than thirty minutes. She realized her company had been there for nearly an hour, and she'd not yet offered them any refreshments. She stood. "Oh, my, what kind of hostess am I anyway? Can I get the two of you some iced tea?"

Erma perked up. "Don't forget the nana pudding."

Sadie's stomach churned. "Erma, can I get *you* some pudding?"

Erma shook her head. "No, darlin'. Doc Pearson says I need to lay off the sweets. I'll take some iced tea, if you please."

"What about you Clyde? Can I get you some pudding or tea?"

Clyde's eyes grew large and his chin dropped. "Uhm . . . uhm . . . just tea, thank you."

She looked toward Jake. "Jake?"

He patted his stomach and shook his head. "I'd better pass on the pudding. I'm still stuffed from lunch and wouldn't be able to appreciate its flavor." He winked at Sadie. "Baby, I would like some iced tea, though."

She started toward the kitchen. They had dodged the crisis for the moment. "Four glasses of iced tea coming up."

Sadie rushed into the den carrying a large silver serving tray that contained four glasses of iced tea, a sugar bowl, sliced lemon, and spoons. The rarely used silver tray had been an elaborate wedding gift and felt out of place in her hands. Her pace slowed when she heard Jake's irritated voice.

Jake wagged his finger. "Would you believe she snapped at us when we asked for her phone number?"

Erma shook her head. "The nerve of some people."

Sadie placed the tray on the coffee table and served the glasses. She took a seat and motioned toward the tea. "You'll need to add sugar," she warned. "Jake and I have started drinking unsweetened tea."

Erma began to load her glass with sugar. A large portion of each spoonful spilled on the tray due to Erma's unsteady hand. The white crystals resembled falling snowflakes in a snow globe as they settled to the bottom. The tea became so saturated with sugar that a half-inch layer formed in the bottom of the glass.

Sadie rolled her eyes at Jake. Doc Pearson would have a fit over Erma's sugar fix. Jake winked back.

Jake squeezed a lemon slice in his tea, releasing a pleasant aroma. "You know my mother loved sweets. She had a real weakness for desserts—apple pie, peach cobbler, and lemon pound cake."

Sadie's mouth watered. When it came to a sweet tooth, she had few rivals.

Jake continued, "She always told us to hold onto our forks after eating our meal because the best was yet to come." He reached for his tea and took a sip. "I want to be buried with a fork in my hand." He chuckled. "Because the best is yet to come."

Erma nearly came off the brown-tweed sofa. "Lord, howdy. Ain't that right? I'll be more than glad to lay down this old body for a new one. The Good Book says our citizenship is in heaven and our Lord Jesus Christ 'shall change our vile body, that it may be fashioned like unto his glorious body . . .' Hallelujah! Praise the Lord."

Clyde pointed a boney finger at Erma. "Old woman, you'd better calm down or you'll be taking a stroll down the streets of gold quicker 'n ya think." He leaned forward. "Speaking of 'kicking the bucket,' what's the matter with the Carving Tree? I've never in all my years seen it look this poor. Do you reckon it's dying?"

Sadie choked on her tea. "Haven't we talked enough about dying?" Her face grew warm following her outburst. She stared at the top of her feet. An awkward silence filled the room. She listened to Clyde's heavy breathing and the constant tick-tock of the mantel clock.

After several moments Jake said, "Did you hear about the judge in Raleigh that has been indicted for taking bribes?"

Sadie adjusted the pillow behind her back and looked up.

Clyde leaned forward and cupped a hand to his ear. "Say what?"

Jake increased his volume. "There is a judge in Raleigh taking bribes. Did you hear about him?"

Clyde shook his head. "Can't say I have."

Jake pointed at the newspaper on the end table next to the couch. "The *Glendale Gazette* claims he accepted over $200,000 in bribe money over the last five years."

Erma sat her glass down. "Land sakes alive. What a hypocrite, a regular ole Judas. He swore to uphold the law, but he's worse than the criminals he judges. I can't stand hypocrites—Lord, help me—people who pretend to be something they aren't."

Sadie shifted uneasily in her seat.

❦ CHAPTER 12 ❦

Clyde propped against the wooden plank fence at the back entrance of the dilapidated barn and watched Mildred eat. The worn-out creature methodically lapped up oats from the wooden trough with her rough tongue. Clyde breathed in the familiar smell of molasses, mildew, and manure, and sighed. "You're one spoiled mule. All that tender green grass and you come in here begging for oats." He leaned over the wooden rail and patted the mare's neck. The late afternoon sun exposed a blizzard of dust particles that danced in the air above the mule. Her coat with its numerous bare spots resembled the carpeted floor mats in their old Dodge.

Mildred raised her head and laid it across the top fence rail. Her nostrils flared as she sniffed at his hand in hopes of receiving a chunk of molasses.

He studied her face. The whites of her eyes had long since yellowed. The mule had seen better days. He rubbed her face. "Ole girl, we're just not what we used to be. Are we?"

She pulled her head away and resumed licking the last kernels from the corners of the wooden trough.

He leaned over the fence to scratch her neck, and the war medal clanked against the top rail. He covered the medal with his hand and felt a gnawing at his soul. "Perhaps . . . we never were."

Sadie washed the serving tray in the kitchen sink and reminisced on the past. She had a clear view of the old red barn from the small window above the sink. Countless times over the years she'd pushed aside the yellow curtains and watched Jake and Frank walk back and forth to the barn.

She shifted her weight from her left leg to her right to ease the constant ache in her foot. It had been good to see Clyde and Erma—except for the banana pudding. But at least Buckshot seemed to appreciate the pudding. Against her better judgment, Jake had given it to the dog. Buckshot had greedily devoured the entire bowl. Apparently, the dog had a cast-iron stomach.

She pulled a clean dishtowel from a cabinet drawer next to the sink and dried the tarnished serving tray. It needed a good polishing, a task usually reserved for Jake. However, he sat on the front porch reading his Bible, which seemed like a good thing since he shouldn't overexert himself. She shook her head. What did Jake find so captivating that drove him to read the King James English for hours at a time?

She found the polish in the back of a kitchen cabinet, poured some of the milky substance on a rag, and wiped it on the tray. The smell of the chalky liquid reminded her of apple cider vinegar that had sat on the shelf too long. She pondered over Jake's comment earlier in the day. He'd said it with a smile on his face. "I want to be buried with a fork in my hand." His comment had taken her breath. Could he, the hardest fighter she knew, be giving up? All the talk about death disturbed her, and Clyde's comment about the poor condition of the Carving Tree just made it worse. A tear meandered down her cheek. What would she do if Jake passed away? He'd always been there, nearly all of her life. How could he joke about such a thing?

She feverishly wiped the silver tray. She stopped and looked at her reflection in the freshly polished surface. A tear dripped onto the tray and ran down the reflected cheek. Erma's words about hypocrites resonated in her head. Maybe, just like the judge in Raleigh, she was pretending to be something she wasn't.

Jake watched with guilt as Buckshot moaned, circled three times, and lay down at his feet. The canine's stomach protruded like he'd swallowed a bowling ball. Jake sighed and laid down his Bible. He should have listened to Sadie. She'd warned him about feeding Erma's pudding to Buckshot. But he hated to throw it out and didn't think Buckshot would eat soured pudding. After all, dogs have a way of knowing when food has gone bad. However, nearly eighteen hours after gorging himself with the pudding, Buckshot moped around in misery.

Two squirrels played at the bottom of the porch steps in the mid-morning sun. They seemed to sense the dog's agony and played a little closer than usual to the porch. Buckshot raised his head and looked at the squirrels. He moaned and dropped his head to the gray plank floor.

Jake sipped some iced tea, leaned forward in the wicker rocker, and placed his hand on the canine's bulging stomach. The dog must really feel bad. Could this be the same dog that lived to catch squirrels, always poised to tear off the porch at a moment's notice in pursuit of the critters? He grinned. Buckshot had never caught one of the creatures, and he wasn't quite sure what the dog would do if he did. He chuckled—most likely pin it to the ground with a paw and lick it to death.

The dog got up and laid his muzzle across Jake's leg. He rolled his sad bloodshot eyes up at Jake and whined.

Jake stroked the dog's head. "Sorry, ole boy. Guess I should have listened to Sadie and not given you the pudding."

The loose skin on the dog's forehead bunched into ridges that resembled multiple rows of eyebrows. The ridges gave Jake the impression that Buckshot was contemplating his words. The dog seemed to accept Jake's apology. He slowly turned and walked to the other end of the porch and flopped down near a small table that contained a black plastic ashtray.

The sight of the familiar tray gave Jake an overwhelming desire to take a draw from a cigarette. He could taste the tobacco. "Boy, I'd kill to have a cigarette," he uttered softly.

He washed the taste from his mouth with a sip of tea and looked across the front yard. Clyde had been correct in his observation the day before. The massive old beech tree looked puny.

He restlessly tapped his fingers on the arm of the rocker and then stood. Both knees ached as they were suddenly called upon to support the weight of his body.

He instinctively patted the empty front pocket of his button-down shirt in search of a cigarette. Jake walked to the table and looked into the ashtray. Three cigarette butts stared back at him. How wasteful he'd been. He could have gotten another two or three draws from each cigarette.

He frowned. What harm could one little cigarette do?

❧ CHAPTER 13 ❧

Megan stared into the tiny bedroom closet and frowned. Women at the local homeless shelter probably owned more clothes. She examined each item before she packed it in a battered and scratched suitcase. Maybe someday her wardrobe would consist of clothes that weren't purchased from the Goodwill store. She closed the suitcase and struggled with one of the latches. She cursed and realized the words from her mouth had come out louder than intended.

She looked to see if she'd disturbed Ethan. He lay sprawled across her bed catching his late morning nap. Numerous cowlicks protruded from his shaggy orange scalp. He'd not awakened. Good—she didn't need to be interrogated by a three-year-old at this moment. He would ask an avalanche of questions. "Whatcha doin', Mommy? What's that box thing? Are them your clothes, Mommy? Are we going somewhere?"

She stood the suitcase up and pushed down on the latch until it snapped shut. "Finally." She turned her attention to Ethan's toys and began to place them in a large cardboard box. A lump formed in her throat, and sadness settled over her. Life didn't seem fair. Ethan had so few toys that she could put his entire collection in a single box. Why did things have to be this way? Why did money have to be such an issue? Why did Ethan's dad abandon them?

She shook her head to refocus. Now whom could she get to keep Ethan? Three people had already turned her down, and she couldn't exactly take Ethan to the audition.

She placed her hands on her hips and glanced around the rickety trailer. For once, renting a furnished trailer seemed advantageous. Moving out would be relatively easy because she owned very little. She walked to the kitchen. The room reeked with the familiar odor of mildew. She let out an exasperated huff. How many times had she scrubbed the wallpaper but to no avail? She picked up the note she'd left on the table and read it aloud once more to see how it sounded.

Dear Mr. Buckhalter,

> *I know I owe you three months rent, but I don't have the money right now. I'm sorry. I've left town in search of a job. I'll do everything in my power to pay you in a few months.*

Megan Thompson

The note lacked elegance, but so did Sam Buckhalter. She laid the note back on the table. It would do.

She held her hand to her forehead and walked around the den in small circles. She had to find a sitter for Ethan, but she'd exhausted every name on her mental list.

After several fruitless moments of racking her brain, she retrieved an envelope from her pocketbook. She pulled five crisp one-hundred-dollar bills from the envelope. The bills felt strange to her hand. She'd handled other people's money at the bank, but she'd never possessed this much cash at one time.

She dropped her shoulders and sighed. It sickened her to think she'd pawned her grandmother's diamond necklace, her share of her grandmother's estate. She'd hoped to have a beautiful wardrobe one day with which to wear the keepsake.

She rubbed one of the bills between her thumb and forefinger. The necklace, worth far more than $500, had caused the pawnbroker's eyes to light up. She hated to sell the family heirloom, but she had no other way to fund her multi-day trip to Charlotte. The audition could be her big chance, and it might be her last.

She noticed several magnetic photographs stuck to the refrigerator door. She'd overlooked them while packing. She studied her favorite photograph, a picture of Ethan taken in the Glendale Baptist Church nursery. His silly expression always brought a smile to her face. Someone else in the photograph caught her eye. In the background numerous children huddled tightly around an elderly woman as she read. "Mrs. Hopkins . . . of course." She couldn't think of anyone more qualified to look after Ethan than a former elementary school teacher. Since Mrs. Hopkins had recently retired, she ought to be available. Based on all she'd heard, Jake and Sadie Hopkins were good people, respected by the church, and a couple with whom she could trust Ethan.

Sadie rushed to the kitchen bay window when Buckshot barked. The sound, the first from the old dog since he'd eaten Erma's pudding the day before, announced the arrival of a stranger's car. A battered Toyota puttered up the rough gravel driveway. Sadie took off her apron and headed for the den. It must be that Thompson girl.

Jake rose from his recliner. "They're here."

She made a pass by the television and turned it off. "Yes. I'm afraid so." She ran her hand over her hair and patted it into place.

Jake slid his arm around her waist as they watched from the screen door. His reassuring touch calmed her uneasiness. Buckshot wagged his tail at them and volunteered a half-hearted "woof" as the car rolled to a stop.

She watched Megan Thompson get out of the car. She'd seen the young woman several times at church on special occasions like Christmas and Easter. She could think of only one word adequate to describe the twenty-something Megan Thompson—gorgeous.

Jake ran his fingers through his wavy silver hair and pushed the screen door open. "Guess I'll give her a hand."

She gave him a harsh look. "Don't go showing off and overexert yourself, Mr. Hopkins. She's a little young for you. Don't you think?"

He grinned, and his brown eyes sparkled. He started down the steps with Buckshot close behind. The dog trotted toward the car with his tail rapidly whipping the air. He circled the car to mark the tires while Megan unbuckled Ethan.

Sadie watched from the front porch with her hands on her hips as Jake made his way toward the car. Megan left the rear door open for Ethan and opened the trunk. The three-year-old leaped from the car yelling, "Wheee!"

Sadie thought she felt the ground shudder when the child landed. He wore a white Big Bird T-shirt and red shorts with large, overstuffed cargo pockets. She shook her head and spoke under her breath, "Trouble has arrived."

"Can I give you a hand?" Jake asked.

The young lady flashed a lovely smile in return. "Why, yes. There's a box of Ethan's toys in the trunk."

Sadie started down the steps. Jake didn't need to be lifting anything in his condition. She watched as Buckshot came around the front of the car and met Ethan face to face. The little boy froze. His eyes resembled large glass marbles.

Buckshot, oblivious to the child's terror, trotted right up to Ethan and poked his cold wet nose against the child's ear. Ethan bellowed a blood-curdling scream, "Momm-mee!"

Sadie stumbled on the bottom step. Megan dropped Ethan's suitcase, and Buckshot nearly knocked Jake off his feet as he ran, with his tail tucked under, between Jake's legs.

Sadie watched Megan gently rock the little boy in the rocking chair in the corner of the den, and her heart broke. How many times had she calmed little Frank in that very rocker? The young woman's brown hair, accented with blonde highlights, reached the middle of her back. With her full-body hair and gentle waves, Megan looked like a hair model in a shampoo commercial. Sadie patted her own thinning hair. What wouldn't she give for hair like that?

When Ethan finally calmed down, Sadie cracked open the screen door to check on Buckshot. The dejected dog huddled in the sunlight in the far corner of the porch. He propped on one hip and leaned against the rail. He held his head low, and his big brown eyes appeared to be full of remorse. The old dog seemed to be broken-hearted by the child's rejection.

"It's okay, Buckshot," she whispered. "You didn't do anything wrong."

The end of the dog's tail thumped half-heartedly against the gray plank floor.

Jake cleared his throat. "Sadie tells me that you need to travel to Charlotte for a few days."

Megan stroked the child's head. "Yes sir. One of the loan officers at the bank has turned in her two-week notice. It's a great opportunity, but I need to complete several days of training." She raked several strands of hair behind her ear. "I appreciate your willingness to keep Ethan." She lovingly rubbed the child's back. "Ethan's a good boy. I'm sure you won't have any trouble with him."

Ethan's head snapped to attention. "Ethan's a good boy," he blurted.

Sadie's jaw tightened. The child had only been in the church nursery a couple of times, but she remembered him well. He'd made a lasting impression on her. "You said on the phone you have some contact information for us."

Megan blindly felt for her pocketbook on the floor beside the rocker. "I don't carry a cell phone." She fished through a side pocket, careful not to disturb Ethan. "I have the number of the motel where I'll be staying." She handed Sadie a slip of paper. "I don't have a number for the bank's training center, yet. I'll call you with the number when I get it."

Ethan climbed down from Megan's lap and began to look around the room. His wide eyes surveyed his new surroundings.

Sadie took a step toward Ethan. She could almost see the gears turning in his head. She wondered what devious thing he was plotting.

Megan touched the little boy's shoulder to get his attention and then pointed at Sadie. "Ethan, this is Mrs. Sadie."

Ethan took several animated steps forward. "Say-da, Say-da, Say-da."

Megan smiled and pointed at Jake. "This is Mr. Jake."

Ethan bunny-hopped around the room, yelling, "Ache and Say-da! Ache and Say-da!"

Megan pointed at the suitcase and cardboard box near the door. "I packed three clean outfits and some of his favorite toys."

Sadie nodded and watched Ethan. He was focused on a small bookshelf near the television where she kept numerous crystal figurines. She positioned herself between Ethan and the crystal. "What does he like to eat?"

Megan stood and inched toward the door. "Oh, he'll eat just about anything." She slipped her purse strap over her shoulder. "He likes to watch TV."

Sadie took a few steps to her right to block the child. The little boy had clearly locked in on her crystal figurines.

Megan pointed at the distracted little boy and said, "We've already had the discussion about what's going to happen and bid our farewells. So, it's probably best if I slip out while he's occupied."

Sadie nodded. Now faced with one of those leave-and-scream scenarios, she wondered why she'd ever agreed to keep the little brat. "I suppose so," she half-heartedly replied. She glanced at Ethan as he approached her delicate treasures.

Jake intercepted the young child. "Little hands should not touch the glass," he said sternly.

Megan opened the screen door and stood in the doorway for a moment. She wiped a tear from her cheek and mouthed the words, "Thank you." She slipped out quietly.

Sadie pushed the wooden front door closed and locked it. She knew the delicate screen door would be no match for Ethan. Normally Buckshot might have betrayed Megan with a bark. However, the broken-hearted dog remained silent. She turned and walked back toward Jake and Ethan. "Jake, I'll get a box to put those in. In fact, there is a lot of childproofing in order." Through the open windows she heard the car start.

Ethan heard it, too. "Mommy?"

He spun around with searching eyes.

His eyes grew wide as he realized his mother had left.

"Momm-mmee," he cried as he ran back to the porch door.

He began to tug on the doorknob.

"I want my Momm-mmee!"

Sadie's heart broke. She recalled the gut-wrenching turmoil of many years earlier as she stood outside the church's nursery and listened to her son's blood-curdling screams—desperate and panic-stricken screams.

She squatted close to Ethan, and her nose detected the faint smell of baby shampoo. "Mommy had to go. But she'll be back to get you soon."

Upon hearing that news, Ethan's screams became even more intense. His pale face grew pink as if sunburned. He dropped to his belly and began to pound the floor with his fists.

She looked, misty-eyed, toward Jake. What had she gotten them into?

❧ CHAPTER 14 ❧

Erma awoke with a jerk and removed her reading glasses. Clyde slept in his den recliner with his head tilted back. His loud snores almost drowned out the sound of the television. His toothless mouth hung open like a dark cavern. His dentures lay on a coaster on the brown stone hearth.

She rubbed the sleep from her eyes and looked at the key-wound mantel clock. It was five minutes after eight and nearly dark outside. She'd been dreaming about Jake and Sadie. Perhaps she should pray for them. They certainly needed prayer. Besides, the Lord had placed them on her mind a lot lately. She battled the recliner for several seconds trying to return the chair to an upright position. Maybe she should just lie there and pray. *Lord, help me get out of this thing.* She rocked forward and pushed down hard with her feet. The chair obeyed and snapped upright. "Thank you, Lord," she whispered.

She pushed with her arms and stood. Countless bones creaked and popped as they engaged to support her generous mass of flesh. Her body ached all over. It seemed like she discovered a new ache every day, the price of a long life. She stood still for several seconds to give her stiff body an opportunity to grow accustomed to the idea of walking.

She shivered. In spite of the warm weather, she always seemed to be chilled. She picked up the ancient afghan that lay across the couch and draped it over her shoulders.

She left the television playing to avoid disturbing Clyde. It seemed like they slept best with the television playing. For the life of her, she didn't know why they owned a television. Most of the shows didn't appeal to them. It often served only as a sleep aid.

She shuffled out of the room and down the hall to their bedroom closet—her prayer room, her place of solitude, her meeting place with God. She switched on the light and closed the door. The odor of mothballs, like strong smelling salts, burned her nostrils. She gazed at the carpeted steps in the back of the closet. "Lord, I'm going to live by faith. I'm going to get down on my knees and trust you will raise me up again." As she carefully and slowly lowered her tired aching body to her knees, her eyes locked on a verse written on the back wall. *I can do all things through Christ which strengtheneth me.* She folded her hands, bowed her head, and began her prayer of intercession.

Megan switched the headlights to bright and focused on the dark road ahead. She feared that deer might be grazing on the shoulder of the road. She'd already seen two carcasses lying at the edge of the highway, victims of fast-moving vehicles. She gripped the wheel tighter. She sure didn't want to collide with a deer.

She chewed on her lip. Had she done the right thing by leaving Ethan with the Hopkinses? An annoying rattle in the dash intensified her anxiety. The couple, well respected by both the church and the community, should provide a safe haven. Sadie

Hopkins had been an elementary teacher for more than forty years. She would certainly know how to handle children. Yet, Ethan would see them as strangers. She dimmed her headlights due to an oncoming car. She felt guilt pooling in the pit of her soul. She shouldn't have lied to the Hopkinses about the purpose of her trip.

She applied pressure to the dash in an effort to silence the irritating rattle. Her treatment of Sam Buckhalter also brought conviction. He'd been very sympathetic of her financial difficulties, always giving her a little more time. And now, three months behind on her rent, she was skipping out on him. How low could she stoop?

She returned her headlights to high beam. Perhaps she could land a modeling job. The thought almost offset her guilt. She hoped for an opportunity that would bring positive changes to their lives. Maybe, she would be able to afford the lifestyle Ethan deserved. What had she ever done to deserve this precious little boy? Rambunctious, spoiled, and at times quite a handful, Ethan remained the one bright spot in her life. All he really needed was a good father figure.

She pounded the dash with her fist, and the rattle subsided for a moment. The lazy bum that had helped bring Ethan into the world had long since departed. Boy, he'd been a mistake. Whatever had she seen in that loser? She'd placed her faith in him only to be betrayed. She'd surrendered everything. But he'd left her as soon as he learned of her pregnancy, avoiding the responsibility of parenthood. He'd disappeared off the face of the earth as far as she knew. Perhaps his flight had been for the best. What a lousy role model he would have made for Ethan.

Ethan certainly deserved better than the lot he'd received in life. He deserved more than she could give him—more than a box of broken toys, more than secondhand clothes, and more than a roach-infested home. Somehow, it didn't seem fair.

The rattle in the dash returned. Regardless of whether or not she landed a modeling job, she had some important decisions to make.

Jake relaxed in the den, exhausted. He drew in a deep, cleansing breath and exhaled slowly. After nearly two hours of Ethan screaming and crying like an injured wild animal, the little boy had finally calmed down.

He looked across the dimly lit room at Sadie. Her head was tilted back in the armchair, and her eyes were shut. The crow's feet at the corners of her eyes seemed deeper than usual, and the roots of her brunette-colored hair appeared grayer. She'd had a hard day. In fact, the last two weeks had been especially difficult for her.

He studied the pudgy little three-year-old balled up on the couch. Ethan's sleeping position resembled that of a crawling baby. His head was awkwardly supported by a throw pillow that lay across his forearms.

Jake rubbed his eyes. He'd just witnessed the worst tantrum he'd ever seen. No wonder the child lay exhausted. It seemed like children today were hopelessly spoiled, mostly because parents were reluctant to set boundaries and to punish their kids. If Ethan was his child . . . If that was his grandchild . . . He swallowed deeply. And there lay the problem. They had neither child nor grandchild. His spirit fell, and a deep sadness flooded his soul. Frank had been seeing a young lady seriously before his death. Jake and Sadie had believed that Lisa Elvington would be the next Mrs. Hopkins, that their son would soon announce the engagement and start a family of his own. He and Sadie had long awaited the day when they would be known as Grandfather and Grandmother or Paw-Paw and Maw-Maw. But everything changed with the accident. Frank, in the prime of life, had been yanked away from them, and with him their hopes of grandchildren had faded as well.

He struggled to swallow as he pushed the pain down again. He wiped away a tear that trickled down his face. It had been a difficult time in their lives. Sadie had taken Frank's death hard, real hard. In fact, it had been a time when he was truly concerned for their marriage. Sadie had grown so bitter toward God that he didn't know if she would ever forgive Him. It had taken her a long time to put Frank's death behind her to the point where they could move on with their lives.

The little boy coughed, and Jake snapped to attention.

Sadie also perked up. She whispered from the armchair, "I guess we should try to put him to bed. I'll turn down the covers in Frank's room. See if you can get him to use the bathroom."

Jake stood and stretched his tight lower back. "Man. I always get the tough jobs. I sure hate to wake up this feisty young'un." He pulled the child to an upright position. Both Ethan's clothing and the couch felt warm and wet. Jake sighed deeply and whispered to Sadie, "I guess trying to get him to use the bathroom is no longer an issue."

✿ CHAPTER 15 ✿

Megan fiddled with her car keys as she anxiously approached The Right Look Modeling Agency receptionist.

The middle-aged receptionist gave her a tired look and asked, "May I help you?"

Megan laid her purse on the counter. "I'm here to see Mr. Parrish."

The receptionist rolled her weary eyes. "Honey, Mr. Parrish is out of town."

Megan dropped her shoulders. "Oh, well, Mr. Parrish told me to come in for a ten o'clock audition."

"Name?"

"Megan Thompson."

The receptionist checked the schedule and then pointed to a lobby filled with women. "You're in luck. Have a seat, and we'll call you when ready."

The lobby resembled a doctor's waiting room that was filled with attractive female patients. The air, saturated with the intermingled scents of two dozen fragrances, reminded her of a department store perfume counter. The walls contained poster-sized pictures of female models, which had been taken from television commercials and magazine advertisements. Jonathan Parrish and his agency appeared quite successful.

She surveyed the girls in the room while pretending to study the posters. All of the girls were "blessed," and many wore outfits that left little to the imagination.

She received several hateful looks as she gazed around the room. What an unfriendly bunch.

The girl seated to her right dropped her pocketbook, and its contents spilled on the floor. Her face grew red. She cursed under her breath and then dropped to one knee and began to retrieve her personal items.

Megan leaned and picked up a tube of lipstick that lay at her feet and handed it to the girl. "Hi. My name is Megan Thompson."

The girl took the lipstick and smiled, revealing a perfect set of teeth. "Thank you. I'm Carmen Davis."

Megan tucked a loose strand of hair behind her ear. Carmen's warm smile provided a welcome reprieve from the cold harsh room. Carmen appeared to be close in age to Megan. Her short black hair framed dark brown eyes, a delicate nose, and softly curved cheekbones. Her best feature, however, was her dynamic smile.

Carmen returned to her seat and began to rearrange the items she'd hurriedly tossed in her pocketbook. She pulled out a small zippered pouch that bore the snake and staff medical emblem.

Megan strained to read the small print on the blue vinyl pouch.

Carmen caught her studying the pouch. She whispered, "It's an insulin kit. I'm a type 1 diabetic."

Megan dropped her gaze to the floor. She felt a blush spread over her face. "Oh."

Carmen returned the pouch to her pocketbook. "It's okay. I've learned to live with it. My pancreas shut down when I turned fourteen. Ever since then I've had to give myself injections in the stomach several times each day. It's the reason I only pursue face-model jobs."

Megan looked up and smiled. "Well, you certainly have a great face and smile for that."

A lady bearing a clipboard opened a side door and called, "Megan Thompson."

Megan glanced at her watch. It read twenty-five minutes past her ten o'clock appointment. The auditions must have been running long. "Nice to have met you."

Carmen nodded. "Ditto."

Megan walked to the door. She felt the piercing stares of nearly every girl in the room—little daggers of hate and envy—directed toward her back.

Once the lobby door shut, Megan's escort introduced herself. "I'm Lydia. I'll guide you through your audition today." She was a blue-eyed, blonde-headed beauty, obviously a model herself.

Megan pushed several strands of hair behind her ear. "It's nice to meet you, but can I ask you a question?"

"Certainly. Shoot."

"All the girls in the lobby looked like they wanted to kill me when you called my name. Why is that?"

Lydia pointed at the clipboard. "You have an appointment for an audition. They don't. Many have simply gathered in hopes of an opportunity to strut their stuff in the event the auditions move faster than scheduled or there is a no-show."

Megan nodded. "Oh, that certainly explains those looks."

Lydia looked at a slip of paper on her clipboard, "Jonathan, uh, Mr. Parrish said you've never auditioned before. He was quite impressed with you and asked me to give you a few tips. I hope you don't mind."

Megan smiled. "Wonderful. This is all new to me, and I can use any help you can give me."

Lydia pushed a door open at the end of the hall and motioned for Megan to step through. "This is the dressing room. You will be modeling three outfits—an evening gown, a swimsuit, and a casual outfit." She pointed at the numerous racks of clothes. "The outfits are grouped according to size. You'll have about thirty minutes to select your outfits."

Megan glanced at her feet. "What about shoes?"

"Barefoot." Lydia motioned toward a door at the far end of the room. "The door to the runway is over there. When it's your turn, walk slowly down the runway. When you get to the end, stop for a second and slowly turn around." She demonstrated the full turn. "Pause just a second and smile at the judges, then turn and walk back to the dressing room. Just walk naturally. Don't twist any more than usual. The judges know raw talent when they see it. Try not to be nervous. There are only four judges, two women and two men. There will also be a cameraman in each of the two rear corners of the room recording your audition." She nodded toward a curtain in one corner. "The dressing area is behind that curtain. You'll have ten minutes to change into the next outfit and return to the runway. You can wear the outfits in any order." She pointed toward the gowns. "I suggest you wear the evening gown first and dazzle them with your natural beauty. Wear the casual dress next and make them think you could be the alluring girl next door. Hit them last with the swimsuit and knock them dead with your figure. Okay?"

Megan chuckled. "Thanks for the vote of confidence. I'll try."

Lydia turned as she headed through the hall door. "Remember, thirty minutes. I'll give you a signal when it's time. Good luck."

Megan immediately went to a rack that contained five evening gowns in her size. She rubbed her hand over a blue silk dress and marveled at the soft delicate fabric. A green tea length and a low-cut pink gown with a matching vest also hung from the rack. But a strapless red satin gown caught her eye. She'd always been told red was her color. She pulled the gown from the hanger and faced the mirror. She held the dress to her shoulders and tossed her hair.

The runway door swung open, and a curly black-haired beauty wearing a business dress suit rushed behind the curtain in the corner.

Megan turned her attention to the casual outfits. The selection would be easier since these outfits were more typical of the clothes she normally wore. She sifted through a dozen outfits in her size. The garments released the sweet fragrance of fabric softener. She decided to go with a lacy blue sundress.

The curly black-haired beauty emerged from the curtain in a string bikini. She adjusted the skimpy bottoms as she disappeared behind the runway door. "Talk about baring it all," Megan whispered.

She held the sundress against her chest and viewed herself in the mirror. It would have to do. She moved to the next rack. Now for the most difficult part—choosing a swimsuit. Twenty swimsuits in her size hung from the rack. However, the disturbing revelation was they were all string bikinis. They left little to the imagination. Apparently, the judges wanted to see each girl's complete package.

The curly black-haired beauty returned through the door. She gave Megan a half-frown as if to say things could have gone better. "You're up next. I'll be out in a sec."

Megan nodded. She'd judged the woman prematurely. None of the swimsuits offered much coverage. She chose a beige swimsuit, one that made her naturally olive skin appear darker. She held the swimsuit against her leg. On the negative side, she'd not been in the sun this spring and lacked the deep tan most of the girls displayed. On the positive side, she didn't have any tan lines. She gathered the three outfits and stood by the curtain waiting her turn to change.

Lydia poked her head in through the door. "Megan, you're up as soon as the judges finish scoring the last audition."

Megan smiled nervously. "Thanks, I'll be ready." Or would she? Apparently, Curls had fallen asleep in the dressing area. Megan certainly didn't want to give the judges a bad first impression by being late. She slipped behind a rack of gowns and disrobed. She wiped her sweaty palms on a dress on the rack and then slipped on the red gown. She returned to the mirror and combed her fingers through her hair. She admired the gorgeous gown.

Curls came out of the dressing area in a hurry as usual. "All yours," she said as she exited the room.

Megan grasped the gown with both hands and twirled in front of the mirror. She watched the fullness of the gown swirl through the air. She felt like Cinderella in her enchanted gown.

Lydia cracked open the door once more. "They're ready. Good luck." The door closed.

Megan drew in a deep, cleansing breath and exhaled slowly. "Be yourself. Walk naturally." She pushed open the runway door and whispered, "Here goes nothing."

She stepped onto the runway ramp and squinted under the bright lights. It was not at all what she'd expected. The ramp, crude and hastily built with unfinished plywood, creaked with each step. Two folding tables were positioned at the end of the twenty-foot ramp, one on either side. One male and one female judge sat at each table. Two cameramen, one in each of the back corners, videotaped the audition.

She tried to make eye contact with the judges as she walked down the runway and presented them with her best smile. They each looked totally disinterested, as if they were bored with the whole process.

She paused at the end of the ramp and turned around slowly, making sure the beautiful dress swirled through the air. She made eye contact with the judges again and then turned and walked back up the ramp. No music, no applause, no comments—just the creak of the rough plywood runway. She hurried behind the dressing room curtain. "Oh, that went well," she sarcastically muttered.

Megan changed back into her personal clothes and reflected on her three trips down the runway. Her second walk had been just as discouraging as the first. However, she had noticed a little life in the male judges when she entered the runway the third time in the string bikini. One judge had leaned forward and the other had sat up a little straighter.

Lydia called from the other side of the curtain, "Megan, someone will be in contact with you later today to let you know whether the agency wants you to audition further. Where can we reach you?"

Megan slipped on a shoe. "I'm staying at the Motel-8 on Market, Room 112."

"I've got Motel-8 on Market, Room 112. I wish you the best. I've got to instruct the next girl. Just follow the exit signs."

Michael pushed away from the judge's table and crossed his arms. "My vote is no."

Patricia removed her glasses and laid them on the table. "I like her. She has nice body lines and a beautiful face."

Carl raked his hand through his silver hair. "I agree." He traced Megan's curves in the air with his hands. "I think she's stunning."

Marjorie tore open a candy bar wrapper. The smell of peanuts and chocolate filled the air. Michael's stomach growled.

Marjorie pointed the candy bar at Michael for emphasis. "The thing I like most about her is the air of innocence. A great face and body sell products, but beauty coupled with the look of innocence sells even more."

Michael glanced toward the ceiling. The light from the high-intensity bulbs burned his eyes. "I disagree. I've seen her kind before. She's got the body type of a Playboy Bunny. My vote is no. Thin is in. It's what fashion agents are looking for."

Marjorie exhaled sharply. "I don't understand you, Michael. You need to consider the other marketing avenues." She pointed at her plump cheeks. "Think about the cosmetic market. Why, her face, her complexion, or even her hair alone could sell a cosmetic product."

Michael shook his head. "No. She doesn't work for me."

Carl stroked his goatee. "What about the male-oriented market? With a little bit of tan and a string bikini, she would make a great hood ornament."

Michael glanced at his watch. "I'll give you that one. She's got a great figure, but they come a dime a dozen."

Patricia tossed her clipboard on the table. "I think we're wasting time here. You know the rules. Our selections must be unanimous, and it's obvious that Michael is not going to budge on this one. We have a tight agenda. Let's move on." She pointed at Michael. "Since you're the odd man out, you get to contact Ms. Thompson and tell her that we don't need her services any further. Understand?"

Michael covered his mouth with his hand and pretended to yawn. When he was able to suppress his grin, he dropped his hand and replied, "Sure thing."

Michael swirled the restaurant's finest wine in his half-empty glass and savored its fragrance. He glanced out the large window at the shimmering lake next to the restaurant. The setting sun cast a long reflection across the surface of the water. He enjoyed the finer things of life—the things that only money could buy. He placed his cell phone on the elegant white tablecloth as the waiter returned with his entrée.

The penguin-suited waiter placed the main dish before him and spoke with a French accent, "Your filet mignon, sir—medium rare, of course. Will there be anything else?"

Michael waved his hand at the waiter as if shooing a fly. "No, Pierre. I'm fine."

He sliced into the meat and a pool of red juice formed on his plate. The aroma of the garlic-based marinade filled his nostrils and his mouth watered. He dipped a sliver of meat into the restaurant's famous sauce, but before he could enjoy the flavor of the meat, his cell phone began to vibrate. He snatched up the phone and checked the number. It belonged to his California contact. He'd been anxiously awaiting this call. "This is Michael."

A low raspy voice on the phone responded, "Boss saw the video. She's perfect. Get her out here as soon as possible. Make the usual arrangements."

Megan hung up the motel phone and wiped a tear from her face. She already missed the little voice on the other end. She felt all alone in the drab little room. She switched on the remaining lamp. Why were motel rooms always poorly lit? Were the owners trying to hide the badly soiled carpet and heavily worn furniture? Oh well. She could be sleeping in the Corolla.

She picked up a hamburger wrapper and fast-food paper sack and tossed them in the trash can. She kicked off her shoes and flopped down on the king-size bed. She felt as if she could get lost in the huge bed. She inhaled deeply in an effort to relax. What a day! It had been a whirlwind.

She sat up and began surfing through the cable channels. She couldn't make up her mind because she was accustomed to only having a few poor quality channels from which to choose. She paused on a channel broadcasting a commercial with a well-known model. Could it be possible for her to be that model?

She chuckled doubtfully. Based on the judges' responses earlier in the day, there would be little chance of that. She'd been humiliated by their indifferent stares and felt like she'd been paraded before them like a choice side of beef. She pushed her embarrassment aside. She would just have to wait for their call. If she didn't receive word by checkout time, she would call the agency. She certainly couldn't afford to stay in the motel another night unless they wanted her to audition further or could offer her a job.

She flopped back on the bed and stared at the ceiling. Who was she kidding? The audition had been a waste of time and money—money she didn't have. Hundreds of girls walked through the doors of that modeling agency each month. How could she possibly expect to land a job?

The motel phone rang, and she jumped. She snatched up the phone and hesitated briefly to regain her composure. "Hello."

"This is Michael Brinks with The Right Look Modeling Agency. I'm calling for Ms. Megan Thompson."

Megan's heart pounded with excitement. Okay, this is it. Here it comes. She drew in a calming breath and then exhaled slowly. "Yes. This is Megan."

"Ms. Thompson, I'm one of the judges from your audition earlier today." He cleared his throat. "I regret to inform you that we can't use your services at this time."

The energy drained from her body, and she leaned against the wall for support. She shouldn't be surprised. After all, she'd expected this result.

The man continued in a formal tone. "However, we believe you have a lot of potential and a lot to offer. I took the liberty of sending your audition video to several other modeling agencies. One in California seemed quite impressed. They want you to audition in person—all expenses paid, of course. If you're interested, I can make the necessary arrangements."

She felt renewed energy course through her veins. She pushed away from the wall and raked her fingers through her hair. "When?"

"I suggest we get you on a plane early Sunday morning."

She was speechless. Her wary conscience wrestled with her impulse to say, "Yes."

"Ms. Thompson, these opportunities are rare and short-lived. I'll leave an envelope with the receptionist at the agency. It will contain your airline ticket and all the necessary arrangements for your travel. The agency is only open until noon on Saturdays. Therefore, you'll need to pick up the packet before twelve tomorrow. Just give me the word, and I'll make it happen."

She heard herself answer, "Yes." She hadn't thought it through, but the words just rolled off her tongue.

❧ CHAPTER 16 ❧

Sadie sipped her morning coffee and stared out the den window at Jake. He sat quietly on the front porch with his coffee and Bible. His thin lips moved slightly as he read the scripture. She struggled to understand what he found so interesting about the Bible that he would treat it like food and water. She admired his strong faith in God—a faith she wished she could claim.

Ethan sat in front of the television eating dry cereal, his toys scattered all over the den floor. She relished the peace and quiet. The last forty-eight hours had been quite a challenge. In fact, she and Jake had decided against attending church because they didn't want to introduce Ethan to yet another change. She would be glad when Megan returned and picked up her son.

She inhaled the fresh morning air that infiltrated the room through the open window and looked toward the Carving Tree. The leaves on the tree had continued to yellow, and the layer of leaves on the ground had grown thicker. If the tree didn't show signs of improvement soon, she would definitely have to take action. However, she didn't know what action she would take.

Rrriinnggg! The rotary telephone on the den desk startled her. Who could it be at this hour of the morning? "Hello. This is Sadie."

The voice at the other end of the line replied, "Mrs. Hopkins, this is Megan Thompson. I just wanted to check on Ethan."

Sadie turned and glanced back toward the television and the little boy on the floor. "Why he's doing just fine. Would you like to talk to him?"

After a brief hesitation Megan replied, "No ma'am. I'm in a hurry. I have an appointment, but I need to ask a favor. The training will run a few extra days, and I was hoping you'd be willing to keep Ethan a little longer than originally planned."

Sadie felt her knees go weak. She slumped into the desk chair.

"Mrs. Hopkins, do you think you could do that?"

Sadie twisted her eyeglass lanyard.

Megan pleaded, "It would be a great help to me and could make the difference in my getting the loan officer position."

Sadie sighed, closed her eyes tightly, and forced herself to say, "Yes."

"Oh, thank you very much, Mrs. Hopkins. I really appreciate it. It's reassuring to know Ethan is in good hands. I'll be in touch. I really need to run. Bye."

Sadie propped her elbows on the desk and laid her face in her hands. She barely knew Megan Thompson and her son, yet she and Jake had been roped into keeping the little boy. Why in the world did she allow herself to get into this mess? It had to have been the desperate sound in the young mother's voice. She knew she should tell Jake that they were stuck with the flame-haired brat a little longer. She heard a commode flush, the slamming of the hall bathroom door, and the pitter-patter of Ethan's feet on the hardwood floor as he ran back into the den and dropped in front of the television. She stood and straightened her aching back, then walked toward the porch door. As she passed by the hallway, she saw a shimmer on the hardwood floor. "What in the . . . ?" And then it hit her. Water was flowing from under the bathroom door. The water, only a quarter inch deep, raced across the floor like a miniature tidal wave. "Jake, the commode is overflowing!"

She stubbed her toe on a toy as she splashed across the hardwood floor. "Oh, for the love of Pete." She threw open the bathroom door. Something blue had clogged the toilet bowl—a hand towel. She snatched the towel from the bowl and the commode began to drain. Her pink bedroom slippers sopped up the water like a dry sponge. She felt the nasty water ooze between her toes.

Jake arrived at the door. He looked pale and out of breath. "What is it?"

"Ethan tried to flush a hand towel down the commode. Just look at this mess." She grabbed several towels from the hall linen closet, and they began to mop up the water.

He cleared his throat. "That boy and I need to have a meeting behind the woodshed."

"Jake, we don't have a woodshed. Besides, you know we can't spank him. We don't have his mother's permission. Things are different now."

He rubbed the back of his neck. "I guess you're right. Well, at least we only have one more day with the young'un."

She reached out and touched his arm. "Megan called a few minutes ago, and she's asked that we keep him a few extra days."

Jake's pale face suddenly grew red.

Megan stood on a small balcony, captivated by the moonlit ocean and the warm, invigorating breeze. She raked her wind-blown hair away from her face and listened to the rhythmic sound of the waves breaking against the rocky shoreline below.

She'd heard of Laguna Beach but never expected to visit. She inhaled the salt air and marveled at the fullness and wonder of her day. She'd been like a child on the airplane with her face glued to the window, studying the terrain of the country below. There had been lots of mountains and rolling land, the Mississippi River, and other large bodies of water. There had been large expanses of flat land that reminded her of a giant checkerboard. The white-capped mountains and rugged beauty of the Southwest with its plateaus and canyons had left her speechless.

The travel arrangements had been well planned. Everything had gone according to the information in the envelope. She had landed in Los Angeles around eight p.m. It had taken nearly an hour to get to the hotel. Thank goodness she'd not been forced to drive on the massive freeways during rush hour.

She stepped back into the room but left the sliding door open to enjoy the ocean breeze. The luxurious room had a king-size bed with four pillows and a massive flat-screen TV. To top it all off, room service had delivered an exquisite meal. She didn't know much about this modeling agency, but they sure knew how to treat a girl right. She picked up a pillow, hugged it to her chest, and sniffed its fresh fragrance. Ahh. She could grow accustomed to this lifestyle.

Sadie wiped the makeup from her face, frowned at the image in the bathroom mirror, and said in a matter-of-fact tone, "Maude called earlier today. She missed us at church." She leaned around the partition that separated the bathroom sink from the master bedroom. "She isn't a happy camper. She feels like Mabel has betrayed their friendship."

Jake lay on the bed propped up by several pillows. He folded his hands behind his head. "How so?"

She applied anti-wrinkle cream to her face. "Mabel went to the tractor pull with Sam Peterson."

"Uh-oh."

She washed and dried her hands. "I told her that Mabel has just as much right to date Sam as she does."

He laughed. "I bet that went over well. How'd she respond?"

"Actually, she didn't say a word, but I could tell the steam was building. She hung up when I told her she should call Mabel and apologize because this thing over Sam wasn't worth the destruction of their friendship." She turned down the sheet. Jake lay there in his usual bedtime attire, nothing more than boxer shorts. She gasped and covered her mouth. She stared at his badly swollen legs. "Jake . . . your legs . . . they're huge!" She reached down and touched one of his shins. The fluid migrated away from her fingertips like catsup in a convenience packet. She pulled her hand away leaving an imprint in the gel-like tissue. "Jake, we need to get you to a hospital."

He pulled the sheet over his legs. "I forgot to take my water pill this morning." He removed one of the pillows from behind his back and patted the bed beside him. "Come on to bed, woman. I'm off my feet now. My legs will be fine by morning."

She shook her head. "I still think you need to see a doctor, Jake."

"Come on to bed. We'll address it in the morning."

She sat on the edge of the bed and fumed. She knew from the sound of his voice that she couldn't change his mind. She kicked off her slippers and turned off the light. "Stubborn mule."

She pulled up the sheet and rolled over toward Jake. She could see the silhouette of his face in the darkness. "You know it bothers me how a loving God allows a good person like you to get sick. Why does he let bad things happen to good people?"

Jake remained silent for several minutes, and then he quoted a verse. "Yea, though I walk through the valley of the shadow of death, I will fear no evil for thou art with me, thy rod and thy staff they comfort me."

She sat up in bed abruptly. "The shadow of death! Jake Earl Hopkins, is that supposed to comfort me?"

He chuckled and pulled her to a prone position. "The 'Valley of the Shadow of Death' refers to a real place, a slot canyon in the Holy Land. Because of the narrow width and high surrounding walls, shadows conceal much of the canyon floor. Hidden in the shadows, robbers and thieves would lie in wait for unsuspecting travelers. The 'Valley of the Shadow of Death' doesn't just refer to death. It refers to traveling through unknown circumstances. The verse could be interpreted: Though we walk through uncertain times, though trials and tribulations, the Lord promises to be with us, to protect us, and to guide us. He doesn't promise that we won't experience bad circumstances, but He does promise to help us through them."

He kissed her forehead. "Let's leave it up to God and get some sleep."

She rolled over on her right side and backed into the "spooning" position. His breathing soon grew deep and slow, and she knew he'd crossed over into a peaceful rest. Peace escaped her. She wrestled with his answer and the scripture that he'd quoted. She still had the unresolved question about how a caring and loving God could allow bad things to happen to good people, and *they* were good people.

Her mind replayed the image of the Carving Tree earlier in the day. The tree looked even worse than before. She decided she would call the county agricultural agent in the morning. Her dad had once called the agent for help with a troublesome crop. The agricultural agent had collected several soil samples that the county lab had used to determine the nutrients needed to make the crop grow. Yes, she would call first thing in the morning.

On top of her concern for the health of both Jake and the tree lay the burden of caring for Ethan. She believed that with a little discipline, Ethan would not be such a terror. However, they had not been given the authority to spank the young boy, and now they had to care for the spoiled brat even longer.

She pressed her back against Jake more tightly. She took comfort in the warm embrace of his arm that lay across her midsection. She inhaled the faint fragrance of his aftershave and soon drifted to sleep.

❧ CHAPTER 17 ❧

Jake pushed the temptation to the back of his mind and watched the sunrise from his wicker rocker on the front porch. Buckshot lay near the top of the porch steps, his old body cocked and ready to charge off the porch in pursuit of an unsuspecting squirrel.

Jake closed his eyes and drew in a slow, cleansing breath. He savored his favorite time of day. He enjoyed the cool morning air, the first rays of sunlight, and the birds singing.

He'd often sat here early in the morning before work and puffed on a cigarette. Man, he sure could use a cigarette. The smell of smoke, the warmth in his lungs, and the taste of tobacco beckoned to him. Sadie had thrown away an entire carton of cigarettes. She'd checked every place where he'd stashed them—all the drawers, cubbyholes, and hiding places—and thrown them out. She'd stoutly warned him like one of her fourth graders not to touch a cigarette again. According to her, cigarettes caused his predicament.

He stroked his chin between his forefinger and thumb. She'd been thorough in her attempt to eliminate his supply of cigarettes, but he knew of one place she'd missed. The glove compartment in the truck contained a partial package of cigarettes.

Buckshot walked over, laid his muzzle across Jake's leg, and looked up at him with his sad eyes.

113

Jake scratched behind the dog's ears. "Old boy, I want a cigarette so bad I can taste it. I want it just about as bad as you want one of those squirrels."

At the mention of squirrels, the lazy dog raised his floppy ears and wagged his tail. The loose skin above Buckshot's eyes bunched, forming rows of eyebrows, as if the dog had understood his words.

He picked at a loose strip of cane on the arm of the chair. It would be easy to slip out to the truck and smoke a cigarette before Sadie got up. She would never know, and what she didn't know wouldn't hurt her. He rubbed the back of his neck. However, one problem existed. He'd given her his word, and as a practice he kept his promises. Not only that, if she caught him smoking, she would be as angry as a swarm of yellow jackets whose nest had just been disturbed. Though gentle by nature, she could make his life quite miserable. He recalled the anger and bitterness in her voice the night before as she griped about how a loving God could allow him to be sick.

He supported the dog's head in his hands, leaned forward, and looked directly into Buckshot's eyes. He lowered his voice to a whisper. "You know what I think, Buckshot? I think Sadie has a lot of people fooled."

Sadie pointed toward the Carving Tree and resorted to bribery. "I'll make you some oatmeal and raisin cookies if you'll walk as quiet as a mouse to the big tree. We don't want to wake Mr. Jake from his afternoon nap."

Ethan bobbed his head in agreement and placed his forefinger to his lips.

Buckshot stood and wagged his tail when they stepped off the porch.

Ethan held his little arms up to her as he nervously watched Buckshot. "Carry Ethan," he demanded.

When they arrived at the tree, she put him down, but he wrapped his arms around her legs and whimpered. She broke his embrace and sat on a bed of leaves. He immediately climbed into her lap, seeking refuge from Buckshot.

She wiped the perspiration from her forehead. The early June day baked with sweltering heat and humidity. Thank goodness the tree, like a huge umbrella, provided shade from the brilliant sun.

Buckshot slowly circled the tree in search of a squirrel. Ethan tightened his grip on her neck each time Buckshot passed. Finally, the dog came to where they sat, turned around three times, and plopped down beside them.

After a few minutes, Ethan warmed up to the old dog and slid down to the ground between her and Buckshot. Perhaps the child's curiosity had overcome his fear.

A cloud of dust rolled up behind a white pickup truck approaching in the distance. The truck turned in at the driveway and headed up the hill toward the Carving Tree.

Sadie smoothed back her hair and patted it gently.

Buckshot stood to bark.

"No. Buckshot. Hush," she scolded.

The old dog whimpered.

She apologized to Buckshot. "We don't want to wake Jake from his afternoon nap. He doesn't need to know about our visitor."

The old truck rolled to a stop. The stenciled black lettering on the passenger door read "NC Department of Agriculture." With a dented hood, missing headlight, and gray primer exposed at every edge and sharp bend, the truck looked like it belonged in a junkyard.

The agricultural agent got out of the truck and left the door open as if he were planning on making a quick getaway. He wore tan clothing from head to foot. A cloth patch, sewn above his left shirt pocket, bore the letters NCDA. He spit some brown liquid on the ground and wiped his mouth on his sleeve. "Are you Mrs. Hopkins?"

She stood to greet the man, who appeared to be about thirty-five years of age. "One and the same, but you can call me Sadie."

The man's face lit up. "Why you wouldn't be Mrs. Sadie Hopkins, the fourth-grade school teacher, would you?"

She nodded. She knew what his next line would be. He would ask, "Remember me? I was in your fourth-grade class." Remembering proved tough because she'd taught nearly everyone in the county under the age of forty-six. Unless they had been especially good or especially bad, she had little recollection of any of her students over the years.

The agent wiped his hand on his pants and extended it to Sadie. "Remember me? I'm Robbie Glazier."

She ignored his dirty hand and held a forefinger to her lips, pretending to be in deep thought, and then brightened up. "Why, yes. Robbie Glazier. I do remember you. It's been a long time, hasn't it? And how long have you been the county agent?"

He pulled off his cap. "Coming up near fifteen years." He wiped his brow on his sleeve, leaving a tobacco stain across his forehead. "Still teaching?"

She glanced to check on Ethan. "No. I just retired this spring."

Robbie put on his hat and adjusted it. "Retired. You don't say. Wish I could retire." He tilted his head back and looked up in the tree. "Is this your sick beech tree? It's looking mighty yeller."

She grimaced and corrected him. "It's looking mighty yellow."

"You noticed the color, too, did you?" He chewed on his tobacco for a moment. "Not to mention all those leaves laying around on the ground. Yeah, your tree ain't doing too good."

She squirmed at his grammar, embarrassed to be known as his former teacher. "You mean to say that the leaves are *lying* on the ground and that the tree isn't doing *well*."

Robbie furrowed his brow as if confused. "I believe that there is about the biggest beech tree I've ever seen." He squirted a stream of tobacco spittle on the ground through a gap in his front teeth. "Got a lot of writin' on it, too."

She placed her hand on the tree. "I've never seen it look this poor before. I'm growing quite concerned it might die. Do you have any idea what could be wrong?"

He rubbed his chin. "There could be a number of reasons, ma'am. Could be insect infestation, poor nutrients, bad pH, not enough water, too much water, or there may be toxins in the soil. Has your husband fertilized this area lately?"

She surveyed the large green hillside and then shook her head. "No, he hasn't fertilized the yard in several years. The fescue grows too fast as it is."

Robbie removed his cap and wiped his forehead on his sleeve again. "Tree like that is bound to have some pretty deep roots, and the season ain't been especially dry. Don't think it's a water issue. I'll collect some soil samples and look 'round and see if I can find any insect holes in the trunk. Of course, it's always a good idea to look at some of the leaves that have dropped. Could be some kind of blight."

She glanced around and saw Ethan with two fistfuls of Buckshot's fur, clinging tightly to the dog's back. He'd definitely overcome his fear of Buckshot. Ethan took two steps and attempted to throw one leg over Buckshot's back. But the stumpy little leg couldn't overcome the dog's height and fell harmlessly back to the earth. Unsuccessful in his first attempt, the persistent little boy took two more steps and tried again while the dog circled the tree.

Robbie returned with several soil kits and knelt to collect some samples. "How long have you been living here, Mrs. Hopkins?"

She scratched her head. "Just about all our married lives. I guess it's been more than forty years."

Robbie slowly surveyed the landscape while on his knees. "Beautiful place you have here. Wish I had a spread like this."

She glanced down the long driveway toward the mailbox. "It's nice and quiet . . . sometimes . . . a little too quiet."

The agent crawled to a new location and nodded toward Ethan. "Grandchild?"

Her stomach churned. "No. I'm afraid not. I'm just keeping him for a friend."

Robbie wrote some information on an adhesive label and placed it on the collection box. "Children?"

She kicked at a stick on the ground. "No. Jake and I only had one son. He would have been forty this year, but he was killed in an accident at Camp Lejeune when he was twenty."

Robbie looked up. "Sorry to hear that, ma'am." He stood to his feet and brushed off his knees with his free hand. "I don't see anything abnormal on the leaves laying on the ground."

She rolled her eyes. "You mean *lying* on the ground."

Robbie cocked his head to one side. "Yeah, a lot of times, if there's a blight, it'll be pretty obvious from the leaves laying on the ground. These leaves look okay."

She frowned at his atrocious grammar.

Robbie walked around the tree and surveyed the bark. "Don't see no signs of insect damage neither. No bores or nothin' like that. Boy, this tree sure is covered with a lot of graffiti. Some of these are pretty old. See how the carved letters expanded over time as the tree grew." He stopped in front of their carving and traced the heart shape with his finger. "This one's really neat. Took somebody a lot of time to carve it. Got an arrow piercing the heart and everything. It says, 'Jake + Sadie.' Did your husband carve this one?"

She reached out and touched the carving. "Yes. He revealed it to me on the day he proposed."

Robbie laughed. "Why ain't that nice."

She corrected him, "*Isn't* that nice."

"Yeah, whatever." He spit out the wad of tobacco. "Still a teacher at heart, I see. Beware. It's hard to teach this old dog new tricks."

Both Ethan and Buckshot trotted toward the nasty tobacco wad.

She stepped between Ethan and the slimy clump. They would have to be more careful where they sat in the future.

Robbie gathered up his soil samples and placed them in a large plastic bag. "I'll send these to the lab and call you in a few days with the results. Hopefully it's nothing more than a pH or nutrient problem, and we can easily take care of it."

She glanced around to check on Ethan. She found him inspecting one of the dog's floppy ears.

Robbie dropped the soil samples in his truck bed. "Got another appointment down the road a piece. Sure has been good talking to my old school teacher again." He climbed into his truck, started the engine, and puttered down the driveway.

She frowned and waved. "Old is right."

Megan slipped behind the wheel of her rental vehicle and removed her heels. She rubbed her aching feet. Only the day's excitement kept her from stretching out on the seat and taking a nap.

She'd been very impressed with the panel of six judges. Unlike the judges at The Right Look Modeling Agency, these judges had seemed much more attentive. Apparently successful models in the past, they had watched her every move and had taken an abundance of notes.

Carpeted with strip lighting, the runway upon which she'd paraded had been more professional. The selection of outfits had been tenfold that of her previous audition. The experience had been much more positive with one exception. She'd not been able to see those who watched from behind the large one-way glass at the back of the room. The lady coordinating the auditions had tried to put her mind to ease by saying, "Clients often watch models from behind the glass. Remaining anonymous keeps the clients from being hounded by aspiring models in public places." Although it had made sense to her, it remained unsettling to know that unseen strangers had watched her every move.

She brimmed with excitement. She knew she'd captured at least one of the anonymous client's eyes because she'd been given a $100 gift certificate to one of the prestigious cliff-side restaurants at Laguna Beach. Common sense told her that even if the judges did not choose her, she would still have a great opportunity to model if one of the clients liked her. She cranked the car and headed back down the famous coastal highway, Highway 1, to Laguna Beach, exhausted but very hopeful.

Megan excitedly climbed the spiral staircase to the viewing platform above the restaurant. She had a wonderful view of the Pacific Ocean. The full moon on the horizon cast a brilliant reflection on the surface of the water for what seemed like miles. A warm breeze blew off the ocean water and tossed her long hair. She inhaled deeply and savored the moist salt air. She heard the crash of the waves against the cliff below. She'd never spent much time at the beach and had only seen the flat beaches of the North Carolina coast. But here, the water collided with the cliffs. Regardless of the outcome of her audition, she would always remember this trip.

She rubbed her stomach. She'd overeaten, not a wise thing to do for an aspiring model. But then again, how many times in life had she been able to dine in a wonderful restaurant with such a tremendous assortment of expensive dishes from which to choose? She'd even splurged and had a fabulous dessert.

She checked her watch. It read 9:05 p.m. She needed to get back to the hotel, talk to Ethan, and get her beauty sleep, of course.

She headed down the platform steps and scanned the parking lot. Her rental car sat in a dark spot at the far end of the lot beneath a burned out streetlight. She cursed. She had chosen the spot to avoid the dark. She quickened her step and pulled the car keys from her purse. However, before she could reach her rental car, a beat-up white cargo van pulled into the parking space beside it. The van completely blocked her car from view. The headlights of the cargo van went off, and the interior lights came on momentarily. Had someone gotten out of the van?

Chill bumps broke out on her arms in spite of the warm night air. She slowed her pace and looked back for other departing diners. Two men dressed in business suits followed close behind. Apparently, they, too, had parked at the far end of the lot. The two men had probably just completed some big business deal over a wonderful meal. Feeling a little bolder by the presence of the two businessmen, she proceeded cautiously toward her car.

As she approached her car, a very large muscular man stepped from the darkness. She stopped abruptly. With his slick head and large gold loop earring in his left ear, he reminded her of a muscle-bound version of the Mr. Clean cleanser icon.

The chill bumps that had collected on her arms earlier ran up her spine. Mr. Clean stood with his arms crossed and stared at her. He had a peculiar grin on his face. Her heart fluttered wildly in her chest. He appeared to be waiting for her next move.

Without taking her eyes off the stranger, she slipped off her high heels. She clung tightly to her shoes. If she couldn't outrun her attacker, the pointed heels might provide a little defense.

The two businessmen approached, and one asked, "Are you okay, Miss?"

She shook her head. "No sir, I'm not. There is a strange man waiting by my car."

The other businessman stepped forward. "Perhaps I can be of some assistance. Where is he?"

She turned and looked back toward her rental car. The bald muscle man had disappeared.

The businessman turned around and faced Megan. "I don't see anyone."

Before she could answer, the second businessman grabbed her from behind and covered her mouth and nose with a strange-smelling handkerchief. She struggled, but to no avail. The smell on the handkerchief grew stronger. Her body gave way, and her high heels dropped from her hands to the pavement.

❧ CHAPTER 18 ❧

Megan awoke from her drug-induced sleep to the sound of strange voices—women's voices. She blinked her sleep-filled eyes. She felt groggy. It must be early morning. But where was she? She couldn't remember how she got here but recalled being grabbed from behind and drugged.

The large room, apparently part of an abandoned warehouse, felt hot and stuffy. A strong musty odor of mildew permeated the air. She lay still and slowly scanned the room. A stout metal door provided the only entrance. A shower curtain hung in one corner that partially hid a commode and sink. The windowless walls were comprised of cracked gray cinderblock. Several large holes existed where the cinderblock met the concrete floor.

She counted seven other women in the room, all young and attractive. She lay motionless on one of the ten cots and listened to the conversation.

A slender blonde with gorgeous curls said, "I think I'm next."

A cute young Hispanic asked, "How do you know?"

The blonde raked her fingers through her curls. "The guard told me last night not to get too comfortable here. He said I would be on the bidding block in today's auction."

The Hispanic girl replied, "Oh, Lindsey, what are we going to do?"

Megan swallowed hard from the choking sensation in her throat. An overwhelming sense of desperation surged through her body at the thought of a human auction.

Lindsey crossed her arms. "What can we do? You know there's no escape from this hole."

Megan sat up abruptly. "Are you saying we are prisoners here, captives of human traffickers?"

Lindsey turned toward Megan, her blonde curls bouncing. "Look, sleeping beauty has awakened."

Megan frowned.

Lindsey motioned around the room with her hand. "I hate to tell you, sister, but you've just awoken from your sweet dreams into the nightmare of reality."

A brunette with short hair and an athletic build hastily stood on the other side of the room and knocked over the wooden chair in which she'd been seated. She strutted over toward Megan. "No, I'm your worst nightmare." She shoved her finger into Megan's chest and cursed. "If you know what's good for you, you'll stay out of my way."

Megan bit her lip and nodded. She wanted no part of the bully.

The stocky brunette gave her a long, penetrating stare and then momentarily glanced back to the other side of the room. Megan saw a fresh-looking scar behind the woman's right ear just below her hairline. It looked like a small cattle brand. The woman turned back toward Megan and pointed across the room. "Stay away from my place," she said harshly and then stomped back to her side of the room.

Lindsey rolled her eyes and spoke softly, "Don't mind Lola. Her bark is worse than her bite. She gets some kind of perverted satisfaction from intimidating people." Lindsey pointed toward a hole in the wall near the floor. "The rats are a bigger concern than Lola."

Megan shuddered. "Rats?"

Lindsey nodded. "Yeah, they come out of the walls scavenging for food scraps as soon as the lights go out. Just make sure your blanket is not touching the floor. I don't think they can climb the cot's metal legs."

Megan swallowed hard. Rats had to be at the top of her most-feared critter list, right up there with snakes and spiders. She leaned toward Lindsey and whispered, "What was that tattoo on the back of Lola's neck?"

Lindsey pushed her hair aside and presented the back of her neck. "You mean this mark?"

Megan gasped. Lindsey had the same ugly circular mark. The nickel-sized scar had the outline of a shark at its center. The scab was just starting to shrink. "What is it?"

Lindsey dropped her hair back over the mark. "It's the boss's logo. He brands each of his girls just like cattle. It's the trademark by which he is known in the underground slave market."

Jake quietly rocked on the front porch and watched Ethan with amazement. The little red-haired child had been terrified of Buckshot, but now he wallowed all over the dog. Buckshot abandoned

Ethan and walked to the opposite end of the long covered porch. He circled three times and plopped down in a shady spot. The relentless freckled three-year-old crawled across the gray planks imitating the old dog. When he reached his destination, Ethan gave the dog's neck a strong bear hug.

Buckshot cast tired eyes toward Jake, moaned, and relocated a second time.

Jake was grateful that Ethan had befriended the dog because the boy's disposition had greatly improved. His crying for Megan had grown much less frequent.

Jake studied the old beech. It seemed as if the tree had its seasons mixed up. The large beech had lost nearly a third of its foliage and another third of the leaves had yellowed. Tall and majestic for as long as he could remember, the tree appeared to be shriveling away like an old man who faces the inevitable aging process. The beech was a lot like him.

Megan watched the overhead fixtures as the lights in the holding room went off and on several times.

"It's the five-minute warning." Lindsey pushed a blonde curl from her face. "They're going to kill the lights in just a few minutes. You'd better take care of your bedtime business now. It will get pitch dark in here."

Megan stood to go to the bathroom but froze when she saw a large-frame woman push aside the curtain and enter the toilet area. She knew it would not be in her best interest to interrupt Lola. She stooped and tucked the bottom corners of the sheets and blanket under the well-worn mattress on her cot. She didn't want to give the filthy rats passage to her bed. She shivered at the thought. In just a few minutes the place would be overrun with rats, and she wouldn't even be able to see them.

The commode flushed and Lola exited the toilet. Megan took one step toward the bathroom, and the room went dark. The inky blackness, like that of a cavern deep within the earth, consumed the room. She couldn't even find the bathroom let alone make use of it. She felt for her cot and retreated under the cover.

Though she felt hot and stuffy, she couldn't keep from tightly pulling the blanket around her neck. She'd rather drown in her sweat than have one of the nasty rodents touch her. Her skin crawled at the unpleasant thought.

"They're coming," said Lindsey.

Megan listened. But how could she hear anything over her pounding heart? She strained to hear the softest of sounds. A few seconds later, she heard the undeniable click of their toenails against the concrete floor. The sound initially came from her right, from the direction of Lindsey's cot. Then she heard the awful sound coming from her left, then from the foot of her cot—the rats were all around her. She pictured thousands of creatures on the floor beneath her cot, swarming like maggots on a dead carcass, crawling over the top of one another, searching for a route onto her cot. Beads of perspiration rolled down her face, and her upper lip quivered. When she could withstand the fear no longer, she pulled the cover over her head and hid.

Sadie nearly toppled the lamp on her bedside table as she groped for the switch. Who could be calling at this hour? They never received calls after ten o'clock. She turned the switch, and the intense light blinded her like an unexpected camera flash. The phone rang again, and she snatched it from its cradle. She squeezed her eyelids shut and tried to chase the bright yellow floaters from her eyes. Could it be Megan? She hadn't heard from the young mother in two days.

She cleared the sleep from her voice. "Hello."

"Thank goodness. It's you."

She rubbed her eyes and looked at the clock. It read 11:15. "Mabel . . . is that you?"

"I'm sorry for calling this late, but I just don't know what to do." She sniffled. "This thing with Maude has spun out of control."

She covered the phone receiver and whispered, "It's Mabel."

Jake rolled his eyes and buried his face under the pillow.

She got out of bed and slipped on her robe and slippers. "What has she done now?"

"Oh, Sadie, it's terrible. She's spreading vicious rumors about Sam and me—outright lies. I never thought she could stoop this low. I thought she was my friend."

She pulled the bedroom door shut, flipped on the hall light, and walked to the den. "Have you talked to her?"

"I've tried. She avoids me in public, and she hangs up when I call. Sadie, you've got to speak to her. Maybe you can talk some sense into her."

✿ Chapter 19 ✿

Sadie pulled a pencil from the den desk drawer and marked through Thursday on the calendar. Ethan had been with them for an entire week. Megan had originally asked that they look after Ethan for only three days. It had now been more than three days since she'd last heard from Megan. This babysitting job, this favor for Megan Thompson, had turned into a major task.

She placed her reading glasses on the end of her nose and retrieved the phone book from the desk drawer. She found the number of the Glendale Savings and Loan, circled it, and dialed the number on the rotary desk phone. She impatiently tapped the desktop with a pencil and studied the grain patterns in the oak paneling as she waited for someone to answer. She pulled off her glasses and let them drop to her chest by the lanyard. She was disappointed in the young girl. At least Megan ought to be considerate enough to call. She wondered how the young mother could go more than a day without talking to her son. The thought saddened her. Oh, the things she would give for the opportunity to talk with Frank once again. She pictured the handsome young man in full dress uniform sitting across from her at the kitchen table.

Click. A professional sounding voice answered the phone. "Glendale Savings and Loan. Miss Howser speaking. How may I help you?"

Sadie cleared her throat. "Yes. My name is Sadie Hopkins. I'm trying to get in touch with Megan Thompson."

Miss Howser did not respond. Ethan sat in front of the TV yelling, "Say-da, Say-da, Say-da!"

Sadie covered one ear and waited.

Finally the lady spoke. "Megan Thompson doesn't— Did you say Sadie Hopkins? Would that be Mrs. Hopkins, the schoolteacher?"

Sadie rolled her eyes. "One and the same."

"Mrs. Hopkins, this is Pam Howser. You were my fourth-grade teacher. Do you remember me?"

Sadie rubbed her forehead. It suddenly hurt. "Yes. The name does sound familiar. Miss Howser, uh, Pam, I need to ask a favor."

"What can I do for you?"

"Megan Thompson asked me to keep her son while she was away on a business trip. I haven't heard from her in three days. Can you give me a number where I can reach her?"

"Have you tried her home number?"

"Why, no, she's in Charlotte. She's taking some kind of loan officer training for the bank."

Again the line grew silent. Finally Pam spoke, "Mrs. Hopkins, Megan Thompson hasn't worked for the bank in more than two weeks. I let her go."

Sadie placed her hand on the desktop to steady herself. "But . . . but . . ."

"I'm sorry, Mrs. Hopkins. The best I can do is to provide her home phone number."

Sadie donned her reading glasses, jotted down the number, and hung up. She dialed the number.

Beep . . . beep . . . beep. "I'm sorry. The number you have dialed has been disconnected. Please check the number and try again." *Beep . . . beep . . . beep.*

She hung up the phone. Disconnected—what was going on?

She sat, removed her glasses, and let them drop against her chest. She laid her face in her hands. Had Megan abandoned her child?

She heard a knock at the front porch door, but Buckshot failed to announce the visitor's arrival. It must be someone familiar. Sadie smoothed back her hair and gently patted it into place.

The knock came a second time, and Ethan sprung from his place in front of the TV and ran to the door crying, "Mommy. Mommy."

She exhaled a sigh of relief. Wonderful. Megan had returned. She hadn't abandoned her child after all.

Ethan stopped short of the screen door and grew silent. He tilted his little chin upward as he studied the person on the porch.

She had a sinking feeling that it wasn't Megan after all and kicked a toy from her path.

A familiar high-pitched voice came from the porch. "Hi, young man. What's your name?"

Ethan's Kool-Aid-stained mouth hung open, and his eyes grew as large as bright blue golf balls.

When she reached the door, she saw Ernie Simmons, their mailman, standing on the porch. He wore navy shorts, a white short-sleeved button-down, and navy knee-high socks. A large tan mailbag hung from his shoulder.

"Hi, Mrs. Hopkins."

She pushed open the screen door. "Hi, Ernie. What can I do for you?"

He handed her several letters but withheld one. "I have a special delivery letter you need to sign for."

She glanced through the letters and exhaled sharply. "More medical bills."

Ernie detached a light green card from the remaining letter and placed it on his clipboard. He handed her the clipboard and pointed to the location for her signature. "Sign right there."

She placed her signature on the card, and Ernie handed her the letter.

Curiosity satisfied, Ethan returned to the television.

Sadie squinted at the return address and frowned. She extended her arm. The address came into focus, but she couldn't read the small print. She slipped on her reading glasses and read the return address. "It's from Cavanaugh and Associates, a law office in Raleigh. I wonder what it could be."

Ernie shrugged his shoulders. "Must be mighty important seeing as they wanted you to sign for it and all."

She motioned for Ernie to come in. "Can I get you a glass of lemonade or something?"

Ernie tipped his cap. "No ma'am. Got to be going. Making this special delivery has thrown me behind schedule this morning."

She carefully opened the envelope as Ernie drove off and slowly read the letter.

Re: *Motor Vehicle Collision Lawsuit*
        Reference: 21201.24924

Mr. and Mrs. Hopkins:

I am an attorney representing Miss Vanessa Kingsley, whom you rear-ended with your vehicle on May 31st.

As a consequence of the accident, Miss Kingsley has suffered immensely from physical, emotional, and financial stress. Miss Kingsley has missed many days from work due to the whiplash that she suffered during the collision. In addition to the loss of potential income, she has also incurred numerous medical bills and suffered from emotional stress.

The purpose of this letter is to notify you of Miss Kingsley's intent to seek financial restitution to offset her losses. Your presence is requested at a meeting to be held at my office on June 13th at 10 a.m.

Sincerely,
Cavanaugh and Associates
Brantley Cavanaugh III, Esq.

Sadie felt for the back of a chair to steady herself and swallowed deeply. "Lawsuit . . . whiplash and emotional stress."

She sat on the brown tweed couch. Vanessa Kingsley had not been physically injured during the accident. The collision had only left a small paint mark on Vanessa's bumper. The blemish was so small that both parties had agreed not to call the highway patrolman. Yet now, weeks later, Vanessa Kingsley threatened to sue.

Ethan squealed at a cartoon on TV as Jake came out of the bathroom. "Who was that?"

Sadie felt her skin crawl. She dropped the letter by her side and shifted her dress to cover it. "Umm . . . Ernie Simmons . . . He . . . he broke away from his mail route briefly to see how you were doing. He heard at church that you had been in the hospital." She couldn't tell Jake about the potential lawsuit. Ethan's presence had already pushed Jake's stress level to the limit. She didn't want to tell him anything that would cause more stress, including the information she'd just learned about Megan Thompson. "Megan Thompson called," she lied again. "She's going to be delayed a little longer."

Sadie peeped through a den window and saw a spotless white Cadillac roll to a stop. She squinted as the bright sunshine reflected off the car's abundant chrome trim. The sound of the car drew Ethan to the screen porch door.

Gladys Winslow climbed out of her car with a covered cake plate. She set her pocketbook and plate on the hood and tugged at the large pale green polyester dress that had climbed up her pantyhose. The dress resembled Frank's old Boy Scout tent. She gathered her pocketbook and the cake plate and waddled toward the house like a lime-colored penguin on the march.

Sadie grinned. Her love for cooking and warm smile made Gladys the perfect chairperson for the church's hospitality committee.

Ethan poked out his bottom lip, kicked at some toys scattered on the floor, and flopped facedown on the couch.

She sighed. Twice during the last hour a visitor had disappointed the little boy. She held open the screen door. "Hi, Gladys. Come on in."

Gladys stepped into the den. "Hey, Sadie." She lifted the cake plate cover. The strong smell of lemon flavoring greeted Sadie's nostrils.

"I brought you and Jake some lemon pound cake."

Sadie's mouth watered. The perfectly uniformed slices were arranged in a circle on the plate. Each overlapping yellow piece had a thin golden brown crust that had been drenched with a translucent lemon glaze. She swallowed deeply. "My that looks good. You're very kind."

Gladys handed her the freshly baked dessert. The cake plate still felt warm.

"Well, I hope you like it. How's Jake?"

Sadie motioned toward the kitchen. "He seems to be doing a little better. He and Buckshot have taken a stroll to the garden to check on his tomato plants." She set the cake on the kitchen table. "He'll be thrilled over the cake. Your lemon pound cake is one of his favorites."

Gladys slumped off her pocketbook and set it on the table. "Sadie, I need to talk to you."

Sadie glanced into the den to check on Ethan. "This sounds serious. Won't you have a seat?"

Gladys's body engulfed the wooden chair. "Sadie, did you know Maude asked me to kick Mabel off the hospitality committee?"

Sadie gasped and covered her mouth.

Gladys leaned forward. "She told me that she saw a car parked in Mabel's driveway early Tuesday morning . . . and . . . it looked just like Sam Peterson's car." She lifted the cake cover and pinched a piece from one of the slices. "I told her that I didn't need to know such things." She chewed for a moment. "Know what she told me? She said that as chairperson of the hospitality committee, I did need to know. It was my duty to remove Mabel from the committee for inappropriate behavior."

Sadie shook her head. This whole thing had gotten out of hand. "Are you going to do it?"

Gladys licked her fingers. "I told her that I was sure there was some logical explanation. Before taking any action, she and I needed to confront Mabel. She wasn't too keen on the idea." She reached for another pinch of cake. "Sadie, you're good friends with both of these women. Won't you talk to them?"

✵ Chapter 20 ✵

Sadie listened to Jake's slow, rhythmic breathing, but sleep evaded her. She glanced at the digital clock on her bedside table. It provided the only source of light in the pitch-black room. The clock read 2:15 a.m. She sighed. No bright full moon kept her awake tonight. Both the moon and the stars hid behind the clouds. Rather, the events of the prior day held her mind hostage. Megan Thompson had lied to them and may have even abandoned Ethan. How could a mother walk out on her own flesh and blood? Perhaps something dreadful had happened to Megan. Maybe she'd been involved in a car wreck or had been abducted. Without an employer, would anyone else even miss Megan? Should she report Megan as a missing person? She sure would feel foolish if Megan showed up moments after she contacted the sheriff.

The letter from Vanessa Kingsley's attorney disturbed her even more. They couldn't afford a lawsuit with their small nest egg. They had performed the calculations carefully and only retired when they felt as if they had sufficient funds. They had no excess. Vanessa Kingsley was pure evil. Sadie had sensed it the first time she'd met her.

Jake grunted. He rolled over and draped his arm across her midsection. His strong arm had always provided protection. He would know what to do. He always did. She was the teacher. Yet, he understood business and took care of the financial side of things. She often gave instructions, but he made the decisions. She longed to tell him about the lawsuit and about Megan Thompson, but she dared not. She feared the consequences the additional stress would place on his heart.

The weight of responsibility pressed down upon her like a baker's rolling pin flattens dough. She shifted Jake's arm, which suddenly felt like a crushing load upon her abdomen. She needed to tell someone and get help. She lay for what seemed like hours and contemplated her predicament. Finally, a name came to her mind. Perhaps Daniel Smith, a young law student who attended her church, could help. The bright young man had been one of her former students. Yes, she would pay Daniel a visit in the morning.

Jake lay motionless in bed and tried not to disturb Sadie. He knew she was awake and restless. She rapidly wiggled one foot like an eastern diamondback shaking its rattle. He, too, found it hard to quiet his mind.

He lay on his right side with his chest pressed against her back, his left arm draped across her midsection. Although his shoulder ached from the firmness of the mattress, he didn't move. He enjoyed her lilac-scented hair and basked in the warmth of her body. Yet, in spite of the pleasantness of the moment, his heart felt troubled. His mind reeled in turmoil. Contrary to what he'd told Sadie, he was worried. The swelling in his legs and ankles, the shortness of breath, and his lack of energy told him that his time was short.

He could deal with his declining health and could handle the prospect of his approaching death. He recalled the words of the Apostle Paul, "For to me to live is Christ, and to die is gain." He knew where he would spend eternity, and he looked forward to that time. Yet, his heart grieved over Sadie's lost condition.

Of course she wouldn't admit it. Whenever he approached the subject or implied the condition of her soul, she always interpreted his concern as an insult and grew angry. She still lived with the scars from the deaths of her father and Frank. She'd never been able to forgive God for taking them unfairly, as she put it. Because of her grudge, she'd never turned to God for her own salvation.

He felt a rare tear trickle from the corner of his eye into his ear. Those who knew him well knew he didn't cry. But this ran deep, and it tore at his heart. He knew unless things changed, they would not be together for all eternity. *Dear God, forgive Sadie. Convict her heart, her mind, and her soul. Make her acutely aware of her sinfulness and shortcomings. She is a wonderful lady, a good person. Yet, your Word says she can never be good enough to earn her salvation. Convict her heart and her spirit that she might recognize her need, understand the forgiveness you offer, and enjoy the hope you bring. Dear God, I pray you would bring her to the point of salvation even at this moment.*

At a little after nine a.m., Sadie stopped the car in front of Bob's A&E and chewed on her lip. A large sign in the front plate-glass window stated: "Bob's A&E - Celebrating twenty-five years of service." Bob Smith had been operating the store for as long as Sadie could remember. It started out as an appliance and electronics store, but his main staples consisted of paint and hardware.

She slipped out of the car and unbuckled Ethan from his car seat. She firmly grasped one of Ethan's hands and then waved her finger. "Don't touch anything."

She pushed against the glass entry door, and several little bells jingled to announce their arrival. A rush of cool air tainted with an odor of paint thinner flowed from the store. Two men standing at the checkout counter looked up. Bob, the older man, wore casual slacks and a short-sleeved button-down shirt. Daniel, his son, wore faded blue jeans and an orange T-shirt bearing the Campbell University logo.

Bob smiled and approached her. Daniel nodded shyly but remained behind the counter. Bob held out his hand. "Hi, Mrs. Hopkins. How is Jake doing? I heard he was in the hospital."

Ethan tugged against her to pick up a penny from the floor. He immediately dropped it into his already bulging pants pocket.

She tightened her grip on Ethan. "Jake is home again, but this heart thing is forcing him to slow down. You know Jake. He's not one to slow down. I fear he will overexert himself. He's been quite irritable lately, mostly because the doctor made him quit smoking."

Bob leaned back against the counter. "Why, I'm sorry to hear that. I hope his condition improves soon. So, how can I help you this morning?"

She glanced at Daniel. "Daniel is actually the person I came to see."

Bob laughed. "Oh, really."

She pulled back on Ethan. "A short time ago, I rear-ended another lady with our car. I'm hoping to get a little legal advice from Daniel."

Daniel's face turned red. "Legal advice." His voice seemed even more drawn out than usual. "I've only completed one year of law school. I still have two full years ahead of me. I'm hardly qualified to give counsel."

She turned loose of Ethan and waved her hands as she described the accident. "Like I said, I rear-ended a lady with our car. The collision only left a tiny mark on her bumper. Although very irritable, she didn't appear to be injured at all. It had been ten days since the accident, and I'd completely forgotten about it. Until, that is, I received a letter yesterday from her attorney. It said she was seeking financial restitution for her physical and emotional stress suffered from the accident. They want to meet next week in his office."

Daniel scratched his head. "Well, what does Mr. Hopkins say about it?"

She stared toward the back of the store. "Jake doesn't know about the letter yet."

She turned and looked at both Bob and Daniel. "I'm trying to protect him from stressful situations. I'm afraid any additional burdens could worsen his heart condition."

Both men nodded as if they understood her predicament. Daniel seemed to brighten up. "I really don't think you have a problem. The reason you're required to have liability insurance is to cover situations like this."

She breathed deeply and relaxed for the first time since she'd read the letter the day before. She felt relieved, almost energized by the good news.

A thunderous crash came from the front corner of the store as several large clay pots shattered on the floor. Ethan came running from the direction of the crash screaming at the top of his lungs, "Say-da!"

Sadie sat her purse on the sheriff's desk and shook her head. "I believe something bad has happened to Megan Thompson. I haven't heard from her in five days." She pointed at Ethan, who sat in an oversized chair. "She wouldn't abandon her son."

Sheriff Kendall slumped in a large leather chair behind an old wooden desk and polished his pistol with an oily cloth. "I wouldn't get too concerned just yet. I've seen it several times before. A young mother gets overwhelmed with her motherly responsibilities and takes flight. She shows up a week later after her maternal instinct has kicked in." He rolled open the cylinder and looked down the barrel. "Give her a few more days before you file a missing person's report."

Megan jumped when the lock on the heavy metal door unlatched. The door creaked as it swung open. Two burly men brought in a new girl, the first since Lindsey had been taken from the group two days earlier. Duct tape secured her mouth and hands. Her eyes, like those of a captured wild animal, revealed her fear. She couldn't have been more than fifteen years old. The men removed the duct tape, shoved the girl into the room, and slammed the door.

The girl withdrew to a corner of the room and propped her forehead against the wall. Her shoulders heaved as heavy sobs emanated from the corner.

Megan felt the girl's grief. She placed an arm around the girl, and the startled teen jumped. "It's okay. I'm not going to hurt you. I'm a captive too."

The girl turned and wiped the tears from her eyes. "Who are these people?"

Megan pushed the hair away from the girl's face. "I've only been here three days, but what I've been able to piece together is that we're captives of a human trafficking ring. A man known as 'the boss' is operating it. Judging from his hired thugs, he is probably associated with the mafia."

Tears filled the girl's eyes again. "Human trafficking ring— the mafia."

Megan nodded. "There appears to be a steady stream of women that pass through this facility, women who have been abducted from all over the country. From what I can tell, there is some kind of Internet auction held each morning. Girls are being sold to powerful men all around the world." She ran her fingers through her hair. Her own words reiterated her predicament. She'd heard of black-market slavery, but never been exposed to it, nor ever dreamed she would be. She found the concept of human slavery totally foreign to her mundane life. But life had changed. She pointed to a cot. "Come sit down."

The girl took a seat and sniffled.

Megan held out her hand. "I'm Megan."

The girl shook her hand. "I'm Nicole. Isn't there some way to escape?"

Megan shook her head. "Not from this room."

She pointed toward the heavy metal door. "There is only one way out of this room, and they keep at least one armed guard outside the door twenty-four hours a day. It's just a large prison cell. I've concluded the best opportunities for escape will come during transportation to our new owners."

Nicole lay on her side in a fetal position. She trembled.

Megan covered her with a well-worn blanket. "Just rest for a while, and we'll talk later." She stretched out on her cot. It all made sense now. The human trafficking ring explained why someone would pay to fly her all the way across the country to audition. Someone involved in the slave trade had watched her photo shoot from behind the glass. Perhaps, he had even supplied the restaurant gift certificate. It had all been a setup to aid in her abduction. And like unsuspecting game, she'd been caught in the trapper's snare.

She turned on her side and thought about Ethan. She pictured the bundle of energy and longed for him to climb up into her lap, to hear him giggle, and to hear him say, "Mommy." She didn't even have a photograph, for they had taken her pocketbook and everything that defined her. It saddened her that she'd ever considered giving up Ethan. Now she would give anything to have the opportunity to see her precious son. She chewed on her lip. Although things did not look too promising, one way or another, she would get back to her little boy—or die trying.

❧ CHAPTER 21 ❧

Sadie looked out the kitchen window and smiled as Jake and Ethan headed toward the big red barn. Buckshot ran ahead of them, sniffing every blade of grass. Surely the short walk to the barn would not physically stress Jake. Perhaps it would do him good.

She decided to take a casual walk to the mailbox. The sun shone brightly in the cloudless blue sky. Jake's health appeared to be a little better, and even the Carving Tree looked healthier. She sauntered down the driveway. Things were looking up with respect to the lawsuit as well. She'd been encouraged by her conversation with Daniel earlier in the morning.

She tugged on the mailbox door, and it came off in her hand. "We've got to fix this thing," she muttered. Perhaps after Jake improved, he would be able to handle this small task. She retrieved the mail, tucked it under her arm, and then pushed the door back in place. She slipped on her reading glasses and inspected each envelope. Two identical envelopes bore the return address for the North Carolina Department of Motor Vehicles and large bold print that said, "Open immediately." She opened one envelope and carefully read the letter.

To: Licensed Motor Vehicle Operator
Subject: Recertification of Liability Insurance Coverage

The Vehicle Financial Responsibility Act of 1957 requires that all motor vehicles registered in the state of North Carolwina be covered by an automobile liability insurance policy and that the insurance remain in effect with continuous coverage until the registration is terminated. The law is designed to compensate accident victims for property losses and personal injuries and is designed for your protection. North Carolinas's compulsory insurance law is strictly enforced.

Your insurance company recently notified the North Carolina DMV that your policy lapsed on May 30, 2005. You have ten days from the date of this notice to certify that liability insurance was in effect on or prior to the date of cancellation. If continuous liability insurance was not in effect, you must pay a $50 civil penalty on each uninsured vehicle and certify that coverage is now in effect.

Failure to respond to this letter and provide requested information within the required time may result in the revocation of your license plate, as provided by law.

She stared at the letter. Her mind reeled. Their insurance had been canceled the day before the collision. She leaned against the mailbox, and the door fell off. A burning question came to her mind. Would the insurance company still cover the lawsuit? She felt a choking lump forming in her throat. Life's cruel timing had struck again. She shook her fist at the sky and yelled, "Why are you doing this?"

She crammed the letter back into the envelope. Two letters, two vehicles. How could the insurance coverage be terminated without her knowledge? Perhaps the insurance renewal check had been lost in the mail. Surely, the law required that insurance companies provide some kind of advanced notification. Then it hit her.

Jake slowly walked toward the big red barn, his mind reflecting on the past. Buckshot, a hound on a mission, trotted ahead of them, weaving from one side of the path to the other and sniffing every-thing. Jake felt Ethan's strong tug against his hand. The little boy's eyes sparkled with excitement.

Jake remembered walking hand in hand to the barn with little Frank to milk old Bessie. The thought of Frank opened a huge void in his heart, an overwhelming emptiness. He looked at Ethan with compassion. Sadie had admitted earlier that morning she'd not heard from Megan in five days. Had Megan deserted the little boy? What would happen to the small fellow? Would he be carted off by social services to a children's home somewhere? The void in his heart grew larger like a great chasm.

He turned loose of Ethan's hand and slid the two large barn doors open. Ethan immediately bent and collected one of the numerous cigarette butts scattered near the entrance. Jake sighed loudly. Once again, he longed for a smoke, to take a long, slow draw from a cigarette. He could taste the tobacco and feel the warm smoke in his nostrils. No matter how hard he tried to ignore it, the nicotine-induced craving remained, and it seemed to grow stronger with the passage of time. Ethan dropped the cigarette butt in his pants pocket and darted through the open doors into the dark barn. Jake stepped inside and waited for his eyes to adjust from the bright sunshine to the dim light.

Ethan's huge eyes were filled with excitement. He pointed to the hayloft above and said, "Up."

Jake looked at the dangerous hayloft. The gray plank floor, filled with numerous knotholes, looked like it had been sprayed with machine gun fire. The floor abruptly ended twelve feet above the ground. Loose sprigs of hay hung over the edge. "No son. Let's stay down here."

Ethan poked out his lip and pouted. His freckled face turned red. "But Ethan wants up."

Jake looked at the two-foot wide stairs that led to the loft. One side of the stairs was mounted against the wall. The other side was open with no handrail. He shook his head. The risk outweighed Ethan's curiosity. He pointed at a stall. "Look back there where I used to keep Bessie."

Ethan ran to the stall and looked through the slats. "Essie, Essie."

Jake opened the stall door, and Ethan ran over to the feeding trough. He grabbed its side, pulled his nose up and over the edge, and peeked into the trough.

Jake patted the side of the wooden box. "That's where I used to put Bessie's food." He pointed to the back corner of the stall and said, "Over there is where—" He looked down. Ethan had disappeared.

Sadie felt a wave of nausea and grabbed the mailbox post to steady herself. The pieces had begun to fit together. She remembered finding a letter in the mailbox from the insurance company on the day Jake had fallen at the garden. It had been nearly four weeks earlier. She'd dropped the mail when she found Jake lying face down on the ground.

She headed to the garden to find the insurance letter. She walked in a furrow between two neatly plowed rows. The straight and precise rows resembled ridges on an old-fashioned washboard. Already the fast-growing weeds had overtaken the young garden plants. It would kill Jake to see the weeds choking out his garden. She found the mail about one hundred feet from the Resting Place. She picked up the mud-splattered letter from the insurance company, still limp from morning dew and rain.

She sat down at the Resting Place in the tall green grass, slipped on her reading glasses, and carefully tore open the envelope. She eased out the damp letter and skimmed the smeared ink.

Subject: Auto Insurance Policy No. K7908P5

Mr. and Mrs. Hopkins:

Please be advised that the premium for your automobile insurance policy is past due. Effective two weeks from the date of this letter, your insurance coverage will be terminated.

Please remit payment immediately if you want your coverage to remain in force.

She looked at the date on the letter. It had been issued on May 16. She slipped off her glasses and chewed on one of the earpieces. Two weeks from May 16 would be May 30, the day before the accident.

She lay back on the ground and glared at the heavens above. "Oh God, why are you doing this to us? What have we done that is so terrible you would punish us this way?"

She gritted her teeth. She wanted to cry, yet the tears wouldn't flow. God didn't deserve the satisfaction of seeing her weep.

Jake gasped and hurried from the stall. He saw Ethan scampering up the steps to the loft.

"Ethan, stop!"

Buckshot dropped his head and tucked his tail.

Ethan paused and looked at Jake, his blue eyes huge and wild.

Ethan pointed to the loft. "Up."

He crawled up the steps on all fours like a little red-headed monkey.

Jake bounded up the steps, taking two at a time.

Midway up the steps he paused to catch his breath.

His heart ricocheted against the walls of his chest, and his face grew wet with perspiration.

Ethan stood at the edge of the loft. His movement dislodged several twigs of straw and sent them fluttering to the ground twelve feet below. Ethan would be seriously injured, if not killed, if he fell. He had to get Ethan away from the edge.

Adrenaline flowed through his veins, pounding its way through his arms and legs.

He hustled up the remaining steps.

"Ethan, get back," he yelled. "Stay away from the edge."

He reached the top step totally out of breath, his heart pounding and his energy depleted. He dropped to his knees, gasping for air.

Ethan, only inches from the edge, leaned over and pointed at the ground below.

Erma yawned and checked the pot of boiling cabbage on the stove-top. Cooked cabbage ranked at the top of Clyde's favorite dishes. She seasoned it with a slice of fatback and covered it with a lid. She opened the oven to check on the cornbread. A wave of heat warmed her face. The cornmeal batter had risen about one inch in the flat rectangular pan and was browning nicely. Cornbread claimed the top spot on both of their lists. She could hardly wait for lunch. She loved to dip the warm pieces of cornbread into a cold glass of milk. The thought of the combination made her mouth water.

She felt a sudden nudging of her spirit, a prompting to pray. The Holy Spirit would occasionally urge her to pray, but it always occurred when something occupied her mind. And for the life of her, cooked cabbage, cornbread, and milk just didn't seem worthy of a prayer—a blessing for sure, but not a prayer. Yet, God's Spirit compelled her to get on her knees. She slid one of the metal chairs away from the kitchen table, slowly lowered her plump body, and planted both elbows on the speckled green vinyl cushion. *Lord, remember, I am depending on you to help me back up.*

She didn't know what to pray but began anyway. *O Lord, thank you for the many years you have given Clyde and me, don't you know. We've always had enough and our cup runneth over. Forgive us when we fail.*

Lord, I don't know why you've called me to pray. But I feel your Spirit tapping on my shoulder. Who, Lord? What, Lord?

Erma listened for the Lord to respond. The lid on the pot of boiling cabbage rattled rhythmically as steam escaped. Several minutes passed before Jake, Sadie, and Ethan came to mind. *Blessed Lord, I lift up poor ole Sadie at this moment. She worries her little ole head very much. Give her that peace that passeth all understandin'. And Father, if you have a mind to, heal Jake of his heart illness. And Lord, protect that little boy, Ethan. He's a handful, but You made him the way he is. You know his heart. Mold him while he is in Sadie and Jake's care that he might learn right from wrong. Place a guardian angel round him and keep him safe. All this I pray in the name of my precious Lord Jesus. Amen.*

Sadie sat up in the grass and swallowed down the pain. She picked up the mail and stomped back toward the stone house at the top of the hill. As she labored to climb the driveway she muttered, "I'm not sure why Jake had to build at the top of a hill a half mile from the road. I guess he knew I'd be the one to walk to the mailbox."

Just as she passed the Carving Tree, she heard a scream coming from the direction of the barn. Jake's desperate cry sent a chill up her spine.

She ran toward the red two-story barn. She'd not run in many years, and it felt foreign to her stiff body. Her knees and hips ached, and her heart pounded in her ears. She gasped for breath as she darted through the open door and stopped to let her eyes adjust to the dim light. She heard Ethan's laughter and looked up. He stood at the edge of the loft and looked down at her. And at the top of the steps she saw Jake on his hands and knees.

❧ CHAPTER 22 ❧

Sadie sat on the den couch and took a deep, relaxing breath. Jake rested in bed while Ethan watched television. Although tired, Jake appeared to be doing a little better. Regardless of her pleading, he'd refused to go to the hospital or to the doctor. "It is what it is," he'd said. "They can't do anything for me anyway."

She called Daniel on the rotary phone. The voice on the other end of the line answered, "Bob's A&E. May I help you?"

She spoke softly to keep Jake from hearing. She wished they had one of those fancy portable phones. "Daniel, this is Sadie Hopkins."

"Why yes, Mrs. Hopkins." His voice came slow and deliberate. "What can I do for you?"

She'd taught the young man years before. Unlike many of her students, she remembered Daniel Smith very well. He'd been a shy little boy who lacked confidence. During the year that she'd taught him as a fourth grader, he'd been sort of a project. Her goal had been to build his self-esteem. His enrollment in the law school at Campbell University gave her a special thrill. She cleared her throat. "Do you remember our conversation the other day?"

"Yes, ma'am. I certainly do."

"Well, I've just learned some disturbing news. This morning we received several threatening letters from the Department of Motor Vehicles notifying us that we have had a lapse in our liability coverage. Apparently the insurance company did not receive our last payment. I know Jake paid the bill. I saw the entry in our checkbook. We received a cancellation warning notice in the mail on the day that I found Jake in the garden, and, well, I dropped the unopened letter and left it there in the garden. I didn't remember the letter until we received the notification from the DMV. I went back to the garden and found the letter in the dirt."

She wiped the tears from her eyes. "Daniel, the worst part is our insurance coverage was terminated the day before the accident. I don't know what we're going to do. We can't afford a lawsuit." She twisted the cord on the handset and waited for Daniel's response.

Finally, Daniel responded. "Mrs. Hopkins, first you need to call the insurance company and get your insurance reinstated. Explain the situation. You've probably been a long-time customer with them. Is that right?"

She nodded. "About forty years."

"Good. Perhaps they'll show you some grace for your long-term dedication and bridge your lapse in insurance coverage. It wouldn't hurt to beg for mercy. The next thing you need to do is go to the DMV with proof of the reinstated insurance. That should prevent any additional fees. Do you understand?"

She nodded. "Yes, Daniel. I do."

Again Daniel hesitated. "Mrs. Hopkins, I have to tell you that your personal property is at risk at this moment since your auto coverage expired just prior to the accident. Hopefully, the insurance company will show you some grace."

Daniel paused. "It's very important you attend the out-of-court settlement meeting to find out exactly what Vanessa Kingsley is looking for and more importantly, what her attorney is seeking. Lowlife attorneys are constantly trying to line their pocketbooks using frivolous lawsuits. Mrs. Hopkins, you probably should talk to Jake about this."

She looked down at her feet. She thought about the trauma in the barn two hours earlier. Her lip quivered. "I just can't do that, not at this time." She lowered her voice. "I don't think Jake could physically handle it." She ran her fingers through her hair. "Daniel, I need to ask a favor. I know nothing about the legal process or settlement meetings. Would you go with me? Would you represent me?"

She heard nothing but the tick of the mantel clock for several seconds. Daniel cleared his throat. "Mrs. Hopkins, you need to understand I've only completed one year of law school. It's general stuff. I have two more years in which to be trained in the process of representing people. I'm afraid it's like the blind leading the blind."

She swallowed deeply. "I can pay you. I'd rather have someone with a little legal knowledge, whom I can trust, than an expert lawyer who I can't."

Daniel sighed. "Let me pray about it, and I'll give you an answer tomorrow. I would immediately say no if anyone else asked. However"—his voice broke— "I owe you a lot."

Daniel smiled and handed the bagged merchandise to the customer. "Thanks. Have a nice afternoon." He propped against the counter half-standing and half-sitting. Bells jingled as the customer exited into the morning sunshine. He thought about Sadie's request earlier in the day. She'd been very emotional.

He wanted to help Sadie, but the fear of Failure paralyzed him. The demon seemed to lurk behind every door as Daniel pursued his dream of being a lawyer. During the school year, Failure frequently placed doubt in his mind, saying, "You can't do it. You're not good enough. You're not smart enough." Even when he scored well on an exam, he would hear an accusing whisper that said, "You got lucky this time. The score was a fluke, an accident, pure chance." And then when he scored poorly, the voice would scream, "Failure. You can't do this." Failure had been right about Constitutional Law. How could he return to school in the fall?

Daniel glanced at his father, who appeared lost in a sea of shipping boxes. Maybe he should agree to help Sadie. Defeat at this point would be the final nail in the coffin and would close the door to his dream—possibly a good thing. He would push the dream aside and move forward with a not-so-lofty goal. On the other hand, if he succeeded in defending Sadie, it might provide the encouragement he needed to continue his pursuit.

Maybe he should get his father's advice, or better yet, his Father's advice. He prayed. *Dear God, I am such an unworthy creature. I am awed when I consider how you reached down and lifted me from my muck and mire and saved me from sin even when I didn't deserve it.*

Oh God, while growing up in the church, I watched the Hopkinses. I know they are good people. Father, they are deeply in love and concerned for one another even after nearly fifty years of marriage.

Father God, it seems unfair a stranger would threaten the livelihood of this sweet, lovable couple. Lord, I remember how she helped me in school and how she gave me encouragement when others made fun of me. I recall the day when we had show-and-tell. All the other boys wanted to be fighter pilots, firemen, policemen, or race car drivers. Everybody laughed when I said I wanted to be a lawyer because I wanted to help people. Oh, how I remember Mrs. Hopkins's words as she explained to the class that it was a noble thing to desire to help people, and being a lawyer was a great way to do that. Not only did she encourage me at that moment, but she has often encouraged me over the years to follow my dream.

Father God, I know of no other man with greater integrity than Jake Hopkins. I remember the first day my dad allowed me to run the cash register. I mistakenly gave Jake excess change. Having recognized my mistake, he returned to the store several hours later, a round-trip of ten miles, and returned the twenty-dollar bill. Dad never even knew about my mistake. Lord, give me confirmation that I might know whether to help Mrs. Hopkins or not. Help me to know what to do and to step out in faith. Help me to trust you for wisdom that I might provide wise counsel.

Lord, I cling to Proverbs 3:5–6: "Trust in the Lord with all thine heart, and lean not unto thine own understanding. In all thy ways acknowledge Him, and He shall direct thy paths." So, Lord, I ask that You direct my path. In the precious name of Jesus, Amen.

Two Hispanic men startled Megan from her afternoon slumber and pulled her to her feet. The short and stocky men could pass as brothers. Their clothes carried the putrid odor of dead fish.

Instinctively, she resisted the men, but their grip on her arms tightened to the point of bruising. She cried out in pain and yielded to their pull.

The guard in the hall opened the heavy door and let them pass. The door slammed closed behind them and echoed down the long hallway. Since the nightmare had begun, she'd longed to be on this side of the door, but now the holding room seemed safer. The walls of the poorly lit hallway consisted of the familiar cracked cinderblock and flaking white paint.

She resisted their forward motion and demanded, "Where are you taking me?"

The younger man smiled deviously. "Miguel and I have little surprise for the señorita." Both men laughed. Their cruel laughs sent a cold chill up her spine. They pulled her into a dark room and closed the door. Miguel flipped a light switch, and a single low-wattage incandescent bulb cast its meager light throughout the small room.

She gasped. Directly beneath the bare bulb stood an old leather-covered examination table similar to those she'd seen in her doctor's office. Thin leather straps lay on the floor next to the table, each tied to a steel ring anchored in the concrete. What were they going to do with her? She pulled against their grip. "No!"

Their grip tightened, and they laughed. They seemed to enjoy her fear. Miguel locked the deadbolt and dropped the key into his pocket.

The hair on the back of her neck stood on end, and she broke into a cold sweat. Her situation seemed hopeless. They could do whatever they pleased with her.

The two men forced her onto the table. She kicked frantically at the air, while the men, one on either side of the table, tied the leather lashings around her wrists. They pulled the leather straps down tightly until her shoulders burned and her cheek pressed firmly into the grimy leather surface. "Let me go," she cried.

The younger man picked up a propane torch from the corner of the room and opened the valve. She heard the hiss of the escaping gas and detected a rank odor like rotten eggs. He lit the torch and adjusted the valve until the flame burned blue.

Her breathing grew rapid and her heart pounded in her chest. Was he going to burn her? Why? What could they gain from torturing her? Her eyes met the devilish eyes of the man. "No! Please don't."

He picked up a branding iron from the corner and began to heat one end. His eyes appeared wild with excitement. "Eduardo make it nice and red for the señorita."

After several minutes he held the branding iron near her face. The iron glowed orange, and she could feel its intense heat. It had the same logo that she'd seen on the back of Lindsey's neck. She felt faint and sick to her stomach.

Eduardo pointed at the glowing brand. "It's Boss's mark. You be his forever."

Miguel pushed down hard on her shoulders with one hand, and with the other hand he grabbed a fistful of her long hair, pulled it roughly over her head, and held her head against the table by her hair.

Megan screamed, "Nooooo!"

❧ Chapter 23 ❧

Sadie tossed the dishcloth on the kitchen counter when the phone rang. It might be Daniel. He'd promised to call with his decision. She dried her hands on her apron and glanced at Ethan. He sat at the kitchen table eating a breakfast of sugar-coated cereal and drinking milk from a sippy cup. He should be okay for a few minutes. She rushed into the den and answered the rotary phone. "Hello. This is Sadie."

"Mrs. Hopkins, this is Robbie Glazier. I just got the soil samples back from your beech tree and wanted to pass on the results."

"Hi, Robbie. What did you find out?"

"Based on what I see here, both the soil pH and nutrients should be adequate for the tree. I really see no reason for its declining health."

She blew at a curl on her forehead. "But it's obviously sick."

"Yes, ma'am. But it's beyond me. I know a specialist at a local tree nursery. If you'd like, I'll give you his number."

"That would be great." She slipped on her glasses and recorded the number. "Thanks, Robbie."

She rushed back through the kitchen's swinging doors to check on Ethan. He held the sippy cup high in the air above his head. Four streams of milk poured from the cup and flowed down his head and face. Milk pooled on the table and floor.

She covered her mouth. "Oh, Ethan." She grabbed a dishtowel and wiped his face and shirt.

Brriiinnngggg. The phone in the den rang again. She draped the towel over Ethan's head. "Stay put."

She rushed into the den and picked up the phone. "Hello. This is Sadie."

"Good morning, Mrs. Hopkins. This is Daniel Smith."

She drew a calming breath. She'd been awaiting the call. "Good morning, Daniel."

He cleared his voice. "I've thought long and hard about your request and prayed about it, too. I feel God is leading me to represent you at the settlement meeting."

She closed her eyes and leaned her head against the wall. It felt like a huge load had been lifted from her. "Oh, thank you, Daniel."

"Don't thank me. Thank God. He's the one that directed me to do this. I don't know how we'll beat this thing, but I'm confident He will guide us. So, thank God."

She lifted her head from the wall, her eyes open. Yeah, right. God's the one who caused all this mess in the first place. "Well, I'm glad He has led you in this direction."

"Mrs. Hopkins, can you tell me the date and time of your settlement meeting? I believe you said it was in Raleigh, right?"

"Yes. It's in Raleigh on Monday morning at eleven o'clock. I'll come and pick you up at nine o'clock." She thanked Daniel again, hung up, and returned to the kitchen to clean up Ethan and his mess.

Sadie arose from her shady seat beneath the Carving Tree as a late-model pickup rolled to a stop. The faded decal on the passenger door read "Simpson's Nursery." The engine stopped, and a short, pudgy man climbed out of the blue vehicle.

Buckshot jumped up to announce the man's arrival.

She touched the dog's shoulder. "No."

The dog immediately dropped his head, tucked his tail, and whimpered.

She softened her voice. "I don't want you to wake Jake from his afternoon nap."

The short, bald man approached Sadie and held out his hand. "Cal Simpson at your service. You must be Sadie Hopkins."

She held out her hand. "Yes. I'm Sadie. Nice to meet you."

The man pointed a plump finger at Ethan. "And who's this little termite?"

She looked at Ethan, who hopped around on all fours like the grasshopper he stalked. "That's Ethan Thompson. I'm looking after him for a while."

Cal dabbed at the perspiration on his forehead with his handkerchief. "Sure is hot for this time of year. The humidity is downright stifling."

She laughed. "That's why I'm trying to stay in the shade."

Cal looked up into the tree. "Is this here your sick tree?"

"It sure is." Sadie raked her foot through some leaves on the ground. "As you can see, the leaves have been dropping for some time now, and the tree has already lost a third of its foliage."

Cal pulled a small spiral-bound notepad and an ink pen from his front shirt pocket and scribbled some notes. "What we have here is a *Fagus grandifolia* of the *caroliniana* variety."

The Latin words piqued her interest. "And what might that be?"

"An American beech," he replied. "This old tree originally lived in the woods, didn't it?"

She nodded. "A thick forest stood here about forty years ago. How did you know?"

He swabbed beads of moisture from his upper lip with his handkerchief. "Because American beech trees prefer shade. Obviously this tree was well established before the surrounding trees were cut away. American beech trees are typically found growing in old forests alongside sugar maple, yellow birch, or eastern hemlock. The European beech, not the American beech, is the tree commonly grown in yards as an ornamental." He placed a hand on the tree and began to examine the bark as he slowly circled the tree.

She glanced at Ethan. He'd captured the unfortunate grasshopper and had begun to dissect it.

Cal patted the tree and scribbled in his notebook again. "At least there's no sign of beech bark disease," he muttered.

She stepped closer. "What is that?"

"Beech bark disease is the product of both an insect and a fungus. The insect, the beech scale, is a tiny critter under a millimeter in length and yellowish in color. It likes to live in the crevices of the bark with all its relatives. They penetrate the bark with their tiny stylets and feed on the tree. An infested tree will appear to have woolly white tufts located on the bark where the thick colonies gather. Later, a fungus infects the tree through the wounds left by the beech scales. The result is beech bark disease. It can cause yellowing of the foliage, cracking of the bark, formation of cankers, and eventually the death of the tree. Fortunately, I don't see any sign of beech bark disease or beech scales." Cal eased his overweight body to a kneeling position and began to examine the leaves that had fallen.

She squatted down beside him. "What are you looking for now?"

"Beech blight aphids," he said. "They suck the sap from the leaves and leave their excrement behind. We call the excrement 'honeydew.' Sooty molds colonize on the honeydew and turn the surface of the leaves black. I don't see any evidence of beech blight aphids either."

Cal struggled to his feet. He wiped the perspiration from his double chin. "There's no sign of infestation. The results of the soil samples provided by the county agent are normal. I really see no reason for the tree's poor health."

She momentarily gazed at Ethan and saw him tuck the crushed grasshopper into his front shorts pocket. That certainly explained the ever-present stains on his pockets. She obviously needed to do a better job checking his pockets before doing laundry.

Cal scratched his head and looked at his notes. "Perhaps its time is up. As you know, everything is eventually affected by old age."

She raised an eyebrow and tightened her jaw. Why did everyone keep mentioning old age?

Sadie leaned forward in the pew and listened to Pastor Nolan's confession. With his persuasive speech and professional appearance—black suit, white shirt, and red tie—he resembled a successful salesman.

The pastor walked to the side of the podium. "In 1985 I was passed over for a promotion in a major corporation. They promoted someone else who had far less experience. I was devastated. I had poured my life into that job." Pastor Nolan paused. Clyde's heavy breathing filled the silence.

She glanced at Ethan, who sat between her and Erma. His eyes appeared oversized and his mouth hung open.

The pastor continued. "I'm ashamed to admit it, but I harbored bitterness toward the company and the person who received the promotion. Like a deep sore that continued to fester, it refused to heal. In today's passage, taken from Hebrews 12, verses 14 through 17, we find Esau harbored a root of bitterness toward his brother Jacob for stealing . . ."

Sadie looked at her two friends. Mabel sat alone on the third row next to the large stained glass windows that lined the left wall. She wore a soft pink dress that perfectly blended with the light streaming through the colored panels of the window. Maude sat by herself next to the windows on the opposite side of the church, her chin pitched high. Her bold yellow dress and matching hat stood out like an ink spot on a white blouse. It seemed strange to see the two women separated by such a great distance. Since the death of their husbands, the two widows had been best friends, almost inseparable. In their shared grief, they alone had been able to comfort one another.

Pastor Nolan walked back across the raised platform to the pulpit. He raked his fingers through his white hair. "Left unchecked, a root of bitterness is a dangerous thing. It grows like a thorny vine that strangles the life from the rose. We see the result of Esau's root of bitterness in Genesis 27:41. It grew out of control until he sought to strangle the life from his brother."

She shifted in her seat. How could anyone grow so consumed with bitterness that he would seek to murder his brother?

Pastor Nolan pounded the podium and the congregation jumped. Ethan dropped a hymnal. "We must pull up the vine of bitterness, root and all, lest it sprout up again and destroy us!" He waited several seconds to let his statement sink in. His voice softened to a whisper. "Good people, if you're dealing with a root of bitterness, won't you ask God for the power to uproot it this morning, once and for all?" Pastor Nolan pointed toward the ceiling. "Perhaps, the object of your bitterness is God. Somehow, you feel He let you down." He motioned toward an empty wooden cross mounted to the wall. "Jesus didn't let you down. He died for you. He did everything necessary to bring restoration with God. And now, He stands with open arms, ready to receive you."

❧ Chapter 24 ❧

Max leaned forward and started the auction when the last bidder joined the Internet meeting. "Gentlemen, welcome to this morning's auction."

He glanced at his computer screen. "We have a total of six bidders in this auction. Remember the ground rules. Should you win the bid, you have one week to collect the merchandise. You also have the right to reject the merchandise after inspection. Once our deliverymen leave, however, your purchase is considered final. The winning bidder must wire payment, in US currency, to the Swiss bank account number we provide. Delivery of the merchandise will not be made until the appropriate funds have posted to our account. As always, current bids will be shown at the bottom of your screen."

Max double clicked on an icon, and video of a girl's modeling audition began to play on the computer screen. He stretched, and his arms nearly touched the opposing walls of his dimly lit office. He double clicked on a second icon, and information about the girl appeared in a small pop-up in the upper right-hand corner of the screen. He adjusted the position of his microphone. "Today's featured girl is Megan. This twenty-one-year-old beauty is five feet, five inches tall and weighs 123 pounds. She has large brown eyes and a naturally light olive skin color. Her teeth are excellent, and she has a beautiful smile. Her long brown hair is accented with blonde highlights."

The door opened, and Boss entered and stood behind him. His expensive cologne overpowered the room. The tight quarters immediately grew warm.

Max pulled up the video of Megan in the bikini and whistled into the microphone. "As you can see, she has a killer figure as well. Gentlemen, the floor is now open for bids."

Max watched the bids across the bottom of the screen. Bidder Number 4 opened the bidding at $100,000. Max muted his microphone and glanced back at Boss, who watched from over Max's shoulder. "I've never seen the bidding start this high."

The silver-haired Italian grinned with satisfaction and replied with a deep scratchy whisper, "Beauty and the look of innocence—priceless."

The bids raced upward until Bidder Number 4 bid $475,000.

Max enabled his microphone and announced, "Going once, going twice, sold to Bidder Number 4! Gentlemen, that concludes today's auction. Bidder Number 4, if you will remain online, I will direct you to another site where you can make your payment and arrange for delivery."

Boss motioned for Max to mute his microphone. "Who is our winner?"

Max double clicked on the Bidder Number 4 icon and a pop-up of information appeared on the screen. "Sheikh Abdol Hassan Kashani. He is a wealthy Iranian oil tycoon. Guess he wants to add a little diversity to his harem."

Boss nodded. "He is good for it. Proceed with the transaction."

Max clicked a hyperlink that redirected both he and Sheikh Kashani to another website. He entered the Swiss bank account number to which the funds were to be wired. A few minutes later a pop-up from the sheikh provided delivery instructions:

34° 00' 00" N, 120° 00' 00" W
6-20-07
0400

Boss repeated the coordinates. "34 degrees north, 120 degrees west. Where is that?"

Max opened an Internet map application and drilled down on the coordinates. "Approximately one hundred miles off the coast of Los Angeles."

Daniel reluctantly read aloud the brass plaque mounted to the cherry-stained door. "Brantley Jefferson Cavanaugh III, Attorney at Law." He looked at Sadie. She frowned and rolled her green eyes. They looked tired. She wore a conservative over-the-knee black skirt and a long-sleeved white button-down blouse with ruffles along the buttons. She'd worn the same attire for years as a public school teacher. As always, her reading glasses dangled from a pearl-beaded lanyard that hung from her neck. Once a teacher, always a teacher, he mused.

Sadie held Ethan's hand. He was deeply engrossed in the examination of a large paper clip that he'd found in the hallway.

Ethan wore a white Bert and Ernie T-shirt and jean shorts with large cargo pockets.

Daniel took a deep breath and turned the doorknob. "Here goes."

When the door opened, Ethan slipped away from Sadie and darted into a large plush waiting area with a desk, two brown leather sofas, and a coffee table covered with magazines.

Sadie hurried through the door. "Ethan. Come back here," she scolded in a loud whisper.

A young blonde receptionist looked up from her desk with a sour expression. "May I help you?"

Daniel froze at the door. The attractive young lady appeared to be his age and looked like she had been poured into her clothes. Her low-cut blouse begged for his attention. He felt his face grow crimson, and his gaze fell to the floor.

Sadie grabbed Ethan's hand. "I'm Sadie Hopkins." She turned and motioned toward Daniel. "And this handsome young man is Daniel Smith."

Daniel's face grew warmer.

Sadie roughly pulled the defiant child to her side. "And this is Ethan. I have an eleven o'clock meeting with Mr. Cavanaugh."

The receptionist rose from her chair. "Mr. Cavanaugh is expecting you." She frowned at Ethan. "I don't think he is expecting a young child though." She opened a door at the other end of the waiting room. "Right this way."

Daniel felt awkward as he passed through the door, though she never even acknowledged his presence.

Miss Stuck-up led them down a short hallway and into a conference room that contained a long mahogany table and ten black leather chairs. "Take a seat at the table. Mr. Cavanaugh will join you in a moment." She started to exit the room and then paused. She squinted and spoke forcefully to both Daniel and Sadie. "You'd better keep a tight rein on that little boy." She pointed to a large silver tray at the far end of the table that contained a dozen delicate crystal glasses and a matching pitcher with water. "Mr. Cavanaugh is very particular about his crystal."

Sadie frowned at the receptionist and said, "Of course."

The receptionist tossed her hair and raised her nose, then exited the room.

Daniel shook his head. "Boy, she sure is full of personality."

Ethan stood, mesmerized by a large wildlife photograph hung on the wall. Mounted in a gold metallic frame, the photograph captured two male lions in mortal combat. The two magnificent beasts stood on their hind legs and sparred with their monstrous paws like two prize fighters. Their faces had been slashed from their opponent's razor-sharp claws, and their manes were splattered with blood. The caption at the bottom of the photograph written in calligraphy read, "Survival of the fittest."

Daniel inhaled deeply. He wondered if the picture reflected his opponent's philosophy. For some reason, he didn't feel like the King of the Beasts. He felt more like a defenseless antelope, easy prey for a hungry lion. He wondered what had possessed him to attend the settlement meeting with Sadie. He lifted Ethan into one of the high-back chairs located around the table. "Sit here." The large swiveling chair swallowed Ethan, who immediately began to rock his small body back and forth in an effort to make the chair rock. His wild red hair resembled the lions' manes in the picture.

Daniel and Sadie stood when a man and two women entered the conference room. The man wore a gray pinstriped suit, white shirt, and burgundy tie. He appeared to be in his mid-to-late thirties. With his short black hair combed back and slicked down neatly into place, he looked both confident and intimidating.

Daniel swallowed. Obviously, this was Brantley Cavanaugh.

An attractive lady wearing a neck brace followed closely behind the man. This had to be Vanessa Kingsley. Her form-fitting blouse and skirt accentuated her fine figure, but the scowl on her face eclipsed her physical beauty.

The third member of the trio, a thin, pale-skinned lady, entered the room last. Judging from her extremely white skin, she'd never seen sunlight. She donned a tailored navy dress suit that exaggerated her pale flesh and carried a manila folder and clipboard. The tight-faced woman, apparently Brantley's battle-hardened paralegal assistant, showed no hint of emotion. Her long, red, manicured fingernails reminded him of the lions' bloody claws. She looked cold and hard, as if she would pounce and shred the opposition without giving it a second thought.

The trio silently walked to the opposite side of the table and sat beneath the portrait of the lions. They seemed to be all business, their rudeness likely part of Brantley's battle strategy.

Daniel and Sadie sat. He frowned, irritated his opponents had offered no greetings. He looked at Sadie. Her raised eyebrow and tight jaw conveyed her irritation as well. He glanced at Ethan. The little boy studied Vanessa Kingsley, apparently fascinated by the neck brace she wore.

Brantley straightened a stack of papers, then laid the neatly stacked documents on the table. He looked to his left at Vanessa

Kingsley and then he looked to his right at his paralegal assistant. Finally, he looked straight at Sadie and said, "I presume you are Sadie Hopkins."

She nodded.

Brantley motioned with his hand. "Perhaps you'd like to introduce your friends."

Daniel leaned forward to represent his client, but the words stuck in his throat.

Sadie looked at Daniel and said, "This is Daniel Smith." She reached out and touched his forearm. "Daniel is providing my legal counsel."

Brantley's head snapped to attention, and Daniel thought he saw a slight grin cross the man's face.

Sadie pointed at Ethan, who still sat motionless in the big chair with his mouth dropped open, mesmerized by the brace on Vanessa Kingsley's neck. "And this is Ethan. I'm looking after him."

Brantley chuckled. "Might he be providing your legal counsel as well?"

Daniel felt his face burn. He wanted to slide down in his chair and underneath the table. Obviously, Brantley didn't take him seriously. Why would he? This man had practiced law for more than ten years, and the best his opposition could offer was a first-year law student, who had only taken a few introductory legal courses—and who had struggled with those.

Brantley motioned to his tight-faced assistant. "This is Miss Smoot. She is my paralegal assistant." He turned and motioned toward Vanessa Kingsley. "And I believe you've already met Miss Kingsley."

Ethan began bumping the chair's armrests against the table as he swiveled the chair back and forth. The trio on the other side of the table stared at the child with ugly scowls on their faces. Daniel reached over and held the chair still.

Brantley looked back toward his prey. "Let's get on with the meeting, Mr. Smith. My client, Miss Vanessa Kingsley, claims your client, Mrs. Hopkins, rear-ended her car on May 31st. As a result of the collision, Miss Kingsley has experienced a serious case of whiplash."

Sadie interrupted, her voice stern and staccato. "Mr. Cavanaugh, I barely tapped Miss Kingsley's car. In fact, we found no physical damage, just a little scratch on her bumper. Other than being irate, Miss Kingsley seemed perfectly fine the day of the accident. So, I find it difficult to believe her whiplash—if she really suffers from whiplash—resulted from the bump-up."

Brantley held up his hand as if to tell Sadie to put on the brakes. He stared harshly at Daniel. "Mr. Smith, I think it is most appropriate that correspondence remain at an attorney-to-attorney level."

Daniel nodded.

Brantley continued, speaking directly to Daniel. "It is a medical fact that it can take several days before whiplash manifests itself." He picked up a document from the table and held it up. "We have a signed letter from Miss Kingsley's physician stating she exhibits the symptoms of whiplash. As a result of her pain she has been forced to wear a neck brace almost since the day of the accident. As you can imagine this has caused substantial hardship."

Daniel shifted in his seat. He knew they were about to learn just how substantial her hardship had been.

Brantley pushed back his chair and stood. He walked to the end of the mahogany table and poured himself a glass of water. "Not only has she had to deal with physical pain and emotional trauma from her whiplash, she has also missed numerous days from work." Brantley took a long drink from the crystal glass.

Daniel gawked in amazement at Brantley's performance— his ability to remain in control, to speak without emotion, and to effectively communicate his position.

Brantley refilled his glass. "Mr. Smith, my client is seeking restitution in the amount of $100,000 for the physical and emotional stress caused by your client, Mrs. Hopkins. We are prepared to file suit in a civil court in order to collect these damages, if necessary."

Daniel felt his mouth drop open. He looked at Sadie's pale face. Her lower lip trembled. He feared she would break out in tears.

Brantley walked back to his chair. "But because litigation is extremely expensive, our hope is that we can settle this matter out of court and save the expenses associated with a trial."

Daniel rocked back in his chair. Their strategy had become clear. They sought to negotiate an out-of-court settlement, probably for about half the requested amount. They believed Sadie would agree to a lesser amount in order to avoid having to go to court. He looked at the face of each person on the opposite side of the table while he gathered his thoughts. He knew Jake and Sadie did not have that kind of money. He leaned forward and responded, "Mr. Cavanaugh, my client does not have that kind of money. The couple has recently retired. They have no outside income other than the retirement that they are drawing. In addition, Mr. Hopkins has recently experienced heart trouble. As a result they have accumulated significant hospital expenses. Under the circumstances, $100,000 seems to be quite excessive."

Brantley forcefully set his glass on the table and spoke with a stern voice. "Mr. Smith, I'm here to represent Miss Kingsley. I cannot and will not be swayed by the financial troubles of your client."

Daniel studied Brantley and Vanessa's faces as he searched for words. Neither showed any signs of remorse or sympathy. What could he say? What would be the appropriate response from a seasoned lawyer?

Crash! The sounds of a metal tray hitting the floor and glass shattering came from across the room. Everyone's attention immediately shifted to the far end of the long mahogany table. Daniel saw nothing but a small hand clinging to the edge of the table and the top of a carrot-colored head.

Brantley's face turned red.

"My crystal," he shouted.

Brantley raced to the end of the table.

Ethan, realizing he'd drawn the man's attention, spun around to make his escape.

Daniel saw terror in Ethan's wild blue eyes.

Brantley's long arm caught Ethan by the shoulder.

Ethan let go a high-pitched scream. "Momm-meee."

Daniel stood, in part to help contain Ethan and in part to help defend him, if necessary. But Ethan did not need defending.

The three-year-old spun around as Brantley closed in and kicked the man in the shin.

Brantley screamed in pain and let go of the little boy.

Ethan scurried behind Sadie like a cockroach running from the kitchen light.

Brantley hopped around for a second on one leg and then flopped down into a chair, his eyes filled with pain or anger, or perhaps, both.

Ethan peeked from behind Sadie's legs and watched the grown man make a spectacle of himself.

Brantley pointed his long, thin finger at Ethan. "Get that little monster out of here," he screamed. "And don't bring him back."

❦ CHAPTER 25 ❦

Sadie rolled over in bed and stared at the ceiling. Worry always seemed to make her restless-legs syndrome act up. She tried her best to lie still so she would not bother Jake. Then without warning, her left leg, as if it had a mind of its own, would jerk. She looked at the clock. It read 1:30 a.m. It seemed like she had lain here half the night. Her mind kept replaying the settlement meeting. Vanessa Kingsley, Miss Smoot, and Brantley Cavanaugh had been rude, unfriendly, and intimidating. She'd been absolutely flabbergasted by the amount of retribution they sought for a fender bender. How could they ever think they could get away with that kind of robbery? She and Jake had spent all their lives accumulating their small retirement nest egg, and now a single event that had lasted only a few seconds threatened to take away a large portion of their retirement.

Life wasn't fair. In fact, God wasn't fair. Whether it concerned Jake's poor health, Ethan being deserted by Megan, the lawsuit, or the death of Frank many years before, she felt certain of this conclusion: God wasn't fair.

Jake rolled away from her, taking the sheet with him. Her feet, exposed to the night air, grew cold. She tugged on the sheet and covered her bare feet.

She felt a grin spread across her face. There had been one bright spot to her day. She relished the thought of Ethan kicking the pompous Brantley Cavanaugh in the shin. She'd watched with delight as the grown man had winced in pain. After all, he deserved it. She chuckled softly, sending a vibration throughout the bed as she remembered how the three-year-old child had gotten the best of Brantley. Oh, how she would love to share the glorious details with Jake. In fact, she longed to tell him all about the lawsuit. But she couldn't, not yet. She would wait until both his health and their predicament improved.

She checked the clock again. Perhaps she would grow drowsy if she drank a glass of warm milk. It had always worked during her childhood. She rolled over and quietly climbed out of bed. She slid her feet into her slippers, located her housecoat draped over the bedpost, and quietly exited the bedroom. She moved stealthily up the hall and through the den under the cover of darkness until she reached the kitchen. She turned on the hood light over the stove and poured some milk into a pot. When the milk had warmed, she poured it into a coffee mug and turned out the light.

She sat at the table and looked out the bay window. This had always been her favorite spot. It provided a commanding view of their huge front yard that sloped down to the state-maintained gravel road. The view from the bay window perfectly framed their beloved Carving Tree. She sipped the warm milk as she scanned the hillside. She could see the profile of the Carving Tree against the moonlit sky. The many bare branches gave the tree a skeletal appearance and reminded her of the tree in mid-winter. Sadie slowly rotated the cup on the tabletop and reflected on the tree's deteriorating appearance. The tree had been a permanent fixture for many years, a pillar of strength, and the symbol of their love. Now the massive beech was dying, and she didn't know how to save it. The county agent and tree specialist didn't know either. She felt helpless. Perhaps Cal Simpson had been right when he said the tree might be dying of old age. Maybe their time on this earth had nearly expired, and they could do little to extend it.

She dabbed at the corners of her eyes with a paper napkin and contemplated the one thing she could do. She could keep the lawsuit a secret as long as possible and spare Jake's weak heart from the stress it brought. She set her jaw and headed to bed.

She kissed Jake on the forehead and breathed in the familiar scent of the aftershave that defined him. She lifted his left arm, backed up against his chest, and lowered his arm to her abdomen. As if by reflex, he slid his right arm under her pillow and bent his knees slightly to assume the familiar "spooning" position. Somehow, at least for the moment, everything seemed better.

Daniel lethargically handed a customer change and said, "Good day. Come again." The bells on the door jingled as the customer exited the store. Daniel turned and was startled by his father, who propped against the paint counter with his arms crossed. His dad had one of his inquisitive looks.

Daniel closed the cash register drawer. "You spooked me. How long have you been standing there?"

Bob unfolded his arms and dropped them to the edge of the countertop upon which he propped. "Long enough to know something is troubling you."

Daniel cocked his head. "What do you mean?"

Bob pushed away from the counter and stepped closer. "You seem distant this morning, preoccupied with something other than work. I can hear it in your voice when you talk to the customers, and I can see it in your body language."

Daniel's gaze fell to the floor. Both the lawsuit and his feelings of inadequacy had been eating at him. Apparently, others could sense his turmoil.

Bob pulled a wooden stool up to the checkout counter and sat. "Son, I don't mean to pry, but I might just be able to help."

Daniel stared into space. He didn't know anyone wiser than his dad. Perhaps, he could offer some sound advice. Daniel exhaled deeply, took a seat on a second wooden stool, and shared the Hopkinses' predicament.

Bob chuckled at the story of Ethan kicking Brantley Cavanaugh in the shin. "That little boy has a lot of spunk. Serves this Cavanaugh fellow right. It's a crying shame that good people like the Hopkinses are taken advantage of by greedy people like this Kingsley woman and her lawyer." He stared at the ceiling and rubbed his chin.

Daniel watched his dad. He could almost see the gears turning in his father's head.

Finally his dad spoke. "This lawsuit is nothing more than a scam. I'm afraid the only way to beat it is to expose it as such."

Daniel raised his eyebrows. "And just how do we do that?"

Bob grinned. "With a scam of our own."

Sadie held Ethan's hand, took a deep breath, and rang the door-bell. *Ding-dong!* She looked down at Ethan, who was trying to lure a red and black ladybug from the porch rail onto his finger. The paint on the rail had begun to peel. The porch hadn't been painted in at least ten years, not since Paul died. She swallowed deeply. She wouldn't know what to do if Jake passed away. How could she ever live alone?

Ethan held up an open palm that contained the ladybug. "Look, Sayda."

She frowned. Red dirt, like heavy rouge, covered Ethan's face and shirt. She'd not taken the time to clean him up. Rather, she'd come as soon as she'd hung up the phone with another irritated church member. She blew at a low-hanging curl. Enough was enough. Maude and Mabel needed to resolve their differences—before they destroyed the church.

She rang the doorbell a second time and tapped her foot impatiently. The shadow that shrouded the front porch darkened as the sun passed behind a cloud.

The front door cracked opened, and Maude peeped out dressed in a hot pink housecoat, her hair rolled in large curlers. "What a pleasant surprise." She pulled the door wide open. "Y'all come on in."

Sadie stepped in with Ethan and the ladybug. She sighed. The subject of her visit would not be pleasant for Maude.

Maude motioned toward the den. "Make yourself comfortable on the couch."

Sadie sat on the soft leather couch. Ethan dropped to his knees in front of the small coffee table and dumped his red and black playmate on the glass tabletop. Aware the novelty of the brightly colored beetle would quickly wear off, she got to the point. "Maude, we've been friends for a long time. Because of our friendship and my concern for your well-being, I need to talk to you about Mabel."

Maude's face reddened. "I'm not talking to Mabel anymore. She's a traitor. She knew full well I was trying to get Sam Peterson to court me and wooed him behind my back until he asked her out instead."

Sadie bit her lip and watched the ladybug scurry across the tabletop, like a miniature Volkswagen beetle, fleeing the three-year-old finger that pursued it.

Maude crossed her arms defiantly. "I'll never forgive her."

Sadie could see tremendous pain in Maude's eyes. For as long as she'd known Mabel and Maude, they'd been like sisters— and fought like sisters. She softened her voice. "Do you remember Pastor Nolan's sermon last week about Esau and his root of bitterness? Maude, I think you have a root of bitterness, too. Things between you and Mabel are spiraling wildly out of control. First, you stopped talking to her, then you started spreading rumors about her and Sam, and then you tried to get her kicked off the hospitality committee. Don't you see your bitterness is consuming you? You need to uproot it."

Maude frowned. "You sound like you're on her side." Her volume grew louder. "Perhaps you should leave if all you're going to do is make accusations and lecture me."

Sadie touched Maude's arm. "I'm not on anyone's side. I just don't want to stand by and watch the destruction of a wonderful friendship."

Maude pounded her fist on the coffee table. "Wonderful, huh? I think it's best if you leave now."

Ethan screamed and stared at Maude's fist. The ladybug was no more.

Megan jumped when she heard the click of the door latch. She surveyed the poorly lit holding room. Three other girls rose to their feet. Her captors only opened the door for three reasons: to deliver meals, to deliver new girls, or to remove existing girls. She swallowed hard. Lunchtime wouldn't come for several hours, so this could be *her* moment. She touched the tender flesh where she'd been branded five days earlier. Fortunately, the crusty scab that had formed over the burn had greatly reduced its sensitivity. The brand could only be seen when her hair was pulled back in a ponytail. But then again, did its visibility really matter? She had been branded like an ordinary heifer, and she belonged to someone else.

The heavy metal door, like a fortress gate, swung open just long enough for two men to shove a girl into the room. The door slammed shut, sending a loud thud throughout the room.

She gasped. Carmen, the model she'd met at The Right Look Modeling Agency, stood just inside the door. With her chin dropped to her chest and her arms wrapped tightly around herself, she looked like a wilted flower. Her body shook as she wept uncontrollably.

Megan stepped forward and lifted Carmen's chin. "Carmen, it's me, Megan." She looked into the heavily flooded eyes and saw a flicker of recognition. "We met at the modeling agency in Charlotte."

Carmen wiped the tears from her eyes. "Where are we? Why have these men abducted me?"

Megan led Carmen to a nearby cot. "You probably need to sit down for this."

Carmen took a seat on the cot.

Megan raked her fingers through her hair. "We are being held captive by a human-trafficking ring that is probably operated by the mafia. From what I've pieced together, we will be auctioned over the Internet to the highest bidder."

Carmen sat in a stupor.

Megan gently stroked Carmen's hair. "How did you get to California?"

Carmen frowned and shook her head. "I was flown out here for an audition, all expenses paid."

Megan's jaw tightened. "Who arranged your trip?"

Carmen squeezed her eyes shut as if trying to recall the details from the back recesses of her mind. "A judge from The Right Look Modeling Agency. Brinks, I believe."

CHAPTER 26

Jake brought his front-porch rocker to a stop and wiped the perspiration from his brow. It felt hotter than a tobacco barn during curing season. Yep, sitting in a rocker on the front porch in the shade and sipping iced tea was the only place to be on such a scorcher. He yawned. Since his return home from the hospital, he typically napped for several hours after lunch. Now with a full stomach, his only concern at the moment was drifting off to sleep while Sadie talked. He patted his stomach. "I ate too much."

Sadie moaned. "You're not the only one." She leaned to one side of the rocker. "Can you see Ethan?"

Jake rubbed the sleep from his eyes and pointed toward the azaleas at the front corner of the porch. "He's in the azalea bed hunting squirrels with Buckshot."

A familiar two-tone pickup turned into their driveway. The cloud of dust that had been pulled along by the truck drifted past their mailbox. Jake would recognize that old F-150 anywhere.

He pointed toward the mailbox. "Well, looky there. It's Clyde and Erma."

Sadie sighed. "You mean, 'Well, look there.'"

He rubbed the back of his neck. "Yes, Mrs. Hopkins, ma'am."

Sadie cradled her temples. "Heavens, I hope she doesn't bring any more banana pudding."

His stomach churned at the thought. "I'm afraid Erma's generous cooking will be the death of us."

The battered pickup rolled to a stop in the front yard, and Jake saw Clyde slip his dentures into his mouth. Erma slowly eased out of the truck. She wore a bright yellow dress with a pattern of large white daisies. Her yellow hat with its large white brim resembled a daisy as well.

Erma bent to lift a huge plastic bowl from the floorboard of the truck and then squealed when Buckshot greeted her with his cold, wet nose. She almost dropped the bowl. "Land sakes alive! That dog needs to learn some manners."

Jake chuckled to himself and caught Sadie's worried glance. The bowl, covered with a piece of wrinkled tinfoil, looked familiar. He climbed down the steps and greeted Clyde with a warm handshake. "Hi, Clyde. What brings you here?"

Clyde snapped his suspenders. "Just passing by. Thought we'd drop in and check on you." Clyde's unbonded dentures clicked as he spoke. "Erma, here, has brought a little something to kill your appetite."

Jake swallowed hard. Kill was right. "Wonderful! Our church family has been really good to us. People just keep on bringing us goodies to eat."

Sadie greeted Erma, who struggled with the large bowl. "Can I help you?"

Erma handed the bowl to Sadie, her Parkinson's hands shaking more than usual due to the weight of the bowl. "Here, shugah." She pulled off the tinfoil cover and a faint breeze brought the sweet smell of vanilla and overripe bananas to Jake's nostrils.

Erma gave a red-toothed smile. "I brought you some of my nana pudding."

Jake glanced at Sadie and saw concern in her large green eyes.

Ethan jumped out of the azalea bed. "Puddin'. Ethan wants puddin'."

Sadie responded, "No, not now. We just ate lunch. Perhaps a little later."

The little boy crossed his arms and poked out his lower lip.

Jake's mind shifted into gear, and he began to formulate excuses for not eating the pudding. Perhaps he would tell Erma the doctor had forbidden him to eat sweets. After all, the doctor had warned him to watch his diet. Being a diabetic herself, Erma ought to understand. He'd heard her say more than once that the doctor had told her to lay off the sweets and the spuds. But he was not a diabetic, and the doctor had not told him to avoid sweets. Besides, even if he couldn't eat the pudding, Erma would leave it for Sadie and Ethan. He certainly didn't need a sick wife and a three-year-old child with an upset stomach.

Of course, he could be straightforward and honest and just tell Erma that her pudding wasn't edible. He knew that wouldn't go over well. It would simply break her heart, and she would probably never speak to him again. No, Clyde and Erma had been too close over the years to be honest. He felt trapped "between a rock and a hard place," as his dad used to say. *Lord, I need a little miracle here . . . just a small one. I know this is a miniscule problem in the overall scheme of things, but it involves people's feelings. Please work a miracle.*

With her hands full, Sadie motioned toward the house with her head. "It's too hot to stand here in the sun. Let's go in the house. I need to put this pudding in the refrigerator." She looked back at her guests as she started up the steps. "Would you like something cold to—?" Sadie stumbled over the bottom step and launched the big plastic bowl of pudding up and over the handrail into the azalea bed. The bowl landed on a large azalea and flipped several times, dumping its contents on the azalea and the ground.

Jake stepped quickly to her aid and searched her eyes. "Are you okay, honey?"

Sadie winked at him and then lifted her body from the steps. "I'm fine, just extremely clumsy." She apologized to Erma. "I'm very sorry. I've ruined your wonderful pudding."

He recognized the insincerity in her voice and realized that in the wink of an eye, he'd become her accomplice. Her intentional dropping of the bowl hadn't been the answer he'd expected, but he would take it.

Erma waddled over and placed her hand on Sadie's shoulder. "Well, bless your heart. It was just a puddin'. It'll be alright."

Buckshot's tail whipped the air as he sniffed the white egg meringue that coated the tip of an azalea branch. All of a sudden, his tail dropped between his legs. He whimpered and ran underneath the front porch.

Jake scratched his head. "Wonder what got into Buckshot."

Jake smiled and motioned toward the den couch. "Have a seat." While Erma and Clyde claimed a spot on the brown tweed couch, he watched Sadie find a television cartoon for Ethan and then dart into the kitchen with the empty pudding bowl.

Erma affectionately ran her shaky hand over the large Bible that occupied the center of the marble-top coffee table. "Is this your family Bible?"

He adjusted his pillow. "It actually belonged to Sadie's parents."

Erma sighed. "It's beautiful."

Sadie re-entered the room and handed the clean plastic bowl to Erma. "I can't believe I'm so clumsy that I dropped your bowl."

He squirmed in his recliner. The deceitful words flowed from her mouth much too easily.

Erma smiled a red-toothed smile. "That's okay, darlin'. If I had a dolla' for every time Clyde has dropped a bowl of my puddin', I'd be rich."

He covered his mouth to hide his grin. Poor Clyde, he probably had to eat the pudding weekly.

Erma pointed toward Ethan, who sat engrossed in a cartoon. "That's a sad thing about his mother. Is there any news?"

Sadie frowned. "No. I had to file a formal missing persons report three days ago. I think the sheriff still believes she'll show up. I'm afraid she's been in some kind of accident."

Erma looked concerned. "Law, honey, I hope not."

Clyde snapped a suspender. "You know, I remember a bad accident back in the war. A soldier got drunk and flipped his jeep— killed his best friend, don't ya know." Clyde's upper dentures shifted as he talked. "He had the filthiest mouth you've ever heard. Cursed God daily. Yet, he spent three days on his knees begging God to heal his friend. But God saw differently, and his buddy died. Man never was the same."

Erma clasped her hands together, looked toward heaven, and quoted scripture, "But your iniquities have separated between you and your God, and your sins have hid His face from you, that He will not hear."

Jake recognized the verse as Isaiah 59:2, one he'd previously memorized.

Erma pointed toward the ceiling. "You know, God doesn't hear the prayers of an unrepentant sinner. It's plain and simple. You can't expect God to answer your prayer, unless your heart is right."

Sadie frowned and raked the same pile of leaves onto the blanket for a third time. She'd barely stepped back when Ethan jumped into the pile and scattered them. She blew at a strand of hair that teased the corner of her eye.

Ethan giggled and tried to bury Buckshot beneath the leaves.

She smiled. Although she grew tired of raking up the same leaves, it did her heart good to see the child having so much fun. She surveyed the remaining area to rake. She didn't seek to be thorough. She just wanted to reduce the volume of fallen leaves so Jake wouldn't draw a correlation between the condition of the Carving Tree and his own health. Jake had been napping since Clyde and Erma had left. So she seized this opportune time to remove some of the leaves without his knowledge.

She stopped, propped against the rake, and watched Ethan as he tossed the leaves into the air. Her mind drifted back to one of their first years after becoming man and wife. They had been raking up leaves under this very tree. Although it occurred decades before, the image came clearly to her mind.

She quietly slipped up from behind, her bare feet stealthily picking their way through the leaves. She squealed with delight as she dumped a handful of leaves over Jake's head.

The young man spun around, eyes full of excitement. Little sticks and debris stuck to his greased-back hair and clung to his white T-shirt.

She giggled. They had only been married for a few years, but he was the most handsome and wonderful man alive.

He spoke with a serious and stern tone. "You shouldn't have done that."

She took a step back. "Oh, yeah?"

He grinned. "Now you're going to get it."

She spun around to run, but before she could take three steps a strong arm caught her by the waist and lifted her effortlessly from the ground. She kicked her legs as if running in air. "Jake Earl Hopkins, you put me down this instant."

He laughed. "Are you sure that's what you want?"

"Right this minute."

He turned and dropped her into a big pile of leaves, then dove in beside her. They both lay in the pile and laughed.

A handful of leaves peppered her face, and she snapped back to the present. Ethan faced her with wild blue eyes. He reared back to throw another handful of leaves.

She retaliated, surprised at how fast her aged body moved. She caught the carrot-top three-year-old, swept him off his feet, and tossed him in the big pile of leaves.

Ethan giggled.

"That'll teach you," she said.

Ethan held out his freckled arms. "Do again, Say-da. Do again."

She lifted her aching body from a kneeling position. "I've got to finish getting up these leaves." She resumed raking and reflected on Erma's words from earlier in the day. She could still hear her words: "You can't expect God to answer your prayer unless your heart is right." Were Erma's words true? Does God ignore the prayers of an unrepentant sinner? Must a person's heart be right before God answers? She propped against the rake to catch her breath. Erma's words stung. She hadn't been right with God for many years. In fact, she hadn't felt close to God since childhood— since the morning her daddy had died. It had been one of the most painful times of her life. On that day she'd lost all interest in reading her Bible or praying to God—that is, really praying. For years she'd gone to church only to meet the expectations of other people. Perhaps, if she met God's expectations, if she got on the right terms with Him—if she read her Bible more often, repented more often, and prayed more often—God would answer her prayers and heal Jake. Yes, she would give it a try. Surely God would answer her prayer.

❧ CHAPTER 27 ❧

Jake watched in awe from his front porch rocker. The brilliant yellow sun began its climb above the edge of the earth. The clouds on the horizon glowed in multiple shades of orange and yellow. The invigorating chill of the night air began to flee as the morning sun's rays touched his face.

Buckshot lay with his muzzle draped across Jake's foot. Most every dawn would find them here—man and faithful canine. He would sit in his rocker on the east-facing front porch with Buckshot at his feet, sip a hot cup of coffee, and reflect on the Creator. The scriptures often came alive after he'd witnessed this spectacular act of nature. This personal time with God prepared him to face each new day.

The sun had just cleared the horizon when the screen door opened. Buckshot's tail thumped softly against the plank floor. Sadie walked out on the porch in her pink housecoat and fluffy pink slippers. She carried a cup of coffee and her Bible.

He checked to see if his mouth had dropped open and then greeted Sadie. "Good morning."

Sadie smiled, laid her Bible on the porch rail, and sat in the porch swing clasping her coffee mug with both hands. "I've come to study with you," she said.

He didn't know what to say. In all the years they'd been married, she'd never wanted to study the Bible with him. How should he respond?

Sadie patted the seat of the porch swing with her hand. "Come join me, and let's watch the sunrise together."

He studied her face by the light of the early morning rays. Her green eyes were bright and more striking than ever. He moved from his rocker to the porch swing. Buckshot relocated along with him. The old dog circled three times and plopped down in front of the swing with a moan.

Sadie slipped her arm in his. He felt her delicate fingers interlace the fingers of his calloused hand. His pulse quickened at her touch. She laid her head on his shoulder and kissed his cheek. He basked in her affection. In the quiet of the morning they watched the spectacular sunrise.

When the sun rose above the tree line, he broke the silence. "I'm glad you joined me this morning." He squeezed her hand. "You mean all the world to me. There is nothing that I desire more . . . except . . . maybe a cigarette."

Sadie playfully slapped his arm. "Well, you can't have one. Doctor's order. So, that puts me at the top of your list." She paused. "You know, I've been thinking."

He chuckled. "Now I'm really in trouble."

Her eyes danced. "Seriously, I've been thinking that maybe we should all go to church Sunday. You've been cooped up here for weeks. It might be good for you. Yes, I think all three of us should go."

He nodded and reflected on her words. He wondered about her sudden interest in spiritual matters. It gave him hope. Perhaps, she felt the Holy Spirit's conviction.

When the early morning light improved, they picked up their Bibles and began to read silently. He stared at the words on the page. He tried to read, but the voices that screamed within him drowned out his mental pronunciation of the words. The voice in his heart said, "Talk to Sadie." But the voice in his head said, "Wait. Wait on God's timing. Let her initiate the discussion." He listened to the voice in his head. Several times during their marriage, he'd dared to approach the topic. Each time it had made her mad and, in his opinion, driven her even farther from the truth. *Lord, help me to know when the time is right.*

Sadie checked her wristwatch. "It's almost eight o'clock. Ethan is usually knocking down the kitchen door for breakfast by now."

He saw concern on her face.

Sadie stood. "He's too quiet. I better check on him. I'm afraid he's getting into trouble." She laid her Bible and empty mug in the seat of a rocker and slipped into the house.

He rubbed the ache in the back of his neck and stood. Buckshot immediately rose and stretched, ready to follow his master to the end of the earth, or at least to the garden or mailbox. Jake opened the screen door and heard Sadie scream. He rushed into the house and found her in Frank's bedroom scolding Ethan.

He propped against the bedroom doorjamb and surveyed the room as he tried to catch his breath. One wall of Frank's bedroom was covered with red squiggly lines. It resembled heavy crayon marks. He looked at Ethan. The little boy's face contained the same heavy red marks.

Sadie wailed, "And with my favorite lipstick."

He touched Ethan's shoulder. "He's just a child."

Sadie frowned. "He's not my child."

Megan felt powerless to help as Carmen's contorted body jerked from a diabetic seizure. Each spasm, like a miniature earthquake, made the worn-out cot shake and creak. How long could Carmen survive without her insulin injections? She'd complained of fatigue and extreme thirst just after lunch. Within two hours she'd become nauseous and complained of dry mouth. From that point forward, her condition had quickly deteriorated. Her breathing had grown rapid, and she seemed confused. And then the seizures had started.

Megan looked around the room for help, but all the girls, even Lola, had a look of terror and hopelessness in their eyes. Desperate to help Carmen, she pounded on the heavy metal door and screamed, "Help! There's a girl having a seizure in here. She's diabetic. She's going to die." After several minutes of screaming and pounding, the lock on the door clicked. She stepped back. The guard opened the door and let in a large bald man. He carried a large hypodermic needle in one hand.

She gasped. She recognized the man instantly. She'd seen him next to her car the night of her abduction. He must have sensed her recognition because he gave her a slight grin just like he had in the parking lot. Tattoos of dragons decorated his arms, and a large gold-looped earring hung from his left ear. With his slick and shiny scalp and thick chin beard, he resembled the Mr. Clean cleanser icon on steroids.

She pleaded as she backpedaled. "Please help her."

He gave her an apathetic look and then walked to the cot where Carmen's spastic body lay jerking. He pointed the tip of the needle toward the ceiling and ejected a small quantity of liquid. He raised Carmen's skirt, stabbed the hypodermic needle in her upper thigh, and injected its contents. Almost instantaneously Carmen's contorted body went limp. The squeaking cot grew silent. Mr. Clean grinned and headed for the door.

Megan rested on her knees beside the cot and dabbed the perspiration from Carmen's forehead. She didn't know what Mr. Clean had given her, but for the moment Carmen rested.

✿ CHAPTER 28 ✿

Jake awoke in the middle of the night and felt strange.

His heart raced wildly.

His chest heaved like he'd just completed the 100-yard dash.

He craved oxygen, but his lungs couldn't draw in enough.

The suffocating sensation felt like he was trapped in a room filling with water and fighting to keep his nose in the disappearing air space between the surface and the ceiling.

To make matters worse, he felt extremely light-headed. Drops of perspiration poured down his face and trickled into his ears. His saturated clothes clung to his body. He desired to kick off the sheets, but at the moment, he didn't have the strength to do so.

He gritted his teeth and resisted the urge to cry out to Sadie. He'd felt the same way the day he'd fallen in the garden. Dr. Bradford had called it ventricular tachycardia, or VT for short. The doctor had explained that his erratic heartbeat was disrupting the normal performance of his heart, significantly reducing the ventricle's ability to eject blood. However, a major difference existed between this episode of VT and the previous attack. The episode in the garden had been brought on by physical activity. This time it had occurred while at rest.

He swallowed deeply. It didn't take a medical genius to diagnose his deteriorating condition. The doctor had said that VT could also cause loss of consciousness or even sudden death. Could this be the end? Was he dying here and now? He wrestled with the thought. Should he wake up Sadie? Should they call paramedics? He didn't want to worry Sadie unnecessarily. Surely this would pass just like it had in the garden.

He squeezed his eyes tightly shut. *Lord, don't let me die. You know I'm not finished yet. There's still more to do.* He lay perfectly still, repeating the prayer over and over. After a few moments his breathing came a little easier, and the pace of his heart slowed. He felt his energy start to return, and he flipped off the damp sheet. He glanced at the clock. It read 2:20 a.m. Sadie moaned and rolled over on her side. He lay very still so as not to awaken her.

The moon illuminated three portraits on the wall at the foot of their bed. The middle portrait featured Frank in his dress uniform. Sadie had taken Frank's unexpected death extremely hard.

He placed a hand over his heart and monitored the beat. How would he die? Would it occur suddenly from the arrhythmia condition of which the doctor had warned? Or would he die a slow, agonizing death confined to a bed or wheelchair and force his beloved Sadie to watch his condition daily deteriorate? What effect would his death have on her? Would it crush her all at once and send her over the edge? Or would it cause her to slowly waste away? Was Sadie bracing for his approaching death? Might this explain her sudden interest in spiritual things? Had she been thinking about eternity? Could she be under the conviction of the Holy Spirit? The thought rekindled a spark of hope. He rolled over and gently placed his arm across her abdomen. He deeply breathed in the fragrance of her hair and kissed her bare shoulder repeatedly until his eyelids grew heavy.

Megan rolled out of her cot and rushed to Carmen when the guards switched on the holding room's fluorescent lights. The girl's position had not changed since she'd received the injection from Mr. Clean. Megan squatted next to the cot and touched the girl's forehead. Unlike the night before, it felt cool. "Carmen," she whispered close to the girl's ear. "Are you feeling better?" Carmen did not respond. She tapped her shoulder and spoke a little louder. "Carmen, are you okay?" Several girls moaned and changed their sleeping positions. She shook Carmen, but the girl didn't respond. She swallowed hard. Was Carmen dead? She shuddered at the thought. She placed her ear over Carmen's mouth, but she couldn't detect a breath. The room began to slowly spin. She reached for Carmen's wrist to check for a pulse, and then—her world went black.

Daniel paused from his task of sweeping the sidewalk in front of the store and smiled. What a gorgeous morning—brilliant sunshine, low humidity, and a cloudless sky. And to top it all off, he'd devised a plan that might just work.

It had been a slow morning at the A&E, and after three days of scheming, he'd finally been able to finish a mental model of the complete scam. Although simple, the scheme would require some careful planning and help from his dad to execute.

He finished sweeping the pine straw and acorns from the sidewalk and hurried into the store to share the details of the scam with his accomplice. He knew his dad's attention to detail and his logical nature would provide a good test of his plan.

He watched as his father rang up a customer. Typical of his dad, Bob seemed to be in no hurry at all and held a lengthy conversation with the patron. Bob always seemed to take a personal interest in each customer that entered the store. Daniel knew his father was not trying to manipulate people to ensure future sales. Rather, Bob genuinely cared for his customers. He wished he could be more like his dad. He earnestly desired to help others, but he constantly wrestled with feelings of inadequacy. Worrying how others perceived him seemed to be engrained in his nature. Fortunately, this morning he felt a little better about himself.

The bells on the entrance door jingled as the customer departed. Daniel watched his father straighten up the counter. The two men exchanged glances as Bob retied his apron.

"What's on your mind, son?"

Daniel felt a grin creep across his face. "I've contrived a plan to help the Hopkinses, and I think it might just work. I'll need to borrow some equipment from the store, and I'll need your help to make it work."

Bob finished restocking the plastic bags at the checkout counter and leaned back against the counter. "Shoot, son."

❧ CHAPTER 29 ❧

Jake sat at the kitchen table with a hot cup of coffee and a heavy heart. It saddened him that Sadie and Ethan had gone to church without him. He'd been quite encouraged by Sadie's recent interest in spiritual matters and longed to see his many friends, but it had not been a good morning. When it had been time to roll out of bed, his legs had been as huge as fence posts. The water pills just didn't seem to be working anymore. He sipped his steaming coffee. It, too, tasted bitter.

He looked at the kitchen clock mounted above the sink. It read 10:50 a.m. Ethan would be playing in the church nursery, and Sadie would be finding a seat in the chapel next to Clyde and Erma. *Lord, make Sadie attentive to your message this morning. Speak through Pastor Nolan so he might say the word that she needs to hear in order to move her to faith. Amen.*

Sadie slid into the church pew beside Clyde and Erma, out of breath. Ethan clung tightly to her hand. She rolled her eyes. "I was afraid we'd be late for the service."

Erma gave a red-toothed smile. "Is Jake coming?"

Sadie shook her head and leaned close. "Not one of his better mornings. His legs were absolutely huge when he woke up this morning, and he had no energy."

Erma nodded. "Bless his heart. Don't sound one bit like Jake. He's always raring to go."

Sadie pulled Ethan into the seat beside her. "No. It's not like Jake. All his life he's been a morning person—ready to roll out of bed and get an early start on the day—but not this morning. He just wanted to roll over and go back to sleep. I didn't want to leave him, but he insisted Ethan and I come on to church. He promised to rest in bed until late morning."

Erma winked at Ethan. "And why aren't you in the nursery, young'un?"

Ethan stuck out his lower lip at Erma.

Sadie leaned close to Erma. "He threw a fit when I tried to leave him in children's church. He's become quite attached."

For what must have been the tenth time, Sadie looked sternly at Ethan, placed her finger to her lips, and said, "Shhh." Entertaining Ethan during the worship service was certainly not what she had in mind when she'd suggested to Jake that they attend church.

She studied the sanctuary while the organist played the offertory hymn. Glendale Baptist Church, the oldest church in the area, had been built in the late thirties. Six colorful stained glass windows were located on each side of the sanctuary. Each window contained some famous biblical scene, such as the parting of the Red Sea or Jesus healing blind Bartimaeus. Central air had been installed in the sanctuary in the early eighties. The large ventilation ducts had been routed next to the ceiling around the top of the walls, a constant reminder of the parishioners' limited incomes.

A man in the pew directly in front of her draped his arm around his wife's shoulder. Sadie bit her lip. She wished Jake could have attended. It would do him good to hear everyone inquire about his health and promise to pray for his complete recovery.

Ethan stood at the end of the pew with one leg in the aisle. She patted the pew and whispered, "Come sit here."

The little boy said nothing, but his menacing eyes said, "Make me."

She leaned, grabbed his upper arm, and squeezed until her knuckles began to turn white. Ethan whimpered and climbed into the seat beside her. Aaah . . . progress. Just a few days earlier the child would have refused to sit in the seat even with her pressure and would have thrown a tantrum, but the discipline they had applied during Megan's unexplained absence had begun to pay off. After a few old-fashioned spankings, Ethan's behavior and attitude had dramatically improved. Erma had noticed it too. She winked at Sadie when Ethan climbed onto the pew.

Jake studied the Carving Tree from his place at the kitchen table and scratched his head. The tree's health seemed worse than he'd initially thought. There had been a light wind overnight and many of the leaves had fallen from the tree. There couldn't be more than twenty or thirty remaining, and they also had the familiar yellow color. He sipped from his coffee mug, never taking his eyes off the tree. All along he'd expected that the grand old tree would recover and he would wake up one morning and notice new growth on the tree. But it hadn't happened. Each day the condition of the tree deteriorated even more. Now it seemed like a foregone conclusion. It wasn't a question of whether the tree would die. Rather, the question was: When would the tree die?

He spit several bitter coffee grounds from his mouth. The fact that his condition seemed to be deteriorating along with the tree disturbed him the most. His health had been on a downward spiral ever since he'd fallen in the garden. Even though he'd been faithful to take his medication and had given up smoking, he had little to show for his effort. He frowned. Why should he bother to abstain from smoking? What difference had it made? He rubbed the back of his neck. With his course set and his outcome the same, why should his final few days be marred by the misery of not being able to smoke?

He thought about the cigarettes in the truck's glove compartment. He stood and looked out the bay window. The pickup sat an easy distance from the house. He squeezed the back of a chair until his knuckles turned white. He could smoke a cigarette and brush his teeth, and Sadie would never even know the difference. Every fiber in his body urged him to fetch the cigarettes, and before he knew it, he stood next to his pickup. He paused a few minutes to catch his breath. After checking to make sure Sadie wasn't coming up the driveway, he rifled through the cluttered glove compartment. He found the cigarettes and headed back to the house. The familiar package felt strange in his hand. He felt like Adam carrying the forbidden fruit.

Winded, he stopped at the bottom of the porch steps to rest. Buckshot sat on one hip at the top of the steps. His head cocked to one side, and the wrinkled skin above his eyes bunched as if he was contemplating Jake's actions.

"Mind your own business," Jake muttered as he climbed the steps. The old dog looked at him with sad eyes and whined with disapproval. He stopped on the porch and removed a cigarette from the package. He dared not smoke in the house. With her keen smeller, Sadie would know in an instant he'd been smoking. He rolled the cigarette between his fingers. He'd promised Sadie that he'd not smoke again. He should keep his word. He stared at the cigarette and then sniffed it. The tobacco aroma lured him, like fresh red meat to a hungry predator. He placed the cigarette between his lips, and it felt natural.

Sadie shifted in the hard wooden pew and half-heartedly listened as Pastor Nolan began his sermon. She glanced around the old chapel. The room, filled to capacity with ordinary folk, resembled a Norman Rockwell painting. Colored rays of light spilled into the room through the east-facing stained glass windows.

Pastor Nolan propped against the wooden podium. "I grew up on a large farm in the Midwest. Each year during harvest time, I would walk through the golden wheat fields and snack on the mature kernels."

He stepped away from the podium. "I would snap off the full-grown heads of wheat and peel away the outer husks to reveal the golden kernels. Occasionally, I would find heads that contained no kernels, just empty husks. My dad called them 'tares,' imposters. They looked just like the real thing on the outside, but on the inside they were empty."

He moved behind the podium and opened his Bible. "The Bible talks about these imposters in the Parable of the Wheat and Tares. Please stand as we read this great parable recorded in Matthew 13:24–30."

The congregation rose. Ethan scrambled to his feet and stood on the pew. After the reading of the scripture, the congregation sat, and Pastor Nolan began to expound on the truths of the passage.

Sadie tugged on one of Ethan's belt loops until the child sat. Ethan quickly grew bored. He repeatedly opened and shut a hymnal. The hardcover book made a loud slapping noise each time it closed. The couple sitting in front of her turned around and gave her an irritated look.

She placed her hand on the hymnal and gave Ethan one of her harshest "fourth-grade-teacher ugly looks." She retrieved an ink pen from her pocketbook and began to draw stick figures on a bulletin. Ethan immediately caught on and snatched the ink pen. He began drawing his own pictures.

Pastor Nolan continued. "People in the church are a lot like the wheat and the tares. Some have made a sincere decision to follow Christ. They are the real McCoys, the stalks of wheat that bear true grain. Others among us, I fear, are like the tares . . . imposters." Pastor Nolan paused several moments for effect. Clyde broke the silence when he dropped his Bible on the floor. The top of his scalp grew deep red. He glanced around and then picked up his Bible.

Pastor Nolan stepped to the edge of the platform and stabbed the air with his index finger. "Tares . . . they look like Christians, smell like Christians, and act like Christians. But on the inside, they are empty, bearing no fruit at all." His voice softened. "Dearly beloved, perhaps you are a tare. To your family and friends, you look just like a perfect Christian—a deacon, a tither, a Sunday school teacher. You may even work on six church committees. Yet, you have never made a decision to follow Jesus. Consequently, one day you will suffer the same fate as the tares in the parable. On the Day of Judgment you will be consumed by fire."

Sadie's stomach flip-flopped. Clyde moved in his seat and wiped beads of sweat from his bare scalp with a handkerchief.

Pastor Nolan continued. "I challenge you to think back through your lifetime. Was there ever a point in time when you surrendered your heart to Jesus? Was there a moment when you repented of your sin and asked Him to come into your life, to forgive your sins and save your soul? If not, *you* are one of those tares."

She shifted in her seat. The wooden pew had suddenly grown unbearably hard. Most of her life she'd attended church, not because she wanted to, but to meet the expectations of others. A hypocrite, an imposter, an empty and fruitless church member— yes, she fit the description of a tare.

Pastor Nolan began to wrap up his sermon. "In a moment, you'll have the opportunity to come forward. If you are a tare, a hypocrite, or a pretender, I beg you to come, meet me at the front, and get right with Jesus. Come as the music plays and surrender your heart this morning."

She felt a tremendous tug at her heart as the music started. She could not sing the words in the hymnal. They couldn't get past the large choking lump in her throat. She swallowed deeply in an effort to clear the lump, but it wouldn't budge. She had an overwhelming need to go forward. But, what would people think? Sadie Hopkins—lifelong church member—lost.

Her hands trembled and tears filled her eyes. When she could no longer resist the pull, she slid past Ethan into the aisle and began the lonely journey to the front. A moment later Ethan latched onto her hand, his eyes large and frightened.

As she moved down the aisle, a voice screamed in her head. "You're Sadie Hopkins, lifelong church member. People will be shocked to find out you're not a Christian. They'll whisper and talk behind your back. They'll say, 'Sadie Hopkins is nothing but a hypocrite, an imposter, a tare. She has been fooling us for all these years.'" She pressed on toward the front with Ethan in tow. She'd let her emotions overwhelm her, momentarily lost her self-control, and stepped out. Now she had to go through with it or look like an even bigger fool.

Pastor Nolan stood in front of the raised podium ready to receive all who would come. He reached out and took her hand as she met him at the front.

Too choked to speak, she squeezed his hand.

He placed his free hand on her shoulder, leaned close, and prayed softly, "Dear God, I pray you would bring your healing power upon Jake. Give the doctors wisdom to diagnose his illness properly. We know you often work your miracles through medicine. So, I ask that the medication would regulate his heart that he might once again be able to live a normal and full life. May your will be done. In the precious name of Jesus, Amen." He released her hand and tussled Ethan's hair.

She looked at Ethan, at the pastor, and then at her feet. The pastor had misinterpreted her walk down the aisle. After all these years, she'd even fooled the preacher. She started to confess her intent, but Ethan tugged on her hand and the voice in her head said, "Let it go. Let it go." So, they returned to their seats, and she remained an empty tare among the wheat.

Sadie stopped the Impala at the Carving Tree, sat in the stillness of the car, and stared at the beech. The light wind from the prior night had almost stripped the tree bare. She climbed out of the car and walked over to the tree, her feet shoveling through the leaves. The fallen foliage crunched underfoot like crisp potato chips. She placed her hand on the bark and slowly walked around the tree, her hand sliding over the smooth-textured surface. She stopped at the carving and traced the shape of the heart with her finger. Tears filled her eyes. The symbol of their love was dying, but even more disturbing, the one she loved was dying.

She drove on to the house and climbed out of the car. Buckshot greeted her with a wag of his tail, but the tired old dog never stirred from his place at the top of the porch steps. She stopped at the bottom of the steps to tease the dog. "Hey, boy, did you miss me?"

Buckshot lazily thumped his tail on the gray plank floor. He looked at her with big sad eyes, moaned, and raised his hind leg, inviting her to scratch his belly. She climbed the steps, squatted, and scratched the dog's belly for a moment. The dog moaned with gratitude.

She cradled his head in both hands and noted the dog's graying muzzle. He, too, had aged just like the Carving Tree, just like Jake, and just like herself. She looked into his eyes. "You're a good dog." The dog's long, wet tongue kissed her nose. She wiped her nose with the back of her hand. "Oh, Buckshot."

She stood slowly, waited for the ache in her knee to subside, and slipped into the house. Her watch read 1:30 p.m. Could Jake still be in bed? She saw no sign of him in the den or the kitchen. She tiptoed down the hall and eased open the bedroom door. With the blinds still closed, the room looked dark and drab. Jake lay flat on his back with the sheet tucked under his arms. She could tell from his breathing that he was asleep. She stood quietly next to the double bed and studied his wrinkled face and thinning hair. His arms appeared slimmer, and his rough, calloused hands seemed oversized for his body. Both age and illness had taken their toll. The body that once seemed young and strong had grown old and weak.

Overwhelmed by deep sorrow, she blinked back the tears. She knew Jake's approaching death was just as inevitable as the passing of the Carving Tree. Jake's Bible lay open on the bedside table. The sight of the book aroused her anger. *Oh God, why haven't you honored my prayers? I've tried to live a holy life the last several days. I've read the Bible. I've attended church. And lord knows, I've prayed. Why haven't you kept your end of the bargain?*

Jake stirred.

She wiped the tears from her cheeks and took several slow, deep breaths. She had to be strong for Jake. She leaned and kissed his forehead, and his eyes opened. He grabbed the lanyard from which her reading glasses dangled and pulled her head toward his face. Their lips met.

Her heart quickened, and she felt a surge of energy pulse through her body. The touch of his lips still gave her goose bumps.

Their lips parted, and he laughed. "I feel like Rip Van Winkle."

She sat on the edge of the bed. "I was afraid you'd sleep all day."

He stretched his arms. "How was church?"

She thought about her trip down the aisle but chose to withhold it. "Just another Sunday."

He wiped the sleep from his eyes. "How did Ethan do?"

She momentarily glanced at the ceiling and then spoke, "He sat perfectly still and listened attentively to every word Pastor Nolan spoke."

Jake rolled his eyes. "Yeah, I believe that. And where is our young Bible scholar?"

She took hold of Jake's hand and interlaced her fingers with his. "That's the best part. He's with Erma and Clyde for the afternoon to give us some time together."

He laughed and pulled her over beside him. "You mean we're alone?"

She relaxed in his arms, and her face rested against his chest. She detected a faint smell embedded in his shirt, an unmistakable odor. She sat up abruptly, and her face grew hot. "Jake Earl Hopkins . . . !"

✿ CHAPTER 30 ✿

The heavy metal prison door swung open, and Megan stopped breathing. The eyes of every girl locked on the entrance, and all chatter and small talk ceased. A thick layer of anxiety hung in the room. She wiggled her foot nervously. With the exception of mealtime, opening of the door always brought bad things. Mr. Clean and another thug entered the room. The two men, with their huge chests and arms, resembled professional wrestlers.

Megan rose to her feet. She wondered if Mr. Clean knew about Carmen's death. Had he administered a lethal drug on purpose? A frigid reality coursed through her veins, a reality very similar to that which she'd experienced two days earlier when she'd tried to lift Carmen's stiff arm. She grasped the back of a chair to steady herself. The ruthless people in the slave ring placed no value on human life. A type 1 diabetic wouldn't be of much value on the slave market, and her captors couldn't exactly release Carmen. She knew too much and had seen too many faces.

She studied Mr. Clean's partner. He had dark skin and long dreadlocks that reached halfway down his back. He wore a skintight, solid black Under Armour shirt that showed every ripple of his oversized muscles. A massive gold serpentine necklace hung from his neck.

She knew the purpose of their intrusion. Known among the women as the deliverymen, they had come to fetch and deliver one of the unfortunate girls to her new master. Fearful of being selected, she held her breath like every other girl in the room.

It appeared as if the men delayed their mission on purpose. They seemed to enjoy the terrified looks on the girls' faces. Finally, Mr. Clean pointed at her and said, "That's the one."

She stood paralyzed, like in a reenactment of a nightmare, as his words took a moment to sink in. Her pulse quickened and her heartbeat pounded in her ears. They had come for her.

The two men took a step in her direction.

Her first instinct was to scream. But who would hear her cries for help?

They stepped closer.

Her next impulse was to flee. But where could she go?

The thugs closed in.

She considered putting up a fight. However, she knew they would easily overpower her. No. To escape, she would have to outsmart them. She would have to pick a moment when she had the advantage.

She surrendered without a fight but shuddered as each man took hold of an arm. Mr. Clean smelled of perspiration. Dreadlocks smelled like a Christmas tree. His strong cologne made her eyes water. They led her out of the room, and the heavy metal door slammed shut behind her with a thud.

The two men escorted her down the same dimly lit hallway that Eduardo and Miguel had dragged her. She shivered as they passed the small room where she had been branded.

Near the end of the hallway they ushered her into what appeared to be a women's locker room. The damp room smelled musty. Unused lockers, many of which stood open, lined the walls.

They passed a counter with four sinks and a large mirror. The girl in the mirror looked like she'd been lost in the wilderness for a week. She had tangled and greasy hair, smudged makeup, and mascara that had trailed down her cheeks from hours of crying.

They led her past several toilet stalls to showers located at the back of the locker room. Each shower was equipped with a small changing area and a privacy curtain. Mr. Clean handed her a towel, a washcloth, and a change of clothes. In a no-nonsense voice he said, "Shower and put these on. Don't try anything stupid. We're right here."

She stepped into the dressing area and pulled the curtain closed behind her. Black mildew grew from every crevice of the musty shower. She grimaced at the thought of stepping into the nasty shower stall and took her time undressing. Disrobing with only a thin plastic curtain between her and the men didn't seem like the best of ideas. But what choice did she have?

Dreadlocks laughed. "Man, I sure would like to give her a hand."

Mr. Clean quickly reminded him, "You know the rules. Boss doesn't allow the merchandise to be touched. And Boss has a way of knowing—everything."

She slipped out of her clothes with a little less apprehension. For once she appreciated "Boss." Even though she knew the shower and change of clothes were to make her more presentable to her new master, she actually welcomed the hot shower. She'd not bathed since being kidnapped. Her itchy scalp and body odor reminded her of that fact.

Dreadlocks mumbled, "That sheikh fellow is one lucky dude."

She listened with keen interest.

Mr. Clean corrected him, "You mean one wealthy dude. Rumor has it that she brought top dollar."

She adjusted the water temperature and reflected on his words. She'd been sold to a wealthy Arab and would be slipped out of the country and never heard from again. She took her time in the shower as she contemplated her situation. The warm water streamed over her face, offering a small bit of comfort. She had to devise a way to escape. Otherwise, she would never see Ethan again.

The plastic shower curtain rattled. She jumped as someone snatched it down, rod and all. Mr. Clean and Dreadlocks stood, crowded at the stall entrance, grinning from ear to ear. She instinctively backed into a corner and tried to cover herself. The flow of water, which had been such a comfort moments before, had now become a nuisance as the spray relentlessly struck her uncovered face. The men stood just clear of the splatter and stared at her body. Dreadlocks held out a towel and laughed. "Come and get it."

She glared at the men and yelled, "Remember Boss said not to touch the merchandise!"

Dreadlocks reached in and turned off the shower. His evil eyes resembled those of a serpent. "We lied." He offered his hand like a gentleman would help a lady step from a curb. "Boss didn't say we couldn't touch the merchandise." He laughed. "He said not to damage the merchandise."

Humiliated and blindfolded, Megan stumbled down a dark wooden walkway, guided by a thug on either side. Absolutely no light passed through the blindfold tied tightly over her eyes. It had to be just after midnight. Duct tape bound her wrists together. With her mouth packed full of cloth and held closed with duct tape, her loudest scream was nothing more than a muffled whimper. How had life come to this? She wasn't a good person, but then again, she didn't deserve this kind of end.

She could smell the ocean and taste the salt that hung in the air. The horn from a distant buoy moaned every fifteen to twenty seconds. Metal cables clanged against the aluminum masts of sailboats, and water lapped against the hulls and against the posts of the walkway. Apparently, they had taken her to some kind of wooden dock with boat slips.

The trio stopped, and Mr. Clean whispered to Dreadlocks, "I'll hold the boat, and you put her in." Mr. Clean turned loose of her arm, and a few seconds later Dreadlocks lifted her up over his shoulder like a sack of potatoes. She shuddered from his repulsive touch. He grunted as he stepped down and laid her in the bottom of the boat. The strong smell of gasoline and the pungent odor of fish greeted her nostrils, a welcome relief from the putrid cologne. The motor sputtered several times and suddenly jumped to life. She felt the movement of the boat and knew their journey had begun. Where? She had no idea other than it led to her new owner. She guessed he waited in a larger boat offshore.

A few minutes after the boat had left the calm water of the harbor, Dreadlocks picked her up and sat her in a seat, a much-needed escape from the boat bottom's relentless beating. He removed her blindfold and gag. She stared at him with all the hatred she could muster. The liberty the two men had taken had violated her to the very core. The lights on the mainland grew smaller by the second, and her distance from Ethan farther. She could yell for help, but no one could hear her screams over the sound of the engine, and no one could see her desperate plight because of the darkness.

She yelled over the sound of the engine at Dreadlocks. "Where are you taking me?"

He smiled a cocky grin and yelled back, "Hundred miles offshore to your new master."

She hollered, "And who might that be?"

Dreadlocks spit over the side of the boat and yelled, "Some wealthy Arab sheikh that wants to add you to his harem."

The damp breeze from the fast-moving boat, coupled with the news that she'd just received, sent a cold shudder down her back. She felt helpless. Her opportunity for escape was rapidly disappearing. Once under the control of the sheikh, there would be no escape. She would be his slave, his sex toy. Even if she could free her hands, she couldn't overpower the two men. She needed something to give her an advantage, but she saw nothing in the speedboat that could be used as a weapon. She contemplated her dilemma for nearly an hour before concluding she only had one option.

She yelled at Dreadlocks sitting in the seat beside her. "I'm seasick. I'm going to throw up." She lethargically rolled her eyes back in her head as if she might pass out.

Dreadlocks angrily shouted, "Not in the boat. Puke over the side."

She held up her bound wrists and hollered, "I can't hold on to the side."

Dreadlocks reached for her arms. "You can't go anywhere anyway," he yelled. He unwound the duct tape.

With her hands freed, she immediately clung to the side of the boat and hung her head over. She made a gagging sound and pretended to heave. She knew what she had to do. She couldn't live the life of a slave.

She glanced around to see if either of the men watched. Mr. Clean focused on the direction of the boat, and Dreadlocks avoided the sight of her upheaval. His long braids danced in the wind.

She took a deep breath and jumped over the side. She smacked the water hard. Her skin stung from the impact. The seawater flushed her head and burned her sinuses. She gagged and coughed violently until the water cleared her lungs.

The water, like the night, looked inky black. However, compared to her windy ride in the boat, it felt warm and surprisingly pleasant. She wiped the water from her eyes as she treaded the black liquid.

Her heart sank as the speedboat turned and headed back in her direction. The boat slowed to a crawl as it approached her location. Its motor ran at no more than an idle.

Mr. Clean looked in her direction. His large gold loop earring sparkled as it reflected the light from the boat's console. He yelled, "Come on babe, we're forty miles from shore. You don't have a chance of surviving. Give us a holler." He waited a minute and his voice hardened. "You need to give up. We've got all night. We'll find you."

She kept her head low and remained as quiet as possible as she treaded water. Mr. Clean began to steer the boat in slow sweeping circles to reveal as much of the water's surface as possible with the boat's fixed headlight. She was thankful for the cloudy night, which helped conceal her position, and that they didn't have a handheld flashlight.

The slow sweeping headlight from the boat came closer and closer. Just before it reached her location she took a deep breath and with a strong upward stroke of her arms she thrust herself beneath the surface of the water. She could hear the hum of the motor and the chopping of the prop. She counted to ten and opened her eyes and looked toward the dark surface. The salt water burned her eyes, but she didn't care. Upon resurfacing, she exhaled quietly and breathed in the fresh air.

The boat circled and made another pass. This time as the boat approached her location, the engine stopped. The boat drifted less than twenty feet away. The gentle lapping of waves against the boat provided the only sound cover. She hoped it concealed the sound of her breathing and pounding heartbeat.

They stood in silence and listened for her—her breathing, her splashing, even the lapping of the water against her head. They knew she floated nearby.

After a few moments, Mr. Clean spoke again, his voice agitated but controlled. "Come on out, babe, before you're eaten. Don't you know there are great whites in these waters?"

Her spine tingled at the thought of sharks. The prospect of becoming shark bait had not entered into her decision to jump overboard.

Mr. Clean continued his efforts to frighten her into surrender. "These waters are infested with great whites. I've seen them bite unsuspecting harbor seals clean in two. The seals never even knew what hit 'em."

She fought the urge to scream her location, but she'd rather die a quick death than be subjected to a lifetime of slavery.

Dreadlocks spoke in a hushed voice, "We've got to find her. Boss will skin us alive if we don't deliver her. He'll feed us to the sharks himself."

She grinned. It would almost be worth death at sea to know that Boss had painfully exterminated the two filthy rodents.

Mr. Clean whispered back, "She'll be getting tired soon. Before long she'll be begging us to pull her out of the water." He reached over the side, offered his hand to the darkness, and called, "Come on babe. Come take my hand."

She continued to tread water as quietly as possible until the boat drifted past her. She'd rather drown than feel the touch of his hand again.

The motor came to life, and the boat continued to make slow sweeping circles. Each time as the boat moved away, she swam farther from the area. She kept her strokes and kicks underwater so as not to splash. She continued to move beyond their ever-widening patrol. She put one hundred yards between herself and the boat and then two hundred yards. Eventually, she could only see the boat's running lights when she crested the swells. She continued to swim away from the boat with no destination in mind, except away from the boat. After several hours she could neither hear nor see the light from the boat. Only then did she feel completely alone.

❧ Chapter 31 ❧

Sadie sat frozen in the hard wooden pew. She could feel the heat of the old overhead canister lamps. They burned intensely, like a dentist's examination light. Pastor Nolan stood at the front of the church, his penetrating eyes burned white. He screamed at the top of his lungs, "For the Word of God is quick and powerful and sharper than any two-edged sword, piercing even to the dividing asunder of soul and spirit and of the joints and marrow and is a discerner of the thoughts and intents of the heart." He waved the sword, the Bible, for emphasis as he spoke. "Neither is there any creature that is not manifest in his sight; but all things are naked and opened unto the eyes of him with whom we have to do." He began to examine each person in the congregation with his penetrating stare. He started at the front pew and slowly worked his way toward the back of the church, pew by pew. When he came to the third pew, he pointed his Bible at a teenage girl and screamed "Tare! Tare come forth!"

When the young girl realized she'd been discovered, she leaped up and rushed for the rear exit, but several deacons grabbed her and dragged her kicking and screaming out through one of the side doors at the front of the sanctuary.

Sadie covered her mouth. This couldn't really be happening.

Pastor Nolan, eyes ablaze, continued to inspect the members on each pew. Perspiration broke out on her forehead, and her breathing grew shallow. She felt lightheaded.

Just before the pastor reached the fifth pew, a middle-aged man jumped up and ran toward the back of the sanctuary. He screamed, and a moment later two deacons dragged his limp body out through the front side-door entrance of the sanctuary. She looked all around for help. Erma, Clyde, Jake, and Ethan just stared at the pastor and nodded their heads in approval. Pastor Nolan moved closer. Soon he would expose her too. She knew she could not escape his penetrating gaze. Beads of sweat rolled down her face. She wanted to jump up and run, but then everyone would know.

He stopped at her pew. She dared not look at his eyes. He extended his hand over her pew and cried, "There's a tare among us!"

The congregation began to chant in unison, "Tare, tare, tare." Before she could say or do anything, a deacon arrived at each end of her pew.

Pastor Nolan pointed at her and screamed, "She's the tare. Burn her with the rest of the tares!"

She turned to Jake who sat beside her. "Help me!"

Jake slowly turned his head and looked at Sadie. His eyes glowed white. He casually raked his hand through his silver hair and then said, "Burn her."

The congregation cried in unison, "Burn her, burn her, burn her."

Black billows of smoke began to leak from the closed side doors at the front of the sanctuary. The smoke smelled of burning rubber and sulfur. Numerous hands grabbed hold of her.

She screamed, "No, no, no."

The hands shook her, and a voice cried, "Sadie! Wake up, Sadie."

Megan drifted over a large swell and shuddered as she gazed across a dark, empty sea. She'd treaded water for nearly two hours in the warm summer ocean off the Los Angeles coast, and her fingers had shriveled. Sharks, fatigue, or thirst might claim her life, but not hypothermia.

She remembered a trick she'd learned in a Red Cross water safety course that had been taught to her high school swim team. She decided to give it a try. She bobbed in the water as she wrestled to pull off her denim jeans. Upon removal, she snapped the waist, zipped them, and tied a knot in the end of each leg. Holding the jeans over her head with the waistline open, she slapped the open end of the jeans down upon the water, trapping air in each leg. She gathered the waist of the jeans in one hand and held it closed and then draped the other arm across the crotch. It was a crude floatation device, but the tightly knit jeans did a good job of retaining the trapped air. She could float for ten minutes or more before she had to repeat the inflation process.

Swimming seemed pointless because she had no sense of direction in the dark. She would have to wait until sunrise. Since they had left a port near Los Angeles, she would need to swim directly to the east. She rested her hope on the possibility that some fishermen might find her in the morning.

Sunrise would occur soon. Come the first rays of light, she would start swimming toward the rising sun. She wouldn't kid herself. Although she'd been among the best on her high school swim team until her pregnancy had forced her to quit, she knew she couldn't swim forty miles in open water. However, she figured the closer she got to shore the better her chances a fishing boat would stumble upon her.

At first light she would tie her jeans around her waist and start swimming. When she grew tired, she would inflate her makeshift life preserver and rest. She would repeat the whole process until someone found her, she made land, or she drowned.

As she awaited the first rays of the sun, she pondered all the things that had happened to her in such a short time—the auditions, the abduction, the branding, Carmen's death, the sexual assault, and her escape. She thought about Ethan and how she desired more than anything to gather the young boy in her arms and hear him say, "Mommy." How could she have ever considered abandoning her son? How might Ethan feel each day as he watched for his mommy to return, and how might he be suffering from the feeling of abandonment?

A wave sloshed against her face. She gagged on the salty water. She sure had messed up her life and Ethan's too. In fact, her whole life had been one big screwup. She wiped the water from her face. How could she have allowed that worthless high school sweetheart to talk her into bed? He'd made it sound innocent and without consequence. But there had been consequences. She'd become pregnant, and the guy that had claimed to love her would not have anything to do with her. So she'd walked across the stage at her high school graduation with a big belly and a load of guilt. Not only had she failed at choosing a man, she'd also failed at numerous jobs. For one reason or another she couldn't keep a job for very long.

And then there was Ethan, the one bright spot in her life. But even in the area of motherhood, she'd failed. She didn't know how to discipline her son. She couldn't provide for him, and she wasn't sure she really knew how to love him. How does one define love? She remembered hearing about God's unconditional love each year on Easter Sunday and during the Christmas season, but that kind of love seemed impossible. She'd always thought love, like respect, had to be earned. Maybe, if she'd gone to church more, things would've been different. But she couldn't change the past. Perhaps drowning at sea was not such a bad option.

The sky cleared during the early morning hours. With no sources of man-made light and the moon positioned low in the sky, she observed an infinite field of stars. With no obstructions such as trees and buildings on the horizon, the night sky seemed immense. She saw deeper into the universe than she ever had before. A phrase that she'd heard at church as a child came to her mind: "The heavens declare the glory of God."

She watched a meteor streak across the sky. If God really was the creator of all things, as she'd heard in church, He must be a really big God, an all-powerful God. She looked up into the starry sky and yelled, "God, if you're up there . . . if you're real . . . I could really use your help about now." She waited more than thirty minutes for an audible voice from heaven, a rescue boat, or some miraculous sign. Nothing happened. She screamed sarcastically toward heaven, "I thought so."

The words had barely left her lips when something brushed her leg. It felt like sandpaper had been rubbed across her thigh, and the abrasion burned from the salt water. "What the . . . ?" Then it occurred to her. She'd felt the abrasive hide of a shark. As a young girl she'd once touched a dead shark lying on a pier, and the hide had felt like sandpaper. She'd heard that sharks often investigate their prey before attacking—bumping it, nudging it. Instinctively, she spun her body, fearful the predator would sneak up from behind.

Her breathing grew rapid.

Mr. Clean's words came rushing back to her.

Could it be a great white?

She'd seen documentaries that showed how the great white sharks could grow to be huge creatures and could devour human prey with a couple of bites. She remembered her captor's words: "I've seen them bite unsuspecting harbor seals clean in two."

Her pulse quickened.

Adrenaline flowed through her body and energized her tired limbs.

She rapidly rotated her body as she treaded water.

She scanned the surface for any sign of the shark.

Then she saw it.

A large fin broke the surface.

The beast was circling her, sizing up its next meal.

Perhaps, other sharks lurked beneath the inky water.

It would only be a matter of time before one of them took a chunk from her defenseless body—a leg, an arm, most of her trunk—and the feeding frenzy would begin.

She shuddered and remembered that movement often attracts sharks. She slowed her kick and bobbed in the water, hoping the predator would lose interest.

The circling fin disappeared below the dark surface. Had the shark grown bored or was he preparing to strike? Her eyes clouded with tears. "I don't want to die. Not this way." She stared into the murky water and tried to track the shadow of the creature by the light of the stars, but it proved to be useless.

She waited, and her heart pounded. It felt as though her chest would burst at any moment. Seconds passed, but it seemed like hours.

Just when she thought the shark had left, it brushed her leg, this time harder than before.

It pushed her back several feet and rotated her body from the glancing blow.

She screamed, "No! Please God, save me. Don't let me die. I promise I'll become one of those Christians as soon as somebody can tell me how."

❧ CHAPTER 32 ❧

Erma abruptly awoke from a deep sleep and lay perfectly still in bed. She slowly surveyed the dark room for the form of a stranger and listened for the sound of glass breaking or the wooden floor squeaking. She heard nothing but Clyde's heavy breathing. She sniffed the air for the smell of smoke but detected only the odor of her arthritis cream. What had startled her from sleep? She looked at Clyde. Maybe he'd been agitated by a nightmare. But he seemed to be resting peacefully on his back—his toothless mouth gaping open and his breathing a slow, rhythmic pace.

Had God awakened her? More than once during her lifetime, He'd done so in the middle of the night and moved her to whisper a prayer for some needy soul. Each time she would later learn that at the very moment she had prayed, God had ministered to that individual in some fashion.

She stared at the ceiling and listened intently for God's voice, that still, small voice. She didn't hear anything, but Ethan's mother came to mind. *Lord, I pray for Megan at this late hour. I sense the poor girl has a great need. We don't know where she is holed up or why she hasn't come home. So, I lift her up and ask that You would wrap your lovin' arms around her. Protect her, dear Lord. Draw her to you that she*

might know you are the one true God, that she might recognize her need
for you and become one of your own. In Jesus' name, Amen.

She continued to stare at the ceiling and listen for God's
direction. But after a few minutes her eyelids grew heavy, and once
again, she drifted off into the land of dreams.

Daniel reviewed the letter one last time and then hurried from the
stockroom to the front of the store. He wiped the perspiration from
his brow and checked his watch. He had forty-five minutes to discuss the letter with his father before the A&E opened.

Bob stood at the front of the store near the paint supplies.
He sipped from a cup of coffee and studied a new display. He looked
up at Daniel. "What do you think of the display?"

Daniel walked to his father's side and took a long, hard
look. "Two for the price of one. Hey, I'd buy it. Looks like a good
deal to me."

Bob rubbed his chin. "It is a good deal, and hopefully
people will think so."

Daniel handed the letter to his father. "Would you look at
this letter and see if it accomplishes what we want?"

Bob set his coffee cup on the counter and slipped on
his reading glasses. "Well, it certainly looks official on the store's
letterhead. Let me read it aloud so you have the opportunity to hear
how it sounds."

Daniel stared out the front plate-glass window as his father
read.

Dear Ms. Kingsley:

Congratulations! You have won a new TV/DVD Combo. This is not a gimmick or sales pitch. Bob's A&E is celebrating its 25th anniversary. To commemorate this special occasion we are giving away the above gift. Your name was randomly selected from the store's mailing list. In addition to the prize, we would also like to include your name and picture in the Glendale Gazette in an article describing the store's 25th anniversary. Again, this is not a gimmick. Please contact our store at 336-9476 and schedule a time when you can pick up your prize. If we have not heard from you within ten business days, we will randomly select another winner.

Sincerely yours,

Bob Smith,

Owner and Manager of Bob's A&E

Bob handed the letter back to Daniel. "It sounds good to me." He removed his reading glasses and took a sip of coffee. "I do recommend you send it certified mail with receipt acknowledgement. It provides two benefits. First, we'll know she has received the letter, and it hasn't been lost in the mail. Second, it will give the letter more credibility."

Daniel nodded. "Thanks, Dad." He sealed the envelope and headed to the Glendale post office to set the scam in motion.

CHAPTER 33

Having survived a night in the ocean, Megan felt lucky to be alive. She'd flirted with a great white shark, and he'd shown mercy and left her alone. Or, perhaps, God had shown mercy. She clung to her makeshift life preserver, totally exhausted. She'd started swimming at the first glow on the horizon. Now the sun stood directly above. She'd been battling the waves for nearly six hours, and progress had been slow. Unlike swimming across a lap pool, the rise and fall of the swells greatly hindered her advancement.

Her mouth was dry, her saliva thick and tacky. But she knew drinking seawater would be fatal. How ironic. Water filled her whole world at the moment. Yet thirst consumed her thoughts, and she couldn't take the smallest sip. The sun presented another hazard. Her eyes burned from both the salt and the brilliant reflection off the water's surface. Unprotected from the hot sun, she knew severe sunburn would occur within a few hours. How far had she come— two, maybe three miles at best? She chuckled. Only thirty-seven miles remained, assuming the currents hadn't carried her even farther from shore.

She let the air out of her jeans, tied them around her waist, and once again struck out in an easterly direction. After approximately ten minutes, she stopped, inflated her jeans, and rested. A large swell carried her upward. As she floated over the top of the crest, she saw a small fishing boat on the horizon, trolling with a large net in tow. She yelled for help and waved to attract attention, but abruptly stopped when she realized the futility of her actions. The crew would not be able to hear over the boat's engine and would not likely notice her small form. Maybe they would stay in the general area long enough for her to close the gap and be seen. She deflated her preserver, tied it around her waist, and swam in the direction of the boat.

Megan felt like kissing the California soil when the small fishing boat returned to the dock well after sunset. While the fishermen focused on processing their catch, she found the first refuge available, a thirty-foot sailboat tied at the remote end of the dock. She climbed down into the boat's small open-air cockpit and pushed aside a musty canvas sail, which had been hastily crammed into the cockpit. She tried to enter the boat's small cabin, but the hatch was locked. Exhausted and frustrated, she collapsed on the sail and cried.

She shivered from the cool ocean breeze and reflected on how things had changed. Just a few weeks earlier she had stood on a hotel balcony and enjoyed the salt air and ocean breeze. Now, it made her sick to think she would have to spend another night under the stars. She curled up in the small cockpit, pulled the musty canvas over her body, and tried to enjoy its warmth.

The fishermen finished their work, and the dock grew quiet. She listened to the gentle lapping of the water against the boat and constant clinking of the metal cables against the masts. Fearful of recapture, her oversensitive ears magnified every sound. However, totally exhausted from battling the waves, she drifted to sleep.

Sometime after midnight she awoke, startled by voices. She lay as if paralyzed beneath the canvas sail, her ears straining to capture every sound. Through the darkness she could see the silhouette of three people, one large person on either side of a smaller person.

One of the large shapes spoke. "This one won't get away."

The other large shape responded. "Eduardo told Boss that one of his fishing buddies pulled the girl from the water around noon. She survived for more than ten hours."

Megan pulled the canvas up to her eyes. A cold shiver ran down her backbone when she remembered Eduardo, the smelly Hispanic who had branded her.

The trio stopped by a small motorboat in the slip next to the sailboat where she lay. One large shape spoke. "Man, we could make things right with Boss if we could bag her again."

Her blood ran cold as she recognized the two voices, Mr. Clean and Dreadlocks. Her heart pounded violently and her rapid breathing seemed to echo across the docks. Both fear and anger raged through her body. Though dark, she could picture their wicked faces. She remembered the repulsive cedar odor of Dreadlock's cologne, their rough beards against her skin, and their horrendous breath. It made her nauseous, and she wished for a gun. She would kill them without a second thought.

In spite of the darkness she could just make out the girl's blindfold and gag. Duct tape secured the girl's hands behind her back, and rope hobbles around her ankles greatly limited her stride. Obviously, the two men intended on making this delivery.

Mr. Clean grabbed Dreadlocks by the chin and leaned close to his partner. "I'll kill you if you unbind her before we get to the sheikh's yacht. We're lucky Boss didn't have us knocked off for losing the other babe. Fortunately, the sheikh agreed to accept two girls instead."

The whites of Dreadlocks' eyes grew huge, and he broke Mr. Clean's grip. "Don't touch me."

Mr. Clean dropped his flashlight. It fell into the sailboat and struck her ankle. On impact, the light switched on. The flashlight lay on top of the canvas sail, and the beam of light pointed toward her partially uncovered head. She kicked the flashlight from its resting place and pulled the canvas over her head. The flashlight rolled off the canvas onto the floor of the cockpit. She hoped the confrontation between the two men had prevented them from seeing her movement.

The boat leaned toward the dock as Mr. Clean boarded. "Now look what you made me do. I almost dropped the flashlight in the water."

She held her breath and tried to remain motionless. Beads of sweat formed and ran down her forehead into her eyes. Mr. Clean stepped on her calf when he reached for the flashlight. The heel of his work boot gouged into her flesh. It took every ounce of willpower to keep from screaming or moving.

Mr. Clean stood with one foot on her leg for what seemed like an eternity. Her eyes followed the beam of light as he scanned the contents of the small sailboat.

"Kill the light," Dreadlocks whispered. "We don't want to draw attention."

The light went out, and Mr. Clean grunted. The boat tilted toward the dock as he climbed out, and the pain inflicted by his heel subsided.

She exhaled slowly, and tears ran down her cheeks.

The men loaded the girl and cranked the boat.

She felt overwhelming sorrow and regret as the boat pulled away from the dock. She'd wanted to help the girl, but what could she have done? She couldn't overpower the men, and even if she could have distracted them, the girl wouldn't have gotten far with her tethered feet.

❧ CHAPTER 34 ❧

Just before daybreak, Megan scanned the dock for any sign of movement, and then cautiously left her hiding place. She stretched to loosen her shoulders and arms, which had cramped from the small dimensions of the sailboat's cockpit. Already they had grown sore from the prior day's marathon swim. A cool ocean breeze triggered a battalion of chill bumps on her sunburned arms and face. She shivered from both the cool air and the continual threat of recapture. The conversation she'd overheard a few hours earlier confirmed that the slave traders knew she'd survived her ordeal at sea. Since many of the fishermen at the dock knew Eduardo and Miguel, she needed to leave the area before they began to arrive at their boats.

She listened carefully for any sound of activity but heard only the creaking of the dock. She quietly made her way to the parking lot. If she could get to the main highway without being detected, she might be able to flag down a trucker and catch a ride out of town.

When she reached the middle of the parking area, a vehicle entered at the far end of the lot. Its headlights swept across her. She froze, hoping she'd not been spotted. The truck turned slowly to the right, and the headlights swept back across her path.

The pickup suddenly accelerated in her direction.

She ran toward the edge of the parking lot. Each stride inflamed her sore limbs, and bits of gravel pricked her bare feet as she ran across the hard pavement.

The headlights traced her movement, and the truck cut her off before she reached the far side of the lot.

She stopped.

The doors of the pickup opened and the cabin light revealed two familiar faces, Eduardo and Miguel.

She cursed. Not again.

Eduardo pointed in her direction and yelled, "La chica!"

She turned and headed for the street with the men in hot pursuit.

The dawn light revealed a tin building on the right side of the road. Numerous boats were parked out front, some sitting on trailers and some directly on the ground. The lot contained several piles of rusted boat parts and reminded her of the junkyards back home. A faded metal sign mounted on the side of the building read "Dirk's Boat Repair."

She heard the men close behind chattering in their native tongue.

She stopped at the building's front entrance and pulled. The locked door didn't budge.

She turned and saw the men fast closing in.

She ran around the side of the building in search of another entrance.

She found a door at the rear of the building and gave it a yank. The door rattled against the doorjamb but didn't open.

She saw a small tear in the sheet metal siding near the door, a hole through which she might be able to squeeze.

She dropped to her stomach and slithered through the tight hole. But before she reached the safety of the building, she felt a hand clamp down on her ankle. The man began to drag her out.

She grabbed hold of a heavy metal shelf and halted her backward slide. She had to act quickly. She wouldn't be able to resist the pull of two men.

She grabbed a rusty wrench from the bottom shelf, rolled to her back, and swatted at the man's hand.

Miguel cursed and let go of her ankle.

She pulled her legs to safety and crawled to a small space between shelves and wept.

The door rattled violently against the doorjamb as the men tried to break it open. It held. A few seconds later, she heard the rattle of the front door, but it kept her stalkers out. She heard the men's agitated voices. She wished she could understand Spanish. What devious plan were they contriving? Would she be able to hold out until the proprietor arrived? Would he rescue her or sell her out?

All grew quiet. She moved closer to the rear door and listened. Were the men still outside? What were they up to? The morning light streamed through two louvered windows located eight feet above ground. The light revealed the contents of the building. The structure contained lots of counter space, shelving, and large power tools. A small desk stood in one corner cluttered with stacks of paper—and a phone.

She darted to the phone and dialed 9-1-1.

She placed the phone to her ear, but she didn't hear a dial tone. The men always seemed to be one step ahead of her.

She dropped the phone and began to rifle through the desk drawers. Maybe the proprietor kept a pistol close by.

Glass shattered on the concrete floor, and she saw someone knocking out the window panes with a piece of rebar. She had to make a run for it. Staying in the building could only lead to recapture. She needed to make her move while one man focused on the window.

She peeped out the hole where she had entered the building and saw Miguel standing at the corner where he could watch both the rear entrance and the side window. He cradled a bloody hand against his chest.

She slipped to the front door, careful to remain behind the cover of the shelving so Eduardo wouldn't see her from the window. She unlocked the deadbolt and cracked open the door. She had a clear path.

She dashed for the street, past the piles of rusted parts and past the parked boats.

As she reached the street Eduardo yelled, "Ella es escapar!"

She glanced over her shoulder and saw him standing in the doorway.

Megan summoned her last bit of energy and raced to the side of the freeway. The morning rush hour traffic filled the road with the smell of exhaust and the roar of engines.

She glanced and saw the men several hundred yards behind. Fortunate for her, their short, stocky bodies kept them from being fleet of foot.

She frantically waved at the oncoming traffic. Surely someone would stop for a lady in distress, but then she remembered her ragged appearance—barefoot, tangled hair—and knew most people would be afraid to stop. She looked like a drug addict.

Her pursuers had closed the gap to less than a hundred yards with the younger Eduardo leading the way. Miguel lagged behind hindered by his injured hand. She wondered if the impact of the wrench had broken his hand. Served him right.

She jumped up and down and waved her arms at a large oncoming rental truck. It passed. Her heart sank. She didn't have the energy to keep running. But then the truck pulled over to the shoulder and stopped.

With renewed vitality, she sprinted to the truck and yanked open the passenger-side door. The driver must have been over sixty. He had a full silver beard and closely cropped hair. He smiled. "Need a ride?"

She glanced at the Hispanic men. They had stopped fifty yards away, bent with their elbows resting on their thighs, and gasping for breath.

She pulled herself up into the cab and panted the words, "I . . . sure . . . do."

The man held out his hand. "Merle Eckhart. Welcome aboard."

She slid into the well-worn bucket seat and clasped his rough hand. "Megan . . . Thompson." She looked in the side mirror to make sure the slave traders hadn't moved closer. "Glad to . . . be on . . . board."

Merle switched on the left-hand turn signal and pulled the truck back into traffic. "Sorry I made you run so far. Can't stop this rig on a dime, you know." He winked at her. "Where did you get that gosh-awful sunburn?"

She fastened her seatbelt and answered without looking up. "Guess I spent . . . too much time . . . in the water." She surveyed the interior. The old truck had seen many miles. Excessive sun exposure had cracked the dash, and bare metal shone through the rubber-coated floor.

Merle shifted gears. "Where are you headed, young lady?"

She gave an exhausted sigh. "Glendale, North Carolina."

Merle smiled warmly. "It's your lucky day. I'm headed all the way to Nashville."

She felt a glimmer of hope for the first time in a long while.

He leaned to adjust the AC. A small bronze cross dangled from a thin chain around his neck.

She ran her fingers through her matted hair. A cross . . . he must be one of those Christians. She remembered her night in the open sea and her promise to God and then pushed the thought aside. "What's taking you to Nashville? Are you moving there?"

Merle chuckled. "No ma'am. I drive part-time for rental companies. When people make one-way rentals, someone has to drive the trucks back to their home location. You'd be surprised how much they pay me to drive an empty rental truck. It's good money for a retired codger like me, and it gives me a chance to see our beautiful country."

She felt at ease talking with Merle. In addition to his kind and warm nature, he had a special quality about him, a quality she couldn't quite put her finger on. She longed to share her heart with him. It had been a very long time since she'd been able to talk and share with anyone. She held her tongue though. He was, after all, a total stranger that she'd just met.

Jake stepped out on the front porch and studied the red Mercedes-Benz convertible as it rolled to a stop. The car's chrome trim glittered in the sunlight. Obviously, the stranger behind the wheel had expensive tastes. He was probably a salesman or scam artist trying to steal their retirement. Jake chomped on a stick of gum, and it released a cool, fresh sensation. He'd rather have the warm tobacco flavor of a cigarette. He looked at the front yard and frowned. Salesman or not, he hated for anyone to see the shaggy lawn.

Buckshot barked and circled the car as if he'd treed a squirrel. Every few seconds the dog looked at him for affirmation.

Jake whistled and Buckshot joined him on the front porch. He touched the dog's shoulder, and the obedient canine plopped to one hip and leaned against his leg. The man exited the car but cautiously eyed Buckshot. He wore pressed black slacks and a red pullover that bore the emblem of a polo player.

The man waved. "Hello. I'm Michael Brinks from The Right Look Modeling Agency."

Jake rubbed the back of his neck. "Can't say I've ever heard of that agency." Sadie came out on the porch with Ethan in tow.

Mr. Brinks took several cautious steps toward the porch. "We're based out of Charlotte."

Jake glanced at Sadie. "What brings you to Glendale?"

Mr. Brinks took another step toward the porch, his eyes locked on the dog. "I'm looking for Megan Thompson."

Sadie touched Jake's arm and whispered, "Did he say Megan?"

Jake nodded and started down the steps with Buckshot at his heels. "Miss Thompson doesn't live here."

Mr. Brinks froze in his steps. His eyes grew large as Buckshot, tail wagging, sniffed at his leg. "Are . . . are you sure? This is the address she listed with our agency."

Jake planted his hands on his hips. "Don't know why she'd do that." He raised his chin. "What business do you have with Megan?"

Mr. Brinks offered him a business card. "We have a modeling opportunity for her."

Jake took the card. It looked legitimate. He pointed at Ethan. "We haven't seen Megan since she dropped off her son three weeks ago."

Mr. Brinks's head snapped to attention. He studied Ethan, and a slight grin crossed his face. He turned back to Jake. "Well, if you see her, please give her my card. Let her know we have an opportunity for her." He offered his hand. "I appreciate your time."

Jake shook his soft, smooth hand, the sure sign of a city slicker.

Mr. Brinks nodded to Sadie and gave Buckshot a wide berth as he headed to his car. "Have a nice day."

Sadie joined Jake. They watched the red convertible disappear down the dusty gravel road. She shook her head slowly. "I don't have a good feeling about that man."

Neither did Jake.

✿ Chapter 35 ✿

Megan nearly jumped out of the truck seat when she saw it. The side mirror revealed the same old pickup she'd seen earlier in the day. When she and Merle had pulled onto the interstate, she'd hoped the slave traders were left behind, but without question, the stinky fishermen were following them. She wouldn't soon forget the gray truck that had blocked her escape that morning. Its hood and several quarter panels had been sprayed with rust-colored primer but never finished with a gray topcoat. As the pickup came closer, she could just make out the stocky figures of the two Hispanic men. Did they know for certain that she rode in this truck? Had they made note of the license plate when she boarded? Had they contacted Boss? Were they merely tracking her until Boss's men could arrive and take her by force? Or were the two fishermen acting on their own so they could collect Boss's full reward? They must have grown impatient or concerned that they followed the wrong truck, for the pickup began to close the gap between them.

She reclined the bucket seat, slid down below window level, and pretended to be resting. Hopefully, the men would not see her and move on. The hot sun agitated her sunburned face, but she had no option to move. She watched the clock in the dash. Thirty minutes passed and nothing happened. The men didn't blow their horn or try to force Merle to pull over. As far as she knew they had passed and gone on down the road.

Afraid to look, she remained in her position. Overcome by exhaustion and enticed by the comfortable seat, her eyelids grew heavy and she drifted to sleep.

Sadie stood on the front porch and smiled. She felt a renewed sense of hope as she watched Jake climb the long driveway. He carried the newspaper and several letters. Buckshot ran a few feet ahead of Jake. Like a fur-covered pinball, the hound bounced from one object to another and recorded every scent.

Ethan sat in the large porch swing, only his feet and ankles extended past the edge of the seat. He rocked his upper body, but his small mass failed to move the heavy swing. He looked at her with a smirk. "Rock Ethan."

She smiled, shoved the swing with her foot, and watched Jake pass the Carving Tree. There had certainly been a dramatic improvement in his energy level since Sunday when he'd lounged in bed most of the day. He'd performed numerous light-duty tasks during the last four days such as fetching the mail, fixing door latches, and repairing the leaky toilet. To her chagrin, he'd even talked about mowing the grass. His increased activity gave her hope of his recovery. However, she needed to make sure he didn't overexert himself.

Ethan kicked his feet. "Rock me."

She sat beside Ethan and pushed the swing into motion. Ethan giggled. Buckshot ran up on the gray plank porch, tail wagging, and barked.

"Are you excited Jake took you to the mailbox?"

Buckshot cocked his head, and his thick brow bunched.

Ethan climbed down from the swing and hugged Buckshot's neck. The dog slipped from his embrace and left the porch to stalk a squirrel. Ethan followed.

Jake walked up the steps. "Beautiful day."

She patted the seat beside her. "Isn't it, though?"

He laid the newspaper and mail in a wicker rocker and sat next to her.

She interlaced her fingers with Jake's and laid her head upon his shoulder. The rusty chains of the porch swing creaked as they gently swung. He squeezed her fingers, and the warmth of satisfaction flooded her soul. She deeply inhaled the warm spring air and slowly exhaled with contentment. She lifted her head and kissed his cheek. "The simple pleasures of life . . ."

Jake nodded. "Are the best."

Megan awoke with a jump, cautiously raised her head, and looked out the truck window. The truck sat next to a gas pump at a large truck stop. The digital clock on the truck's radio read 1:15 p.m. She'd slept for more than three hours. Her skin felt sticky and hot from the salt, and her clothes irritated her sensitive skin. She longed for a refreshing hot shower. She pulled down the visor and looked in the mirror. With her matted and tangled hair, sunburned face, and eyes with dark circles, she looked every bit of the wreck that she feared. She pushed up the visor in disgust. Merle probably thought she was a drug addict. She looked terrible.

She saw his reflection in a side mirror as he pumped gas. She opened the door and slid out of the truck. "Are we going to be here for a few minutes? I need to use the bathroom."

Merle hung up the gas nozzle. "Take your time. I need a break anyway. My back is rebelling from that truck seat."

She washed the salt from her face at the bathroom sink. She splashed water on her hair and ran her fingers through the tangles. She sniffed her shirt. It reeked of salt and body odor. Her face burned with embarrassment, but what could she do? She had no deodorant, no money, and only the clothes on her back. She made her way to the front of the store and saw Merle standing by the cash register paying for his fuel. He motioned to her from the counter. "My back tells me I need a long break," he said. "Hold out your arms."

She stretched out her arms.

He laid a large folded towel, a matching washcloth, and a small transparent zip-lock travel kit in her arms. The kit contained a toothbrush, a small tube of toothpaste, a comb, and all the essential cosmetics. On top of the pile, he laid a large gray warm-up suit. "You have shower number six," he said. "I put some quarters in the travel kit. When you finish your shower, put your clothes in the washer and meet me in the restaurant."

Her lip quivered and her eyes filled with tears. She wanted to hug him but her hands were full. She wanted to thank him, but the words stuck in her throat. Fearful of making a spectacle of herself, she turned and hurried to the shower.

The hot water streaming down her back washed away the salt and odor. It felt good to be clean again. Her tears, like the shower, flowed fast and hard as she reflected on the unexpected compassion, generosity, and thoughtfulness of this stranger. She stepped from the shower and towel dried. She combed out her tangles and slipped on the gray warm-up suit. The drawstring kept the baggy pants in place, and the bulky sweatshirt provided discreet coverage. She brushed her teeth and ran her tongue across her gums, savoring the clean feeling. A hot shower and a few cosmetics could certainly boost a girl's self-esteem. She dropped her dirty clothes in the washing machine, added detergent, and headed to the restaurant. Merle sat in a booth sipping from a large glass of cola and studying the menu. A second menu lay directly across from him. She slipped into the booth's open seat.

Merle looked up and smiled. "Why there's the sunburned lady now."

She managed to squeeze out two choked words. "Thank you."

Merle flipped a page of the menu. "You're more than welcome." He reached across the table and opened her menu. "Pick out something good to eat. It'll be awhile till supper."

Her eyes overflowed again, and she shook her head. "I don't have any money."

Merle laughed. "Well, Ms. Hitchhiker, don't you think I knew that when you got into my truck without a purse?" He pushed the menu closer to her. "God has been good to me, and it's only right that I share that goodness with others. Go ahead. This one's on me."

She dabbed at her tears with a napkin and then ordered an entrée.

When the waitress brought their food, Merle addressed the waitress. "I'm about to say grace for God's provision. Is there anything for which you would like for me to pray?"

The waitress gave Merle an inquisitive look and her lip quivered. She stared out the window in silence for several seconds. She wiped several tears from her cheeks and spoke softly. "My husband left me last night." She wrestled to keep her composure, and her pleading eyes met his. "Please ask God to bring him home."

Merle turned to Megan. "How about you, Megan?"

She swallowed hard and said, "Thank God for kind strangers." She bowed her head to avoid eye contact.

Merle sat quietly for a few seconds and then began. "Dear God, your Holy Word reminds us of your abundant blessings. 'Bless the Lord, oh my soul, and all that is within me. Bless his holy name.' Father, you are truly holy, and we bless your name. 'Bless the Lord, oh my soul, and forget not all of his benefits.' We thank you for all of your provisions. 'Who forgives all thine iniquities.' Lord, you forgive our sins, every one of them. 'Who healeth all thy diseases.' You lift us up when we're sick—emotionally, physically, mentally, and spiritually. 'Who redeemeth thy life from destruction.' We thank you because you have provided a way for us to escape your coming judgment against sin. 'Who crowneth thee with loving-kindness and tender mercies.' You daily shower us with your great mercy, and you sent your son to die in our place to pay the penalty for our sins because of your great love for us. 'Who satisfieth thy mouth with good things so that thy youth is renewed like the eagle's.' And we thank you for this food set before us, Lord, that it truly might give us the strength of eagles and renew us. We pray for our waitress friend as she struggles with a broken relationship. We ask that you would bring her husband back home and restore her marriage. And Lord, we lift up Megan. We pray she might cross the paths of many kind strangers as she travels back to Glendale. We ask all these things in the wonderful name of Jesus. Amen."

Megan covered a puddle of tears with her plate and wiped her eyes with a napkin.

Megan almost choked on her food when she saw Eduardo and Miguel walking around Merle's rig. Merle must have noticed her distressed gaze. He laid down his fork and watched the men.

Merle jumped to his feet when Eduardo stepped up on the running board and looked into the passenger-side window. "They're up to no good. Wonder what they're looking for?"

Megan took a deep breath. She had to come clean. She had to trust someone. "They're slave traders!" She glanced around the restaurant to see if anyone had overheard her outcry. She softened her voice to a whisper. "They're after me."

Merle's face grew red, and for the first time she saw anger flash in his eyes. He pointed toward the restrooms. "Go hide in the lady's room until I send for you. I'll take care of this!" He laid a twenty next to his plate and stomped out of the diner.

Contrary to his instructions, she stayed by the window and watched the scene unfold. Merle intercepted the two men as they approached the travel center. He pointed toward the rig and said something. If only she could read lips. Eduardo did most of the talking. He waved his hands, most likely to aid his broken English.

Merle shook his head and pointed back toward LA. Eduardo pounded his fist on the trunk of a parked car. Merle proceeded to his truck, and the fishermen headed toward the travel center.

She rushed to the restroom where she waited nearly an hour.

Her heart pounded when a lady opened the restroom door and yelled, "Megan, Merle's ready to leave."

She hesitated. Were the men gone or was this a trap? Merle seemed like a trustworthy person, and yet the promise of money had a way of changing people. Since leaving Glendale, she'd not been able to trust anyone. She thought about his generosity just an hour earlier—the shower, the meal—his heartfelt prayer for the waitress, and the cross that hung from his neck. Weren't Christians supposed to be trustworthy?

She met Merle just outside the restroom.

He smiled. "They're headed back to LA."

She raked the hair away from her face. "But . . . ?"

He laughed. "I convinced them that I had only carried you a few miles to the next exit."

Once again, her tears flowed freely.

✿ CHAPTER 36 ✿

Sadie rolled over in bed and frowned at the clock. It read 6:30 a.m. She'd not slept well. She kept dreaming about the Carving Tree. In the first dream, the majestic tree withered under the hot sun. In the second dream, a hard wind had blown the tree over. And then a logger had sawed down the tree in the third dream. Only one thing could put her mind at ease.

She climbed out of bed, stood for a moment to let the aches subside, and then slipped on her pink slippers and housecoat. She quietly stole out of the room by the early morning light.

She peeped into Frank's bedroom where Ethan snored softly. He lay in a fetal position, with his face on the pillow, his knees pulled toward his tummy, and his little rump poking high in the air. He slept comfortably with no signs of stirring.

She picked her way through a field of scattered toys to the front door. Buckshot lay against the outward-opening screen door, so she nudged the dog with the bottom of the door. He stood slowly, waited a moment, and then stretched each hind leg. His ears and gums flapped as he shook his head to awaken. A cool, moist breeze greeted her as she stepped onto the porch. She drew her housecoat tighter and tied the belt.

She stood on the porch and looked toward the Carving Tree. From a distance the barren tree looked like it did in mid-winter—a skeleton against the gray morning sky. The overcast morning made it darker than usual. In the dim light she couldn't see any leaves on the tree. Compelled to get a closer look, she left the porch. Buckshot wagged his tail and followed, happy to embark on an early morning adventure. The dew-dampened grass soaked her pink slippers, but she didn't care. She picked her way down the rough gravel driveway toward the Carving Tree but stopped short of her destination. A strange gray sedan sat on the side of the road a short distance from their mailbox. She cocked her head and studied the car. Why would anyone park his car on this secluded stretch of gravel road? If the car had broken down, why hadn't its owner knocked on their door? Oh, well, he must have a reason.

Buckshot ran ahead in search of squirrels. Two of the bushy-tailed rodents saw the canine fast approaching and scrambled up the beech tree. They chattered angrily at the dog from a low branch. She stopped and observed the spectacle. The two squirrels, tails bushed, boldly fussed at Buckshot from their leafless wooden perch. She scanned the entire tree but only found three leaves that remained.

The threat of rain made the morning air damper and cooler than usual. She pulled her housecoat tighter and crossed her arms for added warmth. Buckshot circled the tree and sniffed the ground and trunk where the rodents had been. The dog lived a simple and carefree life. It consisted of eating, sleeping, and chasing squirrels. She wished their lives were as simple and carefree as the old dog's life.

One of the three leaves still remaining on the tree fluttered to the ground and joined the thick bed of leaves that had accumulated around the base of the tree. She sighed. The massive beech had been a local landmark for years. Its death would be another of those injustices that had intruded in their lives recently. Her jaw tightened, and she felt a familiar anger prod at her soul. "Why, God? Why are you letting this stuff happen? What purpose does the tree's death serve? Why are you allowing a stranger to sue us for no reason?" Buckshot wagged his tail and cocked his head. She realized she had verbalized her thoughts. A tear ran down her cheek. She softened her voice to a whisper. "Why are you taking Jake's life?" She waited for an answer. She heard nothing but the leaves rustling on the ground.

A second leaf turned loose. She watched as the wind tossed it about. Was this God's response? Was He mocking her? Was He showing her that she was powerless to change His mind? Was He telling her that she had no more control of her life than a leaf blown about in the wind?

She turned and stared at the last leaf. Despair strangled her. The yellow leaf, held fast by the tiniest of stems, danced in the breeze. She wondered how long it would hang on. Its falling would announce the death of the majestic tree. Her chest felt as if a crushing weight lay upon it. She labored to breathe as she watched the leaf.

A sudden gust of wind separated the leaf from the tree. She watched as the wind carried the leaf into the woods across the driveway. A series of small sobs racked her body as reality set in. The Carving Tree, the symbol of their love, had expired.

Sadie heard the sound of a car just before the den phone rang. She grabbed the handset of the old rotary phone before the fourth ring. "Hello."

"Hey, Sadie. It's Maude. Can you talk a minute?"

She surveyed the den. Ethan sat in front of the TV, Jake snored peacefully in his recliner, and Ethan's toys were scattered all over the floor. She wanted to postpone the chat, but she could sense Maude needed to vent. "Sure." As a good friend, she felt obligated to listen. Jake would have to tend to the visitors.

The car engine stopped, and Buckshot barked with a ferocity she'd seldom heard. She walked to the limit of the corded handset while Maude complained about Mabel's treason. She gazed out the den window and saw the gray sedan, the same car she'd seen parked near their mailbox. A wave of apprehension poured over her. She covered the phone receiver. "Jake, we have visitors!"

Jake stirred and wiped the sleep from his eyes. "Huh?"

"We have guests."

Buckshot yelped and then remained silent. Jake glanced at her with concern in his eyes. "I'll check it out."

Maude's voice grew louder. "Sadie? Sadie? Did you hear what I said?"

Sadie kept her eyes fixed on Jake. "I'm sorry. I got distracted."

Jake reached the front door and spoke to someone on the porch. "What can I do for you fellows?"

A stern voice responded. "We're here for Megan."

She strained for a glimpse of the stranger at the door. Did this person have something to do with Megan's disappearance?

Jake rubbed the back of his neck. "She's not here."

"Where is she?"

Jake shrugged. "I don't know. We've not seen her in more than three weeks."

"Back up, ole man."

Jake backed away from the door with his hands raised. A black man holding a gun stepped into their den. He had long braided locks of hair and wore a large gold serpentine chain around his neck. He looked like a pimp's bodyguard. His cologne smelled like her father's cedar chest.

She dropped the phone and gasped.

A large bald white man with a chin beard and gold loop earrings entered next. Even in his prime, Jake would have been no match for the two ruffians and their massive muscles.

Ethan looked up from his place in front of the TV with wide eyes. He ran to Sadie and wrapped his arms around her leg.

Jake spoke with a soft calm voice. "What do you want from us?"

Dreadlocks wiped perspiration from his forehead. "The girl." He pointed toward Sadie. "Go stand with your woman."

Baldy started down the hall. "I'll check the other rooms."

Though she could not see the intruder, his trail of sound—doors slammed and drawers dumped on the floor—revealed his location.

He walked quickly through the den and entered the kitchen. He returned a moment later and shook his head at Dreadlocks. "She's not here. Ain't no sign of her."

The black intruder ran his fingers through his dreadlocks. "What now?"

Baldy slapped a lamp off an end table. He pointed at her. "Where is the girl?"

Tears streamed from her eyes. She shook her head. "We don't know. We told you we haven't seen Megan in more than three weeks."

He seized her arm. Pain raced to her shoulder and fingertips from his crushing grip. He snarled. "Don't mess with me, lady." He pointed at Ethan. "She left her boy with you. I wanna know where she's hiding."

Pow! The sound of the gun rang in her ears. Jake and Dreadlocks rolled on the floor. Baldy released his grip and turned to help his partner. Jake jumped to his feet with the gun. "Stop!"

The two intruders stood motionless. She pulled Ethan to safety and looked at Jake for instructions. His face grew pale and his hand shook. His shoulders rose and fell as he panted for air.

Jake pointed to the phone. "Call . . . call . . . the sheriff."

His weak voice and the strange look on his face made her hesitate. Before she could reach the phone, Jake grabbed his chest and dropped to his knees.

She gasped and ran toward her husband. "Jake!"

The intruders, overcome with surprise, stood motionless. In the quiet of the moment, a faint siren whined. The high-pitched siren rapidly grew in volume like an approaching train. Dreadlocks grabbed his gun, and the two fled out the back door.

She rolled Jake on his back. His brown eyes looked hollow and tired, his rapid breathing shallow and raspy. "Oh, Jake."

He reached up and touched her face. "I love you . . . Sadie . . . You've been . . . a good . . . wife." He lowered his hand. "Don't . . . blame God. He . . . He loves you." His eyes shut.

Sadie cried, "No! Don't leave me."

Jake's eyelids parted slightly like he was squinting into a bright light. "I'll be . . . waiting . . . by the . . . pearly . . ."

Erma cracked a second egg and frowned at the contents in the bowl. A large piece of eggshell floated on the surface of the yoke. "Shucks." She chased the shell around in the bowl with her finger.

"Erma," yelled Clyde from somewhere else in the house. "What did you do with my teeth?"

She pulled her finger from the bowl and wiped it on her apron. The eggshell would have to wait. She shuffled to the kitchen door and yelled back at Clyde, "What did you say?"

Clyde hollered, "My teeth. What did you do with my teeth?"

"Oh for Pete's sake." Erma pulled off her apron and laid it in a chair. "That man would lose his head if it weren't tied on," she muttered as she waddled toward their bedroom. She found Clyde on his hands and knees. He lifted the skirt and looked under their bed. She placed her hands on her hips. "Did you look in the glass next to the sink?"

He rose from his knees with a groan using the bed as an aid. "Say what?"

She spoke a little louder. "Did you look in the glass next to the sink?"

Clyde frowned. "Of course I looked in the glass. That's where I soak 'em."

She held out her hands, palms up. "Well, since you seldom put them where they belong, I thought you might not look there." She glanced toward his bedside table. "What about your bedside table? You've left them there several times before." In fact, he'd left them nearly everywhere at least once.

Clyde's scalp reddened. "Looked there, too." He squinted his eyes. "You sure you didn't move them someplace?"

She detected agitation in his voice. "Now don't pitch a hissy fit. We'll find them directly." Every time Clyde lost his dentures he blamed her. Of course, they always found them exactly where he left them. She rubbed her chin. "Did you check the hearth next to your recliner?"

Clyde scratched his bald head. "Why would they be there?"

She headed for the den. "The way you're constantly taking them out, they could be most anywhere. Why don't you use cement like everybody else who wears false teeth?"

Clyde followed Erma like a puppy. "'Cause I don't need them most of the time."

When they arrived at the recliner, Erma pointed at the dentures lying on the hearth. "Well, look yonder. I guess they sprouted legs and marched right in here." She heard Clyde mumble something as she headed back into the kitchen.

She tied on her apron and began to beat the eggs with a fork. She suddenly felt the Spirit impress upon her a great need to pray for Sadie. She dropped the fork, grabbed hold of the edge of the counter, and squeezed her eyes shut. "Dear God, please be with Sadie at this moment. I sense she is in great need of your comfort. Wrap your lovin' arms round her and give her the peace that passeth all understandin'. Give her the strength to face come what may. Help her, dear God, to 'mount up with wings as eagles . . .' Amen."

She reached for the phone and dialed the Hopkinses' home.

✿ CHAPTER 37 ✿

Sadie grimaced in pain as she stood in the receiving line next to Jake's casket. Her high-heeled shoes stabbed at her tender heels like a baking nail penetrating a potato. Erma's feet had to be hurting even more, given her advanced age and overweight frame. However, her loyal friend—adorned in a black dress with little white polka dots, a large-rimmed black satin hat, and a healthy coat of red lipstick—had stood by her side all evening.

Clyde stood in the corner near the head of Jake's casket and chatted with each person who passed through the receiving line. In his new navy jeans, white shirt, red suspenders, and navy corduroy jacket, he looked more dressed up than she'd ever seen him. Of course, he proudly displayed his war medal on his jacket.

She couldn't recall ever seeing this many flowers packed into a single room. Jake's previous co-workers, people that she didn't even know, had sent many of the arrangements. The strong fragrance of the flowers permeated the room. She was struck by the irony of their sweet, sweet smell at such a bitter moment. This had been one of the most difficult days of her life. For more than forty-five years Jake had been by her side. She couldn't even fathom life without her husband.

She stole a glance past Mrs. Dickson, who stood next in line. For the first time the receiving line no longer looped out of the parlor into the hallway. She appreciated the great show of respect, but she tired of sobbing. Every time she regained her composure, someone would approach her in tears, tell her a story about Jake, or mention how much they would miss him. She would find herself weeping again in their embrace.

After the last person in the receiving line passed, she looped the strap of her pocketbook over her shoulder and walked to the front of the shiny black casket accented in silver trim. Jake looked very peaceful. Under different circumstances she might have mistaken his stillness for deep sleep. She wondered what Ethan would say if he saw Jake lying there in the black box. Ethan had been staying with Ethel Burton, one of the ladies from church, since the prior morning.

Jake wore his favorite dark gray suit and burgundy tie. She always loved to see him dressed in that suit. He looked handsome. She adjusted his tie. She remembered the occasion when Jake had bought the suit. He had jokingly told her, "As outstanding employee of the year, I deserve a new suit—and my own parking space. Don't you think?" She felt the trace of a smile form on her lips.

The mortician had done a good job styling Jake's hair. She tugged down one coat sleeve and re-fluffed the burgundy handkerchief positioned in his jacket's breast pocket. She swallowed hard. This inspection had been part of their Sunday morning routine. She would fluff up the handkerchief in his breast pocket, button down his collar, and cinch the knot of his tie against his neck. Her eyes clouded again. Now she performed the final inspection.

Pastor Nolan moved to her side and placed his arm around her lower back. "He was a fine man, a real man of integrity."

She dabbed at the corners of her eyes with a tissue and nodded as she battled a choking sensation in her throat.

Pastor Nolan continued, "The Good Book says, 'Precious in the sight of the Lord is the death of His saints.'"

Her knees went weak, and Pastor Nolan caught her and guided her into a nearby chair. Erma and Clyde rushed to her side.

Erma leaned close and asked, "Are you all right, shugah?"

Sadie arrived home to a dark and dismal house. When she'd left earlier in the evening, she'd not had the presence of mind to leave on the porch light. Fortunately the full moon lit her path to the door. Buckshot lay against the screen door. His muzzle rested on the floor between his front paws. He didn't even lift his head when she climbed the porch steps. She stooped and patted the dog's head. "Looks like it's just you and me, old boy."

The dog whined softly.

She reached for the door handle, and he jumped to his feet. With his tail tucked under and his head hung low, Buckshot walked slowly off the porch. He looked like she felt, brokenhearted and crushed.

She unlocked the door, entered the house, and switched on the lights in the den. The familiar room seemed twice as large and twice as empty. Her high-heeled shoes echoed on the hardwood floor.

She slumped off the shoulder strap of her pocketbook and tossed it on the couch. She kicked off her high heels, rubbed her aching feet for a moment, and then stretched out on the couch. The mantel clock chimed nine times. Though she felt exhausted, sleep avoided her. She heard nothing but the steady tick-tock of the mantel clock. It had seemed like the longest day of her life, and even now she would swear the relentless tick-tock of the clock was slower than normal. She had lain on her side for fewer than fifteen minutes, yet it seemed like an eternity. Time had slowed down, and she feared life without Jake would be torturously slow.

She turned on the TV and flipped through the three channels but found nothing that caught her attention. The absence of Ethan's noise, which had dominated their lives over the last several weeks, exaggerated the quiet of the house. She left the TV playing. Any sound seemed better than no sound.

She spotted her parents' large family Bible displayed prominently on the coffee table. She flipped through the old Bible and stumbled on a diagram of the family tree. A date had been recorded beside many of the names which indicated when the person had been baptized. She found her own name on the chart and read the note beside it. "Baptized May 5th, 1955." She'd been thirteen years old at the time.

She remembered the day she'd "walked the aisle" as if it had been yesterday. Pastor Godfrey stood in front of the altar, and the pianist played "Are You Washed in the Blood." Jenny poked her in the ribs with her elbow. "Let's do it."

"Do what?"

Jenny tossed her curls casually and replied, "Go down front."

Sadie's pulse quickened. "Why?"

"It's the cool thing to do. Mom said we have to become members before we can take communion like the adults." Jenny grabbed hold of Sadie's arm and pulled her into the aisle.

Sadie resisted, but before she knew it, they were halfway down the aisle. When they reached the front, Jenny told the preacher, "We want to be saved."

The mantel clock struck ten and brought Sadie back to the present. She remembered her shock at Jenny's proclamation to the preacher. She'd not desired to go forward to be saved.

She closed the Bible and laid it back on the coffee table. She dreaded going to their bedroom. There would be no warm body to curl up against and no strong arm around her. She turned on the bedroom light and propped against the doorframe and cried. Why had life suddenly become unbearable? She looked through tear-filled eyes at the portraits hung on the wall at the foot of the bed, a portrait of her and Jake, a portrait of Frank in his dress uniform, and a portrait of her mom and dad. She felt a familiar anger spark to life in her soul. She cursed and stomped back into the den. She picked up the large Bible from the coffee table and flung it against the wall as she screamed, "The three most important men in my life—and you, God, took them all prematurely."

Clyde rolled over for what must have been the tenth time since they had lain down four hours earlier. The bedside clock read 1:30 a.m. He fluffed his pillow and pushed the sheet down to his waist. Erma slept soundly and gave off an occasional nasal snort. But he stared wide-eyed at the ceiling. He typically fell asleep before his head touched the pillow, but not tonight. It had been a tough evening at the funeral home. Jake had been his best friend for the last thirty years. However, Sadie's request while at the funeral home weighed more heavily on his mind than Jake's death. She'd asked him to speak at the funeral in the morning. He couldn't refuse her request, but the thought of speaking in front of the huge crowd terrified him.

He wiped the perspiration from his brow. What would he say? He thought about Jake's qualities and characteristics, the things that made Jake unique. He thought about what first attracted him to Jake fifty-three years earlier.

It suddenly occurred to him what he should say about Jake. Having determined his topic, he turned on his side, breathed in a few relaxing breaths, and drifted off to sleep.

❦ CHAPTER 38 ❦

Sadie shook the water from her umbrella and stood it in the corner of the vestibule. The cold, soaking rain made the day even more miserable. She hoped it would not rain at the graveside service. She inhaled deeply, stepped through the double doors into the small chapel, and stopped abruptly. Jake's casket rested at the far end of the center aisle, positioned in front of the altar. The upper lid stood open, but the lower lid over Jake's legs was closed. The slick ebony surface reflected the overhead lights like a well-polished desk. She felt faint, and her thoughts spiraled out of control. A vision of another casket flashed through her mind, a seven-foot box with an American flag draped over it. The sealed coffin hid a body burned beyond recognition. Six marines stood at attention near the casket. Like department store mannequins clothed in dress blues, they stood motionless, their faces without expression. Frank . . . oh, Frank. Why had God taken her baby prematurely?

The front side door of the chapel opened and startled her. A florist placed a beautiful flower arrangement on the lower casket lid. He left as quickly as he'd entered. She looked at her watch. It read 10:05 a.m., and no one else occupied the chapel.

Though she willed her legs to move, her feet seemed glued in place. She longed to postpone the moment, the final time that she would see Jake's face. She didn't want to say good-bye. Jake had been dead for more than two days. Yet, it wasn't until this moment that she sensed the finality of his departure.

The approaching funeral, scheduled for eleven a.m., made her time with Jake short. So she pushed her feet to move. With each step down the aisle, the length of the casket grew. Numerous flower arrangements, positioned on either end of the casket, crowded the front of the small chapel. Their sweet scent grew stronger as she moved toward the altar. The familiar scene reminded her she'd walked this path before. An image of a crude wooden box choked her thoughts. She gasped at the childhood memory of her father— much younger than Jake—lying in the open coffin. She continued toward the casket uncertain which man she would find there.

Jake's face came into view as she reached the front of the sanctuary. Her breath vacated her lungs, forming a great emptiness in her chest. She reached out and grabbed the silk-lined wall of the open box to steady herself.

Her shortness of breath caused her to remember their first meeting. Jake had taken her breath then as well. Her family had moved to Glendale the summer before her sophomore year in high school. She'd met the good-looking senior the first day in the new school. All the girls seemed to be crazy over him. She replayed the meeting in her mind.

Late for class, she rushed to get the books from her locker. She slammed shut the narrow metal door and stepped blindly in the direction of her next class. She collided with someone, and her books spilled to the floor.

She dropped to her knees and gathered her books. Extremely embarrassed, she avoided looking up. Everyone would be watching the spectacle she'd become. She reached for the last book, but someone else picked it up first. Her eyes traced up the arm. The smiling face of the handsome young man took her breath.

He handed her the book. "I'm sorry. Are you okay?"

Her face burned red. "It . . . it . . . it was my fault. I stepped before looking."

He raked his hand through his greased-back hair. "Lucky for me you weren't looking."

His unexpected flirtation quickened her pulse. She squeezed the books against her chest. Just breathe. Take long, deep breaths.

He held out his hand. "Here, let me help you up."

Sadie took hold of his hand, and he pulled her up. She felt light-headed like she'd gotten up too quickly. Her body swayed and her knees weakened. She propped against the lockers.

The young man took her books. "Are you okay?"

She forced a smile. "I just stood a little too quickly."

He picked up her pocketbook and handed it to her. "Where's your next class?"

She looped the strap of her pocketbook over her shoulder. "Math with Mrs. Broughton."

"I know where her room is. Come on. I'll walk you there."

The front side door of the chapel opened, interrupting her thoughts. A man from the funeral home brought in another flower arrangement, then left as quickly as he'd entered. She looked down at Jake and lost her breath again.

The double doors of the vestibule creaked, and she caught a glimpse of people arriving for the service. She glanced at her watch. It read 10:35 a.m. Where had her time with Jake gone?

Two attendants from the funeral home entered from the front side door of the chapel. They stood silently a few feet away with their hands behind their backs, like two vultures waiting to steal her prey. Her heart melted. She knew they had come to close the casket before the beginning of the funeral service. She'd dreaded this moment.

She dug around in her purse until she found the fork that she'd stashed there earlier in the day. She placed the fork in Jake's top hand and placed both her hands over his. "I hope the best has come." She leaned and kissed his cold forehead one last time. "I love you, Mr. Hopkins."

Sadie sat in the empty front row with Clyde and Erma, the closest thing she had to real family. Neither she nor Jake had any close living relatives. Jake had been an only child, and her sister had died two years earlier. The three rows reserved for the family contained only a few distant cousins and their families. She'd always envisioned an abundance of grandchildren and great-grandchildren attending their funerals. But that had all been short-circuited by Frank's premature death.

Numbed by her anger, she failed to hear Pastor Nolan's words and refused to listen to anything about God and heaven. However, she perked up when it came time for Clyde to speak. He wore the same outfit he'd worn the night before—navy jeans, red suspenders, a white shirt, and a navy corduroy jacket. The Bronze Star hung prominently from his jacket.

Clyde slowly walked to the podium as if he had shackles around his ankles. The intense stage lights bore down on his small frame, and drops of perspiration glistened on his slick head. His hands shook as he unfolded a crumpled piece of paper containing his notes. He flattened out the paper on the podium with both hands. It seemed as if he operated in slow motion, intentionally delaying his speech. Erma shifted nervously in her seat. Clyde tilted the podium microphone toward himself and blew into it.

Sadie touched her fingers to her lips. She felt sorry for Clyde. She wished she'd never asked him to share. He looked uncomfortable and out of place.

He took hold of the podium with both hands and began. "My name is Clyde Coble. Most of you know me." He pointed at Erma. "My wife, Erma, is planted there next to Sadie. I reckon Sadie asked me to share some thoughts because Jake and I are . . . uh . . . were real close."

She felt a wave of emptiness ripple through her body, and the tears returned. Erma placed an unsteady hand on top of her hand.

Clyde continued. "You might say we were best buddies." He pulled out his handkerchief and blew his nose, then laid the soiled handkerchief on the podium. "I wrote down some stuff that I want to tell you about Jake."

He shifted his weight from one leg to another. "I was thirty-one at the time I first met Jake and no longer living with Ma and Pa. Late one summer my Pa lost the entire bundle of cash on the way home from the Winston-Salem tobacco market, more than $500 in an unlabeled envelope." He wiped the perspiration from his forehead with the back of his hand. "Ma and Pa were near wit's end. You see, they depended on the tobacco money to pay their bills each year. I can still see the desperation on their faces and remember the talk of losing the farm. Just when all seemed lost, a twelve-year-old boy turned over the envelope to the sheriff, not a penny missing. The boy impressed me because he'd not given in to the temptation to keep the money." His voice cracked. "From then on Jake had a special place in my heart." His eyes locked on his notes, and his body visibly trembled.

Sadie dabbed the tears from her cheeks. This had to be extremely difficult for Clyde.

After several minutes Clyde looked up. He wadded up his notes and stuck them in his pocket. "When it comes to Jake Hopkins, I don't need to talk from a piece of paper." He wiped his nose with his handkerchief. "Jake was a man of integrity, an honest fella, and the real deal. He never pretended to be somethin' that he wasn't. What you saw was what you got." His voice broke. "I wish I was half the man that Jake Hopkins was."

Clyde stood with both hands grasping the sides of the podium and stared at its surface as if reading from an imaginary document. The audience grew restless as several minutes passed. Finally, he lifted his gaze and addressed the congregation. "Unlike Jake, I've lived a lie for more than sixty-five years."

Sadie furrowed her brow. What secret had Clyde kept for sixty-five years? Erma pulled her hand from Sadie's and leaned forward slightly.

Clyde's boney hands shook as he unclipped the war medal from his jacket. He looked toward Erma. "I'm sorry, Erma, I deceived you for all these years. I've been the worst hypocrite. You see, I didn't deserve this World War II medal or deserve to be called a hero."

Erma covered her red lips with her trembling fingers.

The war medal clinked when he laid it on the podium. He slowly scanned the room. "In 1941 I was part of the light infantry. My squad was fightin' on the front lines against the Germans, and I was in a foxhole with my sergeant and four other soldiers. The rest of our squad was in a different foxhole. During the hot and heavy fightin' an enemy shell exploded close by and peppered us with shrapnel." He moved to the side of the podium and pointed to his right leg. "I took a piece right here. I cut off a shirtsleeve and wrapped it around my thigh to slow the bleeding. The open wound soured my stomach."

He returned to the security of the podium and continued. "Two of the men in the foxhole died instantly, and two suffered some real bad wounds. They kept fading in and out of consciousness. Sarge defended our position while I tried to help them." He stopped and swallowed deeply. "Only twenty years old and a young whippersnapper, I had never experienced battle." He paused. Someone dropped a wooden pencil that rattled loudly on the laminate floor. "Their blood . . . my blood . . . the blood overwhelmed me. I fumbled to bandage their wounds but didn't help much. Sarge, bleeding like gangbusters, continued to defend our position while I cowered in the hole." He stared at the top of the podium for several moments before he continued. His soft voice seemed distant. "Sarge took an enemy bullet right between the eyes. He turned and looked at me for just a moment before he dropped to the ground. I'll never forget the look in his eyes just before the lights went out."

Erma looked pale, as if the blood had drained from her cheeks. Sadie took Erma's cold and sweaty hand in hers.

Clyde wiped his nose with the handkerchief. "I panicked. I knew any second the Germans would pour into the foxhole and finish us off. I didn't know what to do. I took Sarge's pistol and toyed with the idea of saving the Germans a bullet. Just before I could raise the pistol to my head, the other four members of our squad dropped into the foxhole. Our platoon eventually took the piece of ground, and the story circulated among the soldiers that I had defended the foxhole and saved the lives of the two wounded soldiers."

He held up the medal. "They gave me this here medal for being a hero. I should have refused it, but I didn't. It felt good to be a hero. As a young'un, I was smaller than the other boys my age and always the target of their pranks and jokes. As time went on, it became even harder to come clean. The lie became so engrained in me and such a large part of my identity that I even began to believe it." He stepped down from the platform and placed a boney hand on the casket. "Even in his death, Jake has encouraged me to come clean, to remove the guilt of this lie from my soul." He laid the war medal on the casket. "Thanks, ole buddy."

❦ CHAPTER 39 ❦

Daniel, like most of the large crowd, stood under an umbrella in the cold soaking rain. He shuddered in his short-sleeved shirt, wishing he'd worn a jacket. A cold front had entered the state from the north and brought amazingly cool weather for a late June day. Sadie sat in the front row under the blue funeral home canopy. Jake's old dog lay against her legs. Clyde and Erma Coble huddled next to Sadie, their old frames slumped and their faces downcast. Sadie didn't look well. She'd dramatically aged since the last time he'd seen her. However, he marveled at her composure. This had to be incredibly difficult for her.

The crowd consisted of both strangers and familiar faces from Glendale Baptist Church. He assumed many of the strangers had been coworkers with Jake at the furniture factory. Others, like him, were Sadie's former students.

The canopy that sheltered the burial site stood near the large beech tree. Its tightly stretched canvas yielded a rhythmic "popping" sound from the steady rain. He had noticed the old tree before, majestic in stature and covered with carvings. But today the beech looked different with its bare crown. A heavy layer of matted leaves covered the ground beneath the tree's canopy. The cool, wet air and the ground cover made it seem like late October.

A large pile of red clay stood to one side of the beech. The rain on the pile magnified the smell of the fresh soil. The head of Jake's grave occupied space near the foot of the beech. The grave, offset slightly to the right of the tree's center, allowed room for a second grave—Sadie's grave. The plots had been located such that a large heart-shaped carving would be centered over the future headstones. An arrow ran diagonally through the heart, and the phrase "Jake + Sadie" had been inscribed within it. Apparently, Jake had carved the heart many years earlier. Daniel's heart grew heavy. Not many couples could claim such love and devotion.

Pastor Nolan began his graveside remarks. "Dearly beloved brothers and sisters in Christ, we gather here today in honor of Jake Earl Hopkins. It is a sad time indeed knowing we have been separated from our brother Jake. However, we recognize one day soon we will again see his face. Listen to the words of the apostle Paul in his letter to the Thessalonian church: 'But I would not have you to be ignorant, brethren, concerning them which are asleep, that ye sorrow not, even as others which have no hope. For if we believe that Jesus died and rose again, even so them also which sleep in Jesus will God bring with him. For this we say unto you by the word of the Lord, that we which are alive and remain unto the coming of the Lord shall not prevent them which are asleep. For the Lord himself shall descend from heaven with a shout, with the voice of the archangel, and with the trump of God. And the dead in Christ shall rise first. Then we which are alive and remain shall be caught up together with them in the clouds, to meet the Lord in the air. And so shall we ever be with the Lord. Wherefore comfort one another with these words.'"

Pastor Nolan closed his Bible. A smile broke out on his face as he looked at Sadie and each individual that sat in the front row. "We draw great comfort from these words knowing Jake is in a better place. We know his heart is healed, and he is in a place where 'there shall be no more death, neither sorrow, nor crying. Neither shall there be any more pain, for the former things are passed away.'" Reverend Nolan closed in prayer.

Daniel waited for the crowd to disperse and for each person to speak to Sadie. As the crowd thinned, he slipped under the canopy closer to where Sadie sat. He closed his umbrella and waited patiently for a private moment with her.

He leaned forward and listened with keen interest when a woman pointed at the tree and asked Sadie about the carving. Sadie looked mournfully at the woman for what seemed like minutes. Her mouth opened, but no words came forth. Her eyes filled with tears and her lips began to quiver. Erma turned in her folding chair and embraced Sadie. She pulled Sadie's head to her shoulder. Sadie sobbed uncontrollably. The old dog at her feet looked up at her, wrinkled his forehead, and whined softly. No one else spoke to Sadie. They just touched her shoulder as they parted.

Just when he decided to approach Sadie, two gravediggers, who had been waiting in a dilapidated pickup, began to lower the casket. He elected to wait until they left before talking with her. Clyde and Erma encouraged Sadie to go to the house and get out of the cold, damp air, but she continued to sit silently under the canopy. The gravediggers broke down the lifting equipment and began to shovel dirt into the hole. Sadie stared at the grave with a blank look on her face as if her mind was locked in a trance. Daniel felt helpless. It must be extremely difficult for her to watch as the person that she'd loved for nearly fifty years disappeared beneath the soil.

When the gravediggers had finished burying Jake, they cleaned up their equipment and removed all of the folding chairs with the exception of the one in which Sadie sat. As soon as the gravediggers left, the old dog left the security of Sadie's legs and walked over to the burial plot. He sniffed the fresh soil for a moment, then circled three times and lay across Jake's grave.

Clyde and Erma again insisted Sadie take refuge in the comfort of the house, but she did not respond. Erma took off her sweater and draped it around Sadie's shoulders, and then they left for home.

Alone at last with Sadie, Daniel knelt and touched her arm. "I'm very sorry, Mrs. Hopkins." Her eyes appeared vacant, and she didn't acknowledge him. She just continued to stare glassy-eyed at the fresh mound of dirt.

Megan sat up in the truck seat, rubbed the sleep from her eyes, and stretched her arms. "Where are we?"

Merle adjusted the visor to shield his eyes from the late afternoon sun. "Eighty miles from Nashville." He winked at her. "I'm glad Sleeping Beauty has awakened. I was getting bored."

She yawned and looked out the window at the beautiful rolling countryside and the hardwood forests that resembled those near home. Although Glendale still remained a hard day's ride from Nashville, she was getting close to home and Ethan. She glanced at Merle. The old man had been extremely kind to her over the last several days. She didn't know how she could ever repay him. He'd paid for all of her meals and always managed to stop overnight at a truck stop with a driver's lounge.

Merle shifted gears. His wedding band clicked as it made contact with the gear lever.

She rubbed her chin. Why hadn't he mentioned his wife? "Doesn't your wife get lonely while you're on the road?"

Merle's expression soured. "I would give everything if she could. Lindy died nine years ago. You can bet your last dollar that I wouldn't be on the road if she were still living."

She paused. "I'm terribly sorry."

"Quite all right. But since we're discussing personal matters now, I have a question for you." He looked at her. "Megan, how did you become a victim of a human trafficking ring based in LA?"

She studied the top of her hand for several seconds and then shared all that had transpired over the last three weeks except for her shark encounter and plea to God.

Merle remained quiet and listened attentively. When she concluded, he looked her directly in the eyes and spoke with a very serious tone. "Young lady, rest assured, God has something very special planned for you."

She swallowed deeply. Somehow, God kept coming back into the equation. She wiped her eyes with the back of her hand. "Do you have a tissue?"

Merle pointed at the glove compartment. "I don't have any tissues, but there are some napkins from a fast food restaurant in the glove compartment."

She popped the door open and dug around for a napkin. Several index cards fell to the floorboard. "I'm sorry," she said as she gathered the cards from the floor.

Merle shifted gears. "That's okay. They're just Bible verses. Sometimes on long trips, I memorize some of my favorite verses."

She looked at the top card, which had a scripture reference of Acts 3:19. She read the first phrase silently. "Repent ye therefore, and be converted." She chewed on her lip and looked out the window. The words stung. She recalled her desperate cry for help while in the ocean and her promise to God. She tried to swallow the dry lump that had formed in her throat. God had answered her cry for help. He'd taken away the great white shark, and He'd not forgotten her promise. She silently read the next phrase. "That your sins may be blotted out." She squeezed her eyes tightly shut. Blotted out, wiped away, and removed like an ugly stain from a carpet. Could God remove her sin? Could He blot out her guilt? She read on. "When the times of refreshing shall come from the presence of the Lord." Over the last several days she'd been physically refreshed by the cleansing shower, warm meals, and restful sleep, but the refreshment of her soul—to be right with God—was the thing she really desired. She covered her mouth with her hand and propped her head against the window. She wept.

Merle stopped at a rest area a few miles down the road. He parked the truck and helped her down from her seat.

She sobbed with such intensity that she could not stand erect. He pulled her into a comforting embrace, and she laid her head against his shoulder. The torrent of tears flowed like water from a breached dam.

After a few minutes in the warm afternoon sun, he pointed at an empty picnic table located in the shade. "Let's sit down and talk." He grabbed some napkins from the glove compartment and a small New Testament from the center console, and then led her to the table.

She brushed the tears from her eyes and tried to regain her composure. What had come over her? Why did she feel this way? Was it an emotional reaction to the stress that she'd been under? Perhaps after having to remain emotionally strong for so long, her body now released the emotions that had been bottled within her.

Merle reached across the table and tugged at the index card, which she still clutched tightly in her fist. She realized she'd destroyed the card. It set off a whole new wave of tears. "I'm very sorry," she sobbed. "I can make you another one."

He chuckled. "It's just an index card that took me all of two minutes to make." He unfolded the wadded card and glanced at the passage. He sat silently, but she felt his eyes studying her face.

After a few minutes, Merle spoke. "Megan"—he waited for her to make eye contact—"I can see the Lord is dealing with you and drawing you to Him. He desires to save you, to deliver you from your pit of guilt. He stands ready with open arms to forgive you for all your sins."

All the bad things in her life, neatly catalogued in her mind, flashed before her: the shame and embarrassment of a high school pregnancy, her inability to satisfy the man who fathered Ethan, being fired from numerous jobs, the sexual assault, and, worst of all, her failure as a mother. She buried her face in her hands. "God doesn't want me. I'm not good enough."

Merle touched her shoulder. "You're wrong, Megan. Jesus came to save the lost, the hurting, and the downtrodden. He wants you to come to Him just as you are. He'll help you put your life back together after you've come to Him."

She blew her nose on a napkin. "You don't understand. You don't know the kind of person I am. You don't know what I've done."

Merle leaned forward and cocked his head to one side. "No. I don't know what kind of person you are, and I don't know what you've done. But I do know the kind of man that I was before I met Jesus. I doubt your story is any worse than mine. You see, Megan, I'm a recovering alcoholic. I've been dry for more than twenty years. Praise the Lord! But I let that disease rob me of twenty-three precious years. My bondage to alcohol ruined my career, damaged family relationships, and nearly cost me my marriage. Megan, I was a totally different person under the influence of alcohol." He hesitated. His lip began to quiver, and she saw tears roll down his face. "I abused my wife. I almost killed her once in a drunken rage." He paused. "In a way, I guess that my loss of control was a blessing in disguise because I realized how far I'd fallen."

She listened intently, but struggled to imagine how this kind old man could be abusive.

Merle smiled as if he'd just recalled a fond memory. "At my lowest point God placed an old friend in my life, someone I hadn't seen in years, an old drinking buddy. But Jack was different. He'd changed. He'd dried out. He had such an optimistic outlook and hope for the future. Jack shared with me how God had changed his life.

"Megan, I thought I had to quit drinking, go to church, and clean up my act before I could come to Him." He smiled. "But Jack set me straight . . . good ole Jack. He told me that God bids us to come to Him just as we are. If we ask Him to forgive us, to come into our hearts, and to take charge of our lives, He'll do it.

Till this day, I cling to the verse that Jack told me concerning God's forgiveness, 1 John 1:9. 'If we confess our sins, He is faithful and just to forgive us our sins and to cleanse us from all unrighteousness.' Once we've asked Jesus to come into our lives and take control, He'll help us clean up."

Merle held up the crumpled index card. "It's like the verse says. If we repent and are converted, He'll blot out all our sins and forget them. However, it's the last portion of that verse, Megan, that I want you to hear. 'When the times of refreshing shall come from the presence of the Lord.' Megan, when we turn our lives over to Jesus, He gives us great peace and contentment. Like a warm shower washes the dirt and filth away, our souls are cleansed from the guilt of sin and our relationship is restored with God."

Megan felt a gentle breeze that provided relief from the afternoon heat.

Merle touched her hand. "Life is not easy. I won't kid you. A day hasn't gone by in the last twenty years that I haven't had the temptation to drink. But each time God has enabled me to walk away from the alcohol. Megan, He can forgive you too. He can restore you. He can bring healing in your life. With his power, He can help you overcome your circumstances. How about it? Is that a decision you would like to make?"

She stared across the quiet parking lot. She'd never felt emptier or more desperate than she did at this moment. The words of the promise she'd made to God in the open sea echoed through her mind. Certainly, God had placed Merle in her path for this very reason.

❧ Chapter 40 ❧

Sadie struggled to keep her balance as Jake pulled her through the woods of his father's property. The thick underbrush raked at her body, but it didn't seem to slow Jake. Where was he taking her? Curiosity got the best of her, and she resisted his forward motion until he stopped. "Where are we going? You're pulling me through the thicket so fast I'm going to ruin my poodle skirt and saddle shoes. I've never seen you this excited."

Jake turned and flashed a big grin. He ran his hand through his greased-back hair, and looked deeply into her eyes. "I wanna show you something."

She melted. His dancing brown eyes communicated more than he could ever say.

He turned and proceeded, and she went willingly. A few minutes later he stopped at the edge of a small clearing and stood motionless.

She stepped to his side to see what had captured his attention. Standing alone in the center of the clearing was a huge beech. The majestic tree took her breath. Its massive canopy blocked almost all sunlight to the forest floor and eliminated all undergrowth around the base of the tree. The smooth gray bark bore the initials of numerous individuals and the words "John Paul was here." She stared in awe at the enchanted tree. "It . . . it's beautiful. Is this what you wanted to show me?"

Jake's gaze dropped to the ground.

She detected a hint of embarrassment. Not Jake. She'd never seen Jake embarrassed by anything. Why, he was like James Dean— Mr. Cool himself—standing there with his Brylcreem hairdo and package of cigarettes rolled up in the sleeve of his white T-shirt.

Jake lifted his head and stared into space with reflective brown eyes. Her stomach grew queasy as she watched him search for words. This must be serious. "The tree is beautiful," she said in an effort to break the awkward silence.

"Sadie." Jake smiled and took her hand. "There is something else that I want to show you. Close your eyes."

She squeezed her eyes shut. He led her a few steps forward and turned her around. She sensed a little nervousness in his voice as he spoke. "You . . . you can open your eyes now."

She opened her eyes and saw the backside of the tree. A large heart had been freshly carved into the smooth bark. The interior of the heart bore the phrase, "Jake + Sadie." Her heartbeat quickened. An arrow, which had been etched in the bark, diagonally pierced the heart. "Oh, Jake, that's very sweet."

He blushed, took her hands tenderly in his, and looked deeply into her eyes. She saw a flicker of excitement. "Sadie." He hesitated. His soft voice seemed serious. "I . . . I love you. I want to spend my life with you. Will you be my wife?"

A loud clap of thunder broke her trance. The steady "popping" sound of the cold rain on the overhead cloth canopy reminded her of a gloomy future. Her eyes locked on the familiar carving as daylight faded. If only she could turn back time.

She stood slowly. Her body had grown stiff from sitting hours in the folding metal chair. Buckshot lay across the fresh earth of his master's new grave. His muzzle rested on the cold red dirt between his front paws.

She looked at the dark house at the top of the hill. "Come on Buckshot. Let's go to the house."

The dog never stirred. He rolled his sad eyes up at her and then back to the ground. She understood the dog's sorrow. She grabbed her umbrella and started up the muddy driveway. When she reached the porch she looked back down the hill. Buckshot still lay across his master's grave.

Sadie grew troubled as she looked at the face in the bathroom mirror. She reached for a washcloth to remove the makeup from her face. The color of the washcloth didn't match the wallpaper. Erma or one of the ladies in the church had put out fresh linens. She washed her face and all the age marks and wrinkles became visible in the mirror. For the last twenty-five years, she'd gone to great lengths to hide her age—to make people think she was something she wasn't, a younger Sadie Hopkins. The face in the mirror revealed the real Sadie Hopkins. The fake Sadie had washed down the drain.

Clyde's words from earlier in the morning came rushing back to her. She'd been shocked by his confession. He'd lived a lie for more than sixty years. All that time, only God and Clyde knew the truth. She frowned at the old woman in the mirror. "You're just a big hypocrite." She'd lived a lie just like Clyde. She'd joined the church as a young girl with her friend Jenny, not because of a spiritual awakening, but because of peer pressure. So for years she'd played the part of a Christian and fooled everyone, even Jake, initially.

She'd always desired to please Jake. All the years of their marriage, she'd attended church with him, served on committees, and even helped in the nursery. She'd been approached many times about teaching Sunday school because everyone knew she taught fourth grade in the public school. She'd always refused their request and told them that she needed a break from elementary-aged children. In reality, she found it difficult to teach something she did not totally embrace. Yes, she definitely fit the hypocrite mold. She could say one positive thing about Clyde; at least he'd finally come clean.

She slipped off her dress, let it drop to the floor, and put on her nightgown. She would pick up her clothes later. There was no one else to see them or to trip over them during the night.

Someone had laid the last several days of mail on her pillow. She put on her reading glasses, sat on the bed, and sifted through the mail. The stack included several advertisements, an envelope that bore all the signs of a credit card offer, a telephone bill, and at the bottom of the pile, a letter from the Law Office of Cavanaugh and Associates. "Oh great, more *good* news. I don't think I can take any more *good* news today." She laid the letter and her reading glasses on the side table.

She glanced out the bedroom window at the impenetrable darkness, blackness like the bowels of the deepest cavern. The heavy rain clouds hid all sources of heavenly light. Her watch read 11:30 p.m. In spite of her exhaustion, she knew sleep wouldn't come easy.

She turned down the covers and climbed into bed. Jake had always been warm-natured and usually kicked the blanket off at night. But without him, she knew she would get cold. She reached down and pulled up the sheet and blanket. The fresh smell of fabric softener drifted to her nostrils. Someone had changed the sheets and pillowcases as well. She turned off the side table lamp. She had the urge to cry, but there were no more tears left.

She tossed and turned. The clock on the bedside table read two a.m. She'd remained wide awake in her exhausted state. She missed Jake's arm around her abdomen, the familiar "spooning" position, and the fragrance of his aftershave. His aftershave—that strong masculine aroma she'd grown familiar with over the years. She turned on the lamp, slipped out of bed, and made her way to the bathroom. She fetched his bottle of aftershave and sprinkled a few drops on her pillow. The scent permeated the air. "There, that's better." She slipped under the covers, turned off the lamp, and breathed in the familiar fragrance. She imagined his arms around her and the warmth of his body, and soon fell asleep.

❧ CHAPTER 41 ❧

Sadie slept till the bright morning sunshine penetrated the bedroom. The rain had passed. She pulled on her housecoat and bedroom slippers, hung her reading glasses around her neck, picked up the letter from Brantley Cavanaugh, and stomped to the kitchen. The letter called for a strong cup of coffee. She laid the letter on the kitchen table and started the pot. When the decanter had filled, she poured a cup and took a seat at the table.

She slipped on her glasses and sipped her coffee. The letter, dated four days earlier, had been typed on official letterhead that stated: "The Law Offices of Cavanaugh and Associates." She read the letter aloud.

> Re: *Motor Vehicle Collision Lawsuit*
> *Reference: 21201.24924*

> *Mr. and Mrs. Jake Hopkins:*
> *This letter is a follow-up to our previous meeting. My client, Vanessa Kingsley, has agreed a formal lawsuit is not in the best interest of all parties involved. We, therefore, propose an out-of-court settlement in the amount of $50,000. If we have not heard from you by July 5th, we*

will file a formal lawsuit seeking $100,000 in retribution. Please consult your legal counsel and notify my office of your decision.

> *Sincerely,*
> *Cavanaugh and Associates*
> *Brantley Cavanaugh III, Esq.*

Sadie slammed her coffee cup to the table, spilling its contents. "Jake, who does he think he is? This is robbery. He can't . . . !" She removed her reading glasses and looked at the empty chair. She dropped her face into her hands and cried. Countless mornings they had sat here at this very table drinking coffee and enjoying casual conversation. Now she heard nothing but the soft sizzle of moisture as it ran down the outside of the decanter and contacted the hot warmer.

She left her coffee on the table, picked up the letter, and headed for the Carving Tree. She needed to talk to Jake. He'd never even known about the lawsuit, and she felt guilty she'd never told him. She would do it now. She marched out of the house in her bedroom slippers. Buckshot did not greet her at the door. His tan body still lay across Jake's grave. At least the old dog had stayed dry all night under the cloth canopy.

Guilt-ridden, she walked toward the Carving Tree. She should have told Jake about the lawsuit earlier. She hoped he would not be angry with her. Surely he would understand she'd withheld the information to protect his health. She approached the gravesite, but Buckshot never lifted his head from the fresh soil. The dog had been crushed by Jake's death. She'd always heard a dog is a man's best friend, but in this case, Jake was the dog's best friend. "Buckshot, are you missing Jake?" The dog didn't wag his tail or bunch his brow. He never looked up as she approached. She reached to pat his head and disturbed a hoard of flies that had gathered in his mouth. "Oh, God, nooooo . . . not Buckshot, too!"

Daniel nearly choked on his coffee when he heard the name of the person calling Bob's A&E. He stood next to the wooden checkout counter and nervously twisted the cord on the phone's handset. Vanessa Kingsley, Sadie's accuser, had swallowed the bait. He needed to calm down, keep his composure, and play it cool.

He took a deep breath and deepened his voice. "Yes, Miss Kingsley. How may I help you?" He hoped she wouldn't recognize his voice from the settlement meeting at Brantley Cavanaugh's office.

Vanessa responded, "I have a letter from your store informing me that I've won the twenty-fifth anniversary drawing. The letter indicates I need to schedule a time to pick up my prize."

He glanced at the twenty-fifth anniversary banner hanging in the front window. "And what did you say your name was?"

He heard an irritated sigh on the other end of the line and then her obnoxious voice. "Kingsley. Vanessa Kingsley."

"Just a minute. Let me confirm you're the winner." He placed the phone on hold, counted slowly to sixty, and then resumed the call. "Congratulations, Miss Kingsley, you have won the grand prize, a TV/DVD combo. When would you like to pick up your prize?"

The line went quiet for a moment and then he heard her arrogant voice. "I'll be there around two p.m. This better not be a sales gimmick."

He breathed a sigh of relief. "No, madam. I assure you this is not a sales gimmick. Remember, we want to get a picture of you for the *Glendale Gazette* to show you are the winner of the twenty-fifth anniversary drawing. You may want to dress with the photograph in mind."

She exhaled sharply. "Whatever. Just have my prize ready. I won't have all day."

The phone line went dead. He hung up and hurried to the stock room to tell his dad the exciting news and to make sure his father would be in the store in the afternoon. His dad would have to be the main actor because the scam would be a bust if Vanessa linked Daniel to the store drawing.

After talking with his father, he gathered some equipment and headed outdoors. The cold front had passed during the night. In strong contrast to the wet and bitter day before, it had turned hot and sunny.

Sadie chewed on her lip as she dug through the red clay at the foot of Jake's grave. She paused and wiped the perspiration from her forehead. The Carving Tree had always provided a nice, cool place. But now, absent of foliage, it offered no shade. It made her appreciate the canopy that still stood over Jake's grave.

She glanced at the heart-shaped carving that Jake had etched in the tree more than forty-six years earlier. The cuts had broadened with the passage of time as the tree had grown in diameter. Jake had made a commitment the day he'd proposed, had sealed it with his marriage vow, and had remained true to those words for the duration of their marriage. They had witnessed numerous marriages falter and fail over the years; but theirs, like the Carving Tree, had flourished and grown.

She struggled to dig a shallow hole for Buckshot. Life, like the compacted clay, was hard. Her anger toward God returned. She felt like He was rubbing it in—Jake's illness and death, the lawsuit, Megan's abandonment of Ethan, and now Buckshot. Why had God allowed these terrible things to happen? Was it punishment? She didn't know how much more she could bear. Her eyes clouded again. She didn't know if she could face life any longer or if she even wanted to try.

She felt totally alone. She knew the ladies from church only meant to help by taking care of Ethan. However, at this moment, she would welcome his defiant little voice. She broke through the hard crust, and the digging grew easier. Jake would want Buckshot buried at the foot of his grave. After all, Buckshot had spent the majority of his time near Jake's feet. In her mind she could see Jake walking to the mailbox or barn with Buckshot at his heels every step of the way. She could picture Jake rocking on the front porch with Buckshot lying against his feet. She could see the dog reclining in the shade at the Resting Place while Jake hoed the garden.

She dragged the dog's stiff body into the shallow hole. She propped against the shovel to catch her breath and stared down at the lifeless dog. She and Jake had found the puppy at the local animal shelter fourteen years earlier. It had been love at first sight. The little puppy—half bull dog and half golden retriever—had waddled over to them from the far corner of the kennel, his round, full tummy shifting from side to side as his tail whipped the air. They had never even looked at another dog that day but had locked in on the special little puppy.

She stooped and stroked the dog's head. A fresh gash behind one ear served as a memorial to how the dog had stood in defense against their intruders. Buckshot had turned out to be the best of dogs, faithful till the end. The flies scattered as the dirt spilled across the carcass. When she'd filled the hole, she wrote a short epitaph on a concrete paver stone with a black permanent marker. She stood the twelve-by-twelve-inch stone on edge and buried the bottom end several inches in the soil. She stepped back and read aloud the words on the grave marker: "Buckshot—Faithful Until Death."

Hot, tired, and dirty, Sadie slumped into the den recliner, her work clothes stained with red clay. Her parents' family Bible, which she had slammed against the wall two nights earlier, had been returned to the coffee table. A lot of help God had been. He took her father, Frank, Jake, and now even Buckshot. Where was this God of love, grace, and mercy of which Jake had often spoken?

She heard a knock on the screen door but ignored it. Maybe they'd go away. She didn't feel like entertaining company at the moment. The persistent visitor knocked a second time, a little harder. She stood. Her body ached from age and overuse. She glanced around the room. It looked presentable since Ethan's toys no longer cluttered the floor. She sighed. She missed the little fellow.

Ding-dong!

"Hello. Sadie, are you home? It's Maude and Mabel."

Sadie massaged her lower back as she shuffled to the door. "I'm coming." Maude and Mabel? Were they bringing the battlefield to her home? She opened the door. Dressed in matching outfits, the two women resembled junior high girlfriends, Maude in bright purple and Mabel in soft lavender. "Come on in."

Maude's eyes grew wide. "Good heavens."

Mabel's mouth dropped open. "You look like you've been mining ore." She brushed some dirt from Sadie's cheek. "What happened to you?"

Sadie looked at the ceiling and closed her eyes. "I just buried Buckshot."

Maude touched her arm. "Not good ole Buckshot? What happened to him?"

Sadie's eyes filled with tears. "I . . . I found him this morning"—her chin trembled—"lying dead across Jake's grave."

Maude and Mabel pulled her into a tight embrace and the trio wept together for several minutes.

Sadie broke the group hug. She needed to get a grip. She changed the subject. "It's great to see the two of you together. I assume you've overcome *all* your differences."

Maude chuckled. "I don't think we could ever overcome *all* our differences, but I did come to my senses. I sought forgiveness, and Mabel, gracious friend that she is, forgave me."

Sadie smiled. "Thank heavens. I feared the onset of World War III. What changed your mind? Did Sam Peterson move on?"

Maude shook her head. "Actually, you changed my mind. I thought about what you told me two weeks ago—the root of bitterness thing. I decided Mabel's friendship meant more than Sam Peterson's affections."

Mabel laughed. "She made a wise decision, too. The next day I told Sam to take a hike. I discovered he looks better on the outside than on the inside."

Maude pointed to a busted lamp sitting on an end table. "What happened to your lamp?"

Sadie straightened the lampshade. "One of our angry intruders knocked it on the floor."

Maude frowned. "What's the latest on the thugs?"

"They're being held at the county jail. Thanks again for calling the sheriff."

Maude shook her head. "I'd called sooner, but I couldn't hear clearly over the phone. It took me a while to realize you were in danger."

Sadie wiped a tear from her cheek. "Thanks to you, they're off the street."

Mabel nodded. "Thank God for that."

Anger pulsed through Sadie's body. "Thank God? How can you say that?" She felt her face and ears burn. "He's the one to blame for everything. I'm tired of hearing about God's goodness and love. He hasn't done me any favors." She picked up the broken lamp and slammed it to the floor. "He took my daddy, my son, and now my husband." She waved her finger at Mabel. "How can you stand there and tell me to thank God? You're not the one facing a frivolous lawsuit nor have you just lost your husband."

Mabel had a blank stare on her face, and Maude remained silent for once.

Sadie held her forehead. "I'm . . . I'm sorry." She wiped the tears from her cheeks. "Life isn't fair." She dropped her chin to her chest.

Mabel lifted Sadie's chin. "It's okay. You have a right to be angry."

Maude placed both hands on Sadie's shoulders and looked her in the eyes. "Sadie, a lot of bad things have happened during your life, things which have created open wounds. Those wounds can't heal as long as you're bitter toward God. A wise woman once told me to pull up my root of bitterness before it consumed me."

Megan struggled to contain her excitement as she watched the familiar North Carolina terrain from the bus window. Just a short distance remained to home—all because of Merle. He'd smiled, handed her the bus ticket, and said, "It's the least I can do for my new sister in Christ."

She glanced at the small black New Testament in her hands. It had been his parting gift to her. The old leather had cracked, but the binding held fast. Inside the front cover she found Merle's home phone number and a brief note that read, "If you ever need an ear, give me a call."

She wiped the tears from the corners of her eyes. Merle's generosity and genuine concern had been a living testimony of the love of Christ. Because Merle had first met her needs, she'd been willing to listen to his witness. *Thank you, God, for Merle and his desire to share the love of Christ.* A ray of sunshine shone through the bus window and warmed her shoulder.

She watched a mother sitting nearby read to her little boy. The young child, approximately Ethan's age, propped against his mother totally engrossed in the story. Merle's encouraging words circulated in her head. He'd looked her directly in the eyes and said,

"Megan, if you stay close to Jesus, He can help you to be a good mother." She bowed her head. *Dear Jesus, help me to be a good mother to Ethan.*

She couldn't wait to see Ethan. She tried to picture the expression on his face during their coming reunion. Something in her chest tightened. How would Ethan receive her? Would he be thrilled at her return or angry because of her prolonged absence? How would she explain her delay in returning home? Would Ethan ever trust her again?

Sadie sat on the bottom porch step with her arms crossed, an elbow cupped in each hand, while a chorus of crickets and frogs filled the summer night air. She could see the silhouette of the Carving Tree standing like a giant tombstone against the brilliant night sky and the shadow of the funeral home canopy that covered the two graves. The thought of their final resting places left her chilled in spite of the warm night. Her body shuddered and fresh tears began to seize her. She wiped her eyes, exhaled sharply, and gazed into the heavens. The innumerable stars in the immense sky made her feel small and insignificant. If God really existed, and if He created the vast universe, why would He concern Himself with her, a mere speck of dust? The logical answer, she concluded, was He wouldn't. Why would He? After all, she'd pushed Him away nearly a lifetime ago when her father had died. She felt utterly alone. Jake and Ethan were gone, Buckshot was gone, and now even God Himself had abandoned her. The tears streamed down her face, and she went into the house to get a tissue.

She heard nothing in the quiet house except for the ever-present tick-tock of the mantel clock. The stillness of the empty home only magnified her loneliness. She felt completely deserted. For years she'd thought there would be lots of children and grandchildren to keep her company should Jake die first; but with Frank's accident, the hope of grandchildren had vanished. Now she was just an old retired schoolteacher, a widow with no close family. To top it all off, a lawsuit loomed on the horizon that threatened her retirement savings.

She covered her open mouth as a thought crossed her mind. What exactly did she have to live for anyway? She had no husband, no family, no financial security, no dog, and no real relationship with God. Who would even miss her? Who would even care?

She sorted through her options. Jake had hidden a loaded pistol on their closet shelf in case they ever needed to discourage unwanted intruders. It would do the job, and it would be quick and painless. However, she feared guns. It made her shudder to think of holding the revolver. Could she hold the gun steady enough to do its work? What if she missed? She could slit her wrist with a knife or razor blade. However, she didn't think she could do it. She would probably pass out. She got queasy every time the nurse pricked her finger. She pulled open a bedside table drawer and gazed at the numerous medications prescribed for Jake's heart condition. Perhaps the drawer contained the solution.

❦ CHAPTER 42 ❦

Troubled in spirit, Erma awoke from her nap in the recliner. Never had she felt such a need to pray. Clyde lay asleep in his recliner with his toothless mouth gaped open. She didn't bother to get up but closed her eyes and prayed. The Spirit immediately impressed upon her the need to pray for Sadie—to pray for the preservation of her life and to pray for her salvation. *Why, Lord? Sadie's saved . . . Isn't she?* The impression grew stronger. So Erma prayed fervently.

Sadie's hand trembled as she sat a cup of water on her bedside table. The pills couldn't do their job if she couldn't swallow them. Unlike Jake, she'd never been able to swallow a dry pill. Many times she'd seen him swallow an aspirin without a drink to chase it. She extracted four pills from each of the three bottles and studied the colorful assortment in her palm. The pills resembled a handful of candy. Should she take the entire handful at once or only one pill at a time? She opted for the latter. Why risk choking?

She started to put the small white caps on the plastic pill bottles but decided against it. The open bottles would make it clear she'd committed suicide. "Suicide." The word she'd loathed now had a liberating ring to it. She would soon be free of the pain. Suicide—

didn't people who commit suicide always leave notes? She dumped the handful of pills on the bedspread and pulled a pen and a small notepad from her Bible cover. An old bulletin fluttered to the floor. She sat on the edge of the bed to think about the words for the note. What should she write? Who would be the first to find it? How long would her stiff body lay before being discovered?

After a few minutes of thought she wrote her parting message. She read the note aloud, "Life is too hard without Jake. Sadie." Her eyes clouded, and she became more resolute. She laid the notepad on the bedside table next to the open pill bottles. She placed a pill in her mouth, took a sip of water, and swallowed it. "One down and eleven to go."

She stared at the bulletin on the floor. It contained her notes—only two brief bullets—from one of Pastor Nolan's recent sermons. She picked up the bulletin, put on her glasses, and read the first bullet, "Root of Bitterness." These notes were from the sermon that had inspired her advice to Maude. Boy, if anyone ever harbored a root of bitterness, it had been Maude. It had consumed her and almost ended her long-standing friendship with Mabel. She remembered Pastor Nolan's words. "Left unchecked, a root of bitterness is a dangerous thing. It grows like a thorny vine that strangles the life from the rose bush. We must pull up the vine of bitterness, root and all, lest it sprout up again, and destroy us!"

Fortunately, her words to Maude two weeks earlier had a positive impact. Maude had sought forgiveness and renewed her friendship with Mabel. In fact, when Maude and Mabel visited earlier in the day, Maude had offered her the same advice. Maude's words echoed in her mind. "A wise woman once told me to pull up my root of bitterness before it consumed me. What great advice."

Sadie paced the floor and raked her fingers through her hair. The truth hurt. She'd been bitter toward God ever since her father had died. She dropped the bulletin on the bed, and the memory that could never be erased resurfaced to haunt her once more.

A cool rain had fallen most of the night, and a thick layer of condensation covered the window. She hummed a silly tune and drew a picture on the glass to pass the time. A soft moan came from her mother, who slept in a large armchair in the corner of the hospital room. Her head rested against the wall, and her mouth hung open. The rhythmic beat of the heart monitor echoed in the quiet room.

She looked at the window picture. The little girl needed a companion. She drew a small boy next to the girl. She rubbed her chin and studied the couple. She fogged the glass with her breath and redrew their hands together. She gave the little girl a bonnet and the boy a baseball cap. She smiled.

Bbbeeeeeeepppp. The high-pitched, continuous alarm and the frantic screams of her mother suddenly shattered the happy little world created by her finger.

Her mother's desperate cry was drowned out by her own screams, horrific wails from twenty-three years earlier. The words of the news report still burned in her mind. "In local news . . . A tragic accident today at the Camp Lejeune Marine Base claimed the lives of three young marines. Sources indicate a truck hauling ammunitions exploded for some unexplained reason and killed the three marines riding in the truck. Details of the accident will be released following a thorough investigation. The names of the victims are being withheld until next of kin have been notified."

In a moment her whole life had been turned upside down—a knock at the door, a marine in full dress blues, and catastrophic news. Not only had the fruit of her womb and her pride and joy been taken, but also her dreams of grandchildren had been extinguished.

The horrible memory caused her head to spin. She sat on the bed. Perhaps Jake's medication, not the memory, made her dizzy. The bulletin, which lay on the bed, rattled beneath her hand. She read the second bullet, "Reconciliation with God." What words had Pastor Nolan spoken concerning reconciliation? "Bitterness keeps us from being right with God. It breaks our relationship with a Holy Creator." Pastor Nolan had been right. Her bitterness toward God had kept her from ever experiencing true peace. Jake's face during his final moments flashed before her. His brown eyes looked hollow and tired. "Don't . . . blame . . . God. He . . . He loves . . . you." His words rang in her ears and wouldn't leave.

She knew what it meant to be a Christian. Yet, she'd never surrendered her heart to Christ. Like Clyde, she'd lived the life of a hypocrite most of her life. Wasn't pretending to be a Christian just as bad as pretending to be a war hero? Could it be even worse? She deserved to be burned with all the other tares. At least Clyde had come clean. Maybe the time had arrived for her to do the same. She had grown tired of being at enmity with God.

She slipped off the bed and dropped to her knees. She planted her face on the bed and clutched the brightly colored bedspread in her fists. "Oh, God," she cried. "Please, please forgive me." The words began to flow more easily. "For years I blamed you for my father's death and Frank's accident. Recently, I blamed you for Jake's passing away. Lord, I've blamed you for all the bad things that have ever happened in my life. I'm sorry.

"Jesus, forgive me. Countless times I rejected the salvation you freely offer. Lord, I know you died for my sin and rose from the grave on the third day. I now turn from my sin and turn to you. I pray you would forgive me for all the sin that I've committed in the past and will commit in the future. Dear Jesus, I place my faith in you alone, trusting you will guide and direct me each day of my life. Lord, give me meaning and purpose in life. I ask that you would take control of my life. I pray you would save my soul. In Jesus' name, Amen."

She raised her head from the bed. The crushing weight, which she had long carried, was lifted. The deep emptiness—that had been like a giant vacuum that sucked out her life—disappeared, replaced by an overwhelming peace that flowed through her body. The ache of Jake's death remained, but an even greater peace offset it and enabled her to move forward with life.

She bowed her head once more. "Thank you, God, for saving my soul, for giving me peace during a horrible time of heartbreak. Amen."

☘ Chapter 43 ☘

A great peace came over Erma while she lay in her recliner. She knew her prayer had been answered. *Thank you, God. Amen.* She opened her eyes and saw Clyde still asleep in his recliner totally unaware of what had just happened. She snapped the chair to a full upright position, oblivious to its resistance. She jumped to her feet totally insensitive to her body's aches and pains and hurried to the telephone.

Erma listened as Sadie's phone rang numerous times. Her excitement and energy level increased with each ring. Finally, Sadie picked up the phone. Erma heard a few sniffles and then Sadie cleared her throat and said, "Hello."

She could tell Sadie had been crying. She knew why. "Sadie, this is Erma. I apologize for calling so late, but I just got the news. I had to call."

Sadie hesitated. "What news is that?"

Tears rolled down Erma's face, and her vocal chords tightened as she responded, "Welcome to the family of God."

Sadie almost dropped the bedroom phone. "But . . . but . . . how did you know?"

Erma laughed. "Why honey, I've been praying for your soul for the last hour."

Stunned and speechless, Sadie hung up the phone and sat on the bed. "How . . . who . . . ?" The conversation she'd just had with Erma amazed her. She wiped tears of joy from the corners of her eyes and reflected on God's goodness.

Brriinnnggg! The phone on the bedside table rang again. Who in the world would be calling at eleven o'clock? They never received phone calls after 10 p.m., yet the phone had broken the silence twice tonight. Perhaps the Lord had revealed her recent conversion to someone else.

She picked up the phone. "Hello."

"Hello, Mrs. Hopkins, this is Daniel Smith." His voice, typically slow and methodical, sounded staccato and energetic.

"Hi, Daniel." Why would he call at such a late hour?

"I'm sorry to be calling this late, but I have news that just couldn't wait. It's news that I think you will want to hear."

Her pulse quickened, and she covered her heart with her hand. "It's okay, Daniel. I'm still up. What news do you have?"

"It's not official yet, but I received word from Brantley Cavanaugh a little while ago that the Vanessa Kingsley lawsuit will be dropped."

Her voice abandoned her. She squeezed her eyes tightly shut in order to postpone the avalanche of tears, tears of relief. Try as she might to prevent it, the dam burst, and she wept uncontrollably. Her body shook with sobs. After several minutes, she forced out two words. "Praise God!"

"Mrs. Hopkins, I can't go into the details right now, but I'd like to come by first thing in the morning before work to fill you in. I'll be there around 7:30 with some ham biscuits, if that's okay."

As he pulled into the Hopkinses' yard, Daniel felt a deep emptiness. He saw the two gravediggers breaking down the blue canopy that stood over Jake's grave. He expected Jake's old dog to greet him and announce his arrival as he exited the vehicle, but he didn't see the dog. He retrieved a video player, videocassette, and a bag of ham and sausage biscuits from his car.

Sadie smiled and held open the screen door as he approached. "Good morning, Daniel."

He heard joy in Sadie's voice. Perhaps her joy stemmed from the news that the lawsuit had been dropped. Her attitude was in sharp contrast to the last time he'd seen her at the gravesite. She'd been so distraught that she'd not even acknowledged him. It bolstered his spirit to see her in a much better state of mind. "Good morning, Mrs. Hopkins."

Sadie reached for the bag of biscuits. "Let me give you a hand." She peeped into the bag. "Mmmm, they smell good."

He located the television as he passed through the front door. "I need to show you a video. Can I hook up this VCR player to your TV?"

Sadie stopped and turned. "Sure, go right ahead." She held up the bag of biscuits. "I'm going to take these to the kitchen and start the coffee." She disappeared behind the swinging door.

He connected the VCR player to the television, loaded the videocassette, and rewound it. He hurried with excitement to the kitchen.

Sadie smiled when he entered through the swinging doors. He studied her face for a moment. It glowed with a beauty he'd never noticed before.

She pointed to a chair at the table. "Have a seat. I've fixed some coffee. Would you like some orange juice, too?"

He pulled up a chair. "No, thanks. Coffee is fine."

Sadie placed a platter containing the ham and sausage biscuits in the center of the table and poured two steaming cups of coffee. She pointed at a small sugar bowl and cream pitcher. "There's sugar and cream."

The robust aroma of the coffee and the salty smell of the biscuits made his mouth water.

She laid a cloth napkin at each place setting and then took her seat. "Would you bless the food?"

He bowed his head and gave thanks.

Sadie stirred some cream into her coffee. "Tell me the details, Daniel. I'm dying to hear why Vanessa Kingsley is dropping the lawsuit."

He finished chewing. "The video will show you what happened, but I need to provide you with some background first. You have probably seen advertisements recently about Bob's A&E celebrating its twenty-fifth anniversary."

Sadie nodded.

He continued. "We sent a letter to Vanessa Kingsley on store letterhead. It indicated she'd won a random drawing that was held to celebrate the store's anniversary and she needed to schedule a time to pick up her prize, a TV/DVD player." He took another bite, chewed, and swallowed the food. "The scam worked. We captured video proof that she is faking her injury." He sipped his coffee. "If you're ready, we'll watch the video."

Sadie sat on the edge of her seat as the camera zoomed in on a familiar silver Lexus that pulled into a handicapped parking space next to the store. She immediately recognized the car that she'd struck from behind. It belonged to Vanessa Kingsley.

Daniel provided play-by-play commentary. "I was hidden in a thicket across the street with the video camera."

Sadie watched the driver-side door open and out climbed Vanessa Kingsley. She wore a very short black and white skirt with a skin-tight black blouse that highlighted her bust line. Sadie felt her face blush. With the exception of a neck brace, Vanessa Kingsley looked like a "lady of the night" working a street corner.

The camera followed Vanessa into Bob's A&E and remained focused on the store front. After a few minutes, Bob and Vanessa exited the store. He pushed a hand truck containing a medium-sized shipping box which he parked near the back of Vanessa's car. Bob pulled out a small camera from his pocket and motioned for Vanessa to stand in front of the "25th Anniversary" sign in the store's plate-glass window.

Daniel paused the video. "Dad was going to take Vanessa's picture for the *Glendale Gazette* to publicize the store's anniversary and to show who won the drawing. Notice he hadn't loaded the television into her car yet." He started the video again.

Vanessa stopped Bob, removed the neck brace, and posed in front of the sign. Bob fumbled with the camera for several seconds, held up his palm and said something to Vanessa, and then hurried into the store.

The camera zoomed in on the ugly scowl on Vanessa's face. Sadie had seen that same irritated expression before.

"Dad told Vanessa the camera's batteries had died and he'd be right back with fresh batteries," Daniel interjected.

Sadie watched Vanessa, who appeared upset by the delay. She remembered how impatient Vanessa had been on the day of the accident. Vanessa stood with her arms crossed and tapped her foot. Several minutes passed. Finally, Vanessa walked closer to the window. She cupped her hand above her eyes and looked into the store.

"Dad was delaying on purpose," Daniel commented.

More time passed. The expression on Vanessa's face grew even more sour and her lips moved as she spoke to herself.

Daniel laughed. "I wish I could read her lips."

Sadie shook her head. "I don't think I want to know what she just said."

Vanessa tossed her neck brace in the car's front seat and popped her trunk lid open. She moved back to the sidewalk where she stood with her hands on her hips. After a couple of minutes, she marched angrily into the store. She came back out a few seconds later and slammed the store's front door.

Sadie grimaced, glad that she wasn't on the receiving end of Vanessa's fury.

Daniel paused the video again. "Vanessa found Dad on the phone with another customer. He was faking a rather intense conversation. Watch closely. Vanessa is about to reach her boiling point. She wants Dad to hurry up and take her photograph and load the television."

Sadie didn't need for Daniel to tell her that Vanessa had reached her explosion threshold, she could see it in her face. It seemed like Bob was trying to arouse her anger.

Daniel pushed a button and the video resumed playing. Vanessa walked back to the hand truck. She circled it several times as if sizing up the load.

Sadie leaned forward in her chair.

Vanessa scanned the area, apparently to make sure no one would see her actions, then squatted, lifted the box, and sat it in the trunk.

Sadie gasped. "Oh, my. There's nothing wrong with her. She's as fit as an ox."

Vanessa slammed the trunk lid shut and wiped the dust from her hands. She pushed the hand truck to the sidewalk, got in her car, and left in a hurry.

Daniel stopped the video and ejected it. "I called Brantley Cavanaugh late yesterday afternoon and described the video evidence that we had recorded. He said he would discuss the development with Miss Kingsley and get back with me later in the evening. Brantley called back last night and said Miss Kingsley had agreed to drop the lawsuit." Daniel laughed. "Brantley pled innocence. He said he didn't know Vanessa was faking the injury. However, I suspect he was just as guilty as Vanessa. In fact, I'm sure he coached her."

Sadie's eyes clouded again. "Praise the Lord!" She looked earnestly at Daniel. "Thank you very much, Daniel. Your scam was simply brilliant. How can I ever repay you?"

Daniel looked at the ceiling for several moments and then responded. "You have already paid me, Mrs. Hopkins."

She raised her eyebrows. "How so?"

Daniel looked directly at her. His eyes brimmed with tears.

"You've encouraged me since the fourth grade to pursue my dream of becoming a lawyer. When everyone else made fun of my career choice, you always supported it." He glanced at his feet and chewed on his lip, then looked her in the eyes again. "I'm going to tell you something that I've not shared with anyone else." He hesitated as if searching for the right words. "I didn't do well during the final exams at Campbell University this past semester and failed one of my classes. It greatly discouraged me. In fact, for the last month I've contemplated dropping out of law school."

She sighed deeply. "Oh, don't do that, Daniel. You would make a great lawyer."

Daniel smiled. "I've realized there is a real need for honest lawyers to help offset the corrupt and money-hungry lawyers. I have to admit that beating a snake like Brantley Cavanaugh at his own game has boosted my confidence and made me even more determined. But, more importantly, I experienced real joy and satisfaction knowing I made a difference by helping someone. So, thanks to you, I plan to continue my dream. Consider your debt paid in full."

She touched his shoulder. "That's wonderful, Daniel, but what about the cost of the TV/DVD player awarded to Vanessa Kingsley?"

Daniel shook his head. "It's covered too. My dad said it was an honor and a privilege to help such an outstanding couple as the Hopkinses."

A choking sensation rendered her speechless. She bowed her head and silently gave thanks.

Sadie stood on the front porch and enjoyed the fresh fragrance of summer. She waved at Daniel as he drove down the driveway and uttered, "Such a nice young man and smart, too. He'll make a wonderful catch for some lucky young woman one day."

Daniel's car had barely disappeared from sight when another car approached from the direction of town. It slowed, turned into their driveway, and headed up the hill.

She rubbed her hand over her hair and patted it in place. The vehicle resembled the car that belonged to Ethel Burton, the lady who had been keeping Ethan for the last few days. Could she be bringing Ethan back? Sadie moved down the porch steps as the passenger door opened. Megan Thompson stepped out.

Sadie gasped. Megan had returned for Ethan. Thank God! Megan's olive complexion seemed darker than usual, and the skin on her face and arms showed signs of peeling.

Megan opened the rear door and unbuckled Ethan from the car seat.

Ethel made her way toward Sadie, her gait altered by a past stroke. "Hi, Sadie."

Sadie gave her a hug. "Hi, Ethel."

Ethan hit the ground running and hollering, "Say-da, Say-da." He wrapped his little arms around her legs, almost causing her to lose her balance.

She squatted to the child's level and hugged the little boy. She felt warmth flow through her body. She'd missed the little boy, and he'd apparently missed her, too.

Megan approached tentatively. "I heard about Jake. I'm sorry for your loss."

Sadie stood with Ethan still tightly clutching her neck. "Does Ethan know yet?"

Megan shrugged her shoulders. "I tried to explain it to him, but I'm not sure he really understood." She looked toward the graves. "I called a few days ago to let you know I was coming back for Ethan. When I didn't reach you, I called Glendale Baptist Church. That's when I learned Jake had passed away and where to find Ethan. I'm sorry for all that's happened."

Ethel Burton rattled her keys and looked at Megan. "You two women need time to talk. I'll come back after lunch to pick up you and Ethan."

Sadie gazed in admiration at the cloudless blue sky. Her bleak circumstances had dramatically improved during the previous twenty-four hours. She climbed down the porch steps and followed the ruts in the driveway down the hill to the Carving Tree. The blue canopy had been removed. The graves of Jake and Buckshot now lay exposed to the afternoon summer sun.

She walked to the foot of Jake's grave and stared at the carving. "Jake, I don't know if you can hear me from heaven or not, but if you can, I want you to know God and I are now on speaking terms. In fact, I'm your newest sister in Christ." She dabbed tears from the corners of her eyes. "One day soon I'll meet you at those pearly gates. Until then, I look forward to living in heaven with you for all eternity." She studied the top of her feet. "Jake, I'm sorry for keeping the lawsuit a secret from you. With your heart condition, I just didn't want you to have to deal with the stress of a lawsuit. I hope you can find it in your heart to forgive me."

Her eyes shifted from her feet back to Jake's grave. "You probably know by now the lawsuit has been dropped. God worked that out, too. He used that fine young man, Daniel Smith." She raked several strands of hair behind her ear. "Megan is back. She survived a terrible ordeal while she was gone. She was abducted by a human trafficking ring while in Los Angeles. It's why we never heard anything from her. Fortunately, she escaped. She has an amazing story about spending the night in the open sea. Tomorrow, Megan and I are going to talk to Daniel about reporting the slave trade. She also wants to prosecute the two men, who came to our house, on sexual assault charges. I guess God works in some amazing ways. Because of her experience, Megan gave her heart to Jesus while riding home with a trucker. Praise the Lord! Megan and Ethan are going to stay with me for a while, at least until she can get back on her feet. It'll be good to have them in the house. I made another decision earlier today while looking at the retirement collage the school gave me. I've decided to teach part time at the grade school this fall. Thanks to the Lord, I have more to give to the kids now than ever before." Sadie looked up into the warm sunshine. "Jake, I wish I knew if you could hear me. There is much I never got to tell you."

A red-breasted robin landed on a low-hanging branch. The bird studied Sadie, tilting his head first one way and then the other. He sat quietly for a moment and then began to peck at a bud on a bare limb as if the bud was an insect. The outer petals peeled back, and Sadie could see the greenish-white tissue beneath.

"A bud!" Her exclamation startled the bird, and he flew away. Her eyes traced up the branch and found another . . . and another . . . and another. Her eyes flooded with tears as she realized that tiny buds covered the tree. The beech, just like her, had new life. She felt a large grin spread across her face. Even though she and Jake were separated, their love, like the old Carving Tree, lived on.

About the Author

Terry Thomas Bowman is happily married to Karen, his wife of thirty-two years. Terry and Karen make their home near Wilmington, North Carolina. Terry serves as deacon, decision counselor, and adult Sunday school teacher in his church. He has been writing for fourteen years and has had numerous devotions appear in *Open Windows*, *The Upper Room*, and other publications. More than fifty of his Christian inspirational, home-school, and biblical world-view articles have been published, and he has written several award-winning historical fiction short stories. Visit www.ReadTerryBowman.com to see additional works by Terry.

In *The Carving Tree* a majestic old beech containing a heart-shaped carving stands as a symbol of love for the main characters. Terry drew upon personal experience when he selected this symbol of undying love. Prior to proposing to his wife in 1981, he etched a similar carving on a beech tree at the University of North Carolina at Greensboro. Thirty years later they returned to the university and showed their children the living symbol of their love.

CPSIA information can be obtained at www.ICGtesting.com
Printed in the USA
BVOW05s1239050115

381782BV00001B/2/P